Cachebyte

A cache of short stories from within the Ellie Conway
FBI-Byte Series.

I0613196

Cat Connor

Cachebyte © Cat Connor 2024

For information regarding permission email the publisher at 9mmPressNZ@gmail.com, subject line: Permission.

Formatting: 9mm Press
Publisher: 9mm Press, New Zealand
Publication date: April 2024
Country of first publication: New Zealand.

ISBN D2D print: 978-1-0670083-1-4
ISBN ePub: 978-1-0670083-2-1

"If a man dwells on the past, then he robs the present. But if a man ignores the past, he may rob the future. The seeds of our destiny are nurtured by the roots of our past."

– Master Po (Kung Fu Season One Episode 5)

This book is cache of short stories from the Ellie Conway FBI-Byte Series. Some haven't been seen before and others were available in an earlier collection which no longer exists. The stories are from When Ellie met Mac and beyond.

Quad Espresso and a Mochaccino

Standing in the lunchtime queue at the bank wasn't what I wanted to be doing. I conceded it was preferable to listening to Mom's accusations. That particular joy was way up there with burning in hell. Images of my comfortable bed and my quiet house in Mauryville danced through my weary mind.

A furtive glance at my watch caused me to stifle another impatient sigh; twenty mind-numbing minutes of waiting were taking their toll.

The sigh became a yawn.

Why they don't have a fast deposit box like every other damn bank? Why do I have to wait for a teller? What in hells name did I do that was so bad? This is punishment for something serious.

Sometimes I'm a bit slow. I huffed internally at myself. Upsetting mother carries a price, and this is my penance. I would've preferred a couple of Hail Mary's and a few Our Father's at least it would be over by now.

It occurred to me that I wasn't alone in my misery. There were many faces around me sharing my restless annoyance. I yawned again and watched with silent amusement as my yawn spread through the bank.

Sunlight streamed through the large plate glass windows increasing the heat and my irritation. I needed coffee, sleep, or both.

To top the experience off nicely, a bank guard at the counter hadn't taken his eyes off me since I joined the queue. I flashed a smile in his direction. There was no return smile. He just stood there arms folded across his chest glaring at me from under his thick mono brow. Fighting a tide of rising mirth at his unwavering staunch stare became more and more difficult.

I let my black cotton jacket hang open, it was too warm to contemplate doing up buttons, and every fidgety movement brought my holster into view.

He began to alternate his gaze from my hip to my face but never for longer than a split second. I was certain he saw my badge that I so responsibly hung around my neck before leaving the air conditioned comfort of my car. It was tempting to rest my hand on my gun, just to see his reaction. He looked like the jumpy type so I thought better of it. Just because I was bad-tempered, hot, tired, and fed up there was no need to stir trouble in the bank. The mere thought of such a thing lit a spark of enjoyment that pushed away some of my fatigue.

I yawned so widely my eyes watered.

The waiting continued interrupted only by the yawn as it passed from person to person. My mind began to sift through garbage. I blocked out Mom's ignorance and let one of Dad's questions play on my mind, am I happy?

A large woman behind me squawked loudly in my ear, startling me back to reality, "You're holding up the queue, dear."

"Thank you, ma'am."

I approached the counter, slid the check and deposit form over to the teller and as I turned to leave I smiled sweetly at the cranky looking guard. He had to stay, and had I not been wearing a federal badge, I probably would've poked out my tongue; yep I'm all grown up. To prevent myself from flipping him the bird I stuffed my hands into my jacket pockets, and left.

Something delicious floated on the mid-summer breeze, the smell of fresh ground coffee. I quickly located the source of the aroma, Starbucks. As I walked along the hot sidewalk, a display of newspapers caught my eye. I paused recognizing the front-page picture. The caption under the picture read, 'The now familiar faces of Delta A leaving the Richmond FBI building after the arrest of the Mall rapist.' There we all were in glorious color. I quickly read the first paragraph, 'Delta A once again proves their expertise in serial crime. The two women three man team led by SAC Caine Grafton successfully ended a reign of terror with the capture of a suspected rapist after a grueling investigation.' I stopped reading.

I'd lived it no need to read the hype.

The smell of coffee encouraged me to move on.

One order for a mochachino and a quad espresso later, I was sitting in a booth facing the door wriggling to get comfortable in the oppressive heat.

I hauled myself back to my feet and removed my jacket which I lay carefully across the far end of the table.

Sitting back down and feeling much better, I relaxed and waited for my coffee to arrive.

With my legs stretched out across the seat, and my back wedged against the wall I had the perfect spot to watch patrons come and go. I conjured little stories about their lives in the privacy of my thoughts to pass the time.

Then I saw him, tall, dark haired, and good-looking with a twinge of familiarity. I had no idea why he seemed familiar but he warranted more than a cursory glance. I noted a map hanging out of his back pocket and a general air of confusion in his expression; he carried a dark blue cap in his hand. I sat up a little as I heard him order exactly what I had. He took the booth in front of me closer to the door. I could hear the paper rustle as he unfolded the map and spread it on the table.

A young waitress arrived at my table. "Quad espresso and a mochachino?"

"Thanks," I said, smiling.

The girl smiled back, "I think I saw your picture in the newspaper, are you're in the FBI, part of that new Delta team?"

"Yes."

She almost squealed with delight, "Wow it must be so exciting!"

"It has its moments." I smiled; it was hard not to smile at her enthusiasm.

"I'll leave you to your coffee; I think it's really cool what you did."

She bounced away before I could thank her, leaving me feeling appreciated for the first time in a long while.

The dark haired stranger in the booth ahead of me looked up briefly.

Our eyes met. My heart skipped a beat. And he went back to his map. A few minutes later, the same waitress delivered exactly the same order to him.

Map man intrigued me so did his order, I'd never met anyone who had my taste in coffee.

I could feel the smile on my face as I thought about the errand to the bank for Dad that led to being in this particular Starbucks. Maybe I should be honest with Mom more often; that thought led to a mental head slap of giant proportions; yeah that's exactly what I shouldn't do.

For everyone's sake, I'd be best to keep away from her for a while. Cool down time while she decides which version of the truth to adopt now, the real one or her farcical self-serving version. The morning's breakfast conversation rolled through my head, her accusing me of being gay and of having an eating disorder. It must be hard for her to have such a boring child.

With my coffee finished and my mood much improved, I stood slowly and stretched my tired shoulders and back. I slung my jacket over one arm. As I passed the booth containing the man with the map, he looked up. I smiled at the obviously perplexed man with a road map.

He spoke, "You wouldn't happen to know a short cut to Route 64; they forgot to publish the detour signs on my two year old map." I watched his eyes flash from my visible FBI badge to my holster and back to my eyes.

"Actually I can help. Do you mind?" I asked indicating to the vacant seat opposite him.

After all, I am in a helping profession so really I was just doing my duty. Yeah right!

"Please," he replied moving his legs a little so I didn't have to step over them to sit.

"East or west?"

"Virginia beach," he said shrugging.

"East then," I replied, "You need to be two hours

that way!" I pointed somewhat randomly southeast.

He looked even more confused at the mention of compass points.

I turned the map to face me, pulled a pen from my pocket, and quickly wrote new directions. Then I remembered something, "One sec, let me check something I think there was a major accident on Route 64."

I pulled my cell phone from my belt and dialed quickly; "Hey, where was that crash on Route 64?" It was a brief call. I hung up and clipped my phone back on my belt.

"Sorry," I said, "They'll have the road clear in a couple of hours." Am I helpful or what?

He grinned. "Typical."

Before I could stop it my given name fell from my lips. "I'm Gabrielle," I said wondering why the hell I'd said the G word as I extended my hand and hoped it wasn't clammy.

"Pleased to meet you Gabrielle, I'm Cormac." Firm handshake and strong hands which suggested to me he worked with his hands. There was a subtle change in his expression as if he too sensed the familiarity.

"Guess I should've spent a few minutes and got more current directions from map quest," Cormac muttered.

I smiled hoping it didn't appear patronizing. "Even they wouldn't tell you about this accident."

"Maybe so but I should have at least checked and obtained more current directions, but dad reckoned this map was still good." He sighed.

I flicked the edge of his well-worn map. "You know, they have this really cool thing now, called GPS." I fought rising amusement at his surprised expression.

"You're quite a smartass aren't you?"

"Just sayin' – GPS, it's perfect for..."

"People like me who can't read a map?"

I shrugged. "Maybe you could look into something like NavMan or TomTom for future trips."

"Where am I?"

"Starbucks," I said forcing all hint of smartass from my voice. "You're almost at the Richmond University campus. That's one hell of a detour you took."

Cormac erupted in a warm throaty chuckle. "I'm directionally challenged. Only I swear this time I followed Dad's instructions exactly."

So, the inability to navigate is a family failing?

"Let me reiterate – NavMan, TomTom, Garmin, SatNav... all tools for the directionally challenged." I couldn't help but smile. "So you're allegedly going to Virginia beach huh? Vacation?"

He nodded. "Didn't think it would be so hard to get to."

"You're from the northern Virginia." I finally placed his subtle accent.

From the north and his name was Cormac.

Whom did I talk to almost every night, Galileo AKA Mac?

Who coincidentally was vacationing at Virginia Beach this week? I attempted to settle my thoughts and stop them running rampant with the possibilities.

"Yes, Fairfax," he replied draining his coffee, he stared into the bottom of the cup then looked up at me. "You know Fairfax?"

"I know Fairfax, not as well as I know DC, but well enough." It was easy chatting to him, comfortable even and a little voice inside was telling me this was my Mac and another little voice was saying wait a bit before you jump to conclusions and make a fool of yourself.

"We haven't ever met have we?" he asked.

I suspect I didn't hide my surprise at his question

very well, he watched me closely; I could feel his eyes penetrating my skull searching for answers.

He backed off with an apology. "Sorry I didn't mean to sound like I was hitting on you."

I shook off the feeling of nakedness under his penetrating gaze. "It's all right, I was thinking the same thing, and you are so very familiar. I've been sitting here trying to place you."

Map man Cormac and I chatted for a little while about various weird and wonderful subjects, and discovered as we did so that we had more and more in common. Conversation topics and expressions used triggered even greater familiarity; I waited for the revelation as my mind began to assemble everything. I knew eventually it would become clear where and how I knew him. It's one of those tricky situations for someone like me, there is always a chance that the familiarity could be because I have arrested or interviewed the person.

He wasn't giving off any signals or vibes that would cause me to move carefully to the nearest exit.

Cormac ordered us more coffee while we talked, eventually the subject of computers and chat rooms came up.

"You ever been to an MSN chat room?" he asked.

"Most nights," I said. Instantly thinking of the rooms, I liked. The people I called friends that I hung out with on my seventeen-inch monitor. One person in particular sprung to mind again, my heartbeat faster as I wondered about the possibility of Cormac being that someone I already knew.

"I like the poetry rooms." I remembered his hat, my mind threw up images of my computer screen and a little corner of the messenger window where he resided often wearing his hat. I found myself studying him more intently I'm sure my attentiveness was bordering on creepy but then so was his. I had a feeling that this would all fall into place if he just did one thing for me. "This may sound weird but could you put your hat on for me?"

He was most obliging. As soon as I saw him with the cap on his head I was ninety percent sure that it was the same person.

Cormac leaned closer across the table. "I spend most nights in poetry rooms too. What's your nick?" He chewed his lip for a second then added, "You don't have to tell me."

"You want to guess?" I replaced my previous

thoughts with a more reasonable, or realistic view, what were the odds of us knowing each other? It's a big world out there.

"Otherwisecat," he said in a hushed whisper, as if saying the word louder would crack the very seams of our universe.

I closed my eyes for a split second as he repeated, "Otherwisecat."

The whole world was silent as I looked up at him fighting a lump in my throat so I could form one word, "Galileo"

The world changed forever.

Our fingers entwined.

"It's me," he whispered as I raised my eyes to his.

"I can't believe this." I knew my voice was cracking slightly but he didn't seem to notice, or maybe he did and that's why he squeezed my hand a little tighter.

"When did the world get to be so small?" Mac asked.

I had nothing.

A strange silence descended upon our corner of the room, it wasn't awkward. It was just strange. We were coming to grips with this new development in what had until now been an Internet friendship. I had no idea what he was thinking; all I knew for sure is how I felt; stunned, shocked, and delighted all at once. Thrown fatefully into something that was both new and familiar, both scary and yet not.

Mac grinned; we were face to face and I was looking at the best friend I had never met. "Ellie, damn!"

My Mac!

Mac leaned on his elbows capturing me with his smile I felt the danger and yet could do nothing to stop myself from being lost within his hazel gaze. I may re-think the no children in my future thing.

He broke the silence with a question, "So Ellie, what are you doing in Richmond?"

"Work," I replied hoping it was audible; suddenly feeling flushed and trying to avert my eyes. "Just wrapped up a job."

He nodded. "How was it?"

I shook my head indicating I wasn't prepared to go there and simply said, "Bad."

"Your folks live in Richmond don't they?"

"Yes."

"And your brother too." Mac tapped his head and grinned. "Steel trap."

He was the only person I had ever met who really

did have a steel-trap memory, he forgot nothing. Mac's amazing memory was a double-edged sword, he couldn't choose to forget, and like me had plenty of things he didn't want to remember.

"I was almost on my way home and Dad had me stop by his bank for him, so I ended up here."

My mind rolled over thoughts of karma and fate as I re-counted the events that led to our meeting. I was still stunned at meeting Mac slash Galileo. No matter what I tried, I couldn't tear my eyes from him; my mind was taking its own sweet time in accepting that this was real. It's not as if it didn't have some clues and try and figure it out a little early so I was having trouble with it taking so long to catch up now.

"Home is a bit of a drive isn't it?" he commented.

"Yeah, about two hours west give or take." I found myself chuckling as I recalled past conversations; I very rarely get lost unlike Mac the challenge of direction was a constant for him, in that light I shouldn't have been so surprised that he ended up here today.

"What?" he asked.

"I am not directionally challenged."

"Smartass!"

"I wasn't kidding about the GPS ...," I said with a

wink.

It became obvious that Starbucks was nothing more than an extension of the chat room.

"I keep waiting for you to speak in typo," Mac remarked.

Impulse took over and I slapped his arm replying, "LOL."

Day drifted into early evening which became dusk as we lost ourselves in conversation exactly as we always had in the chat room and in our messenger windows. Some sort of magic seemed to be at work, everything felt right. I had imagined running into Mac in Washington DC or even Fairfax and always thought it would be cool, this surpassed even my wild imaginings, and to meet so far out of our comfort zones struck me as miraculous. The weirdest thing was two years ago when we first 'saw' each other over the Internet we both thought the other familiar. This was even possible, we'd probably seen each other in passing; we drove the same roads often; yet lived over three hours from each other. As teenagers, we road dirt bikes and back then, I even lived in Arlington not that far from where Mac grew up. My mind whirred through memories. Who would have thought two years after beginning an Internet friendship we'd be in the same Starbucks in Richmond and meet quite by chance? Thank God for Mac's directional difficulties!

Mac toyed with a napkin then reached into his pocket and produced a pen, he wrote a few lines.

"What are you doing?"

"Nothing much, just scribbling a lil' post-it poem on a napkin." He pushed it toward me. Our fingers touched, warmth flowed. I picked the napkin up and read the poem.

"Where is the shroud, I always knew? I looked but there was only sun, something not seen for so long. Again I ask, what became of the dark? When I awoke in the middle of my night."

He pocketed the pen and smiled at me. "Just a scribble is all."

"You are too modest by far dude and you are indeed the king of all post-it poems." I read it again to myself. "I love this. Can I keep it?"

"Yes, if you must."

I folded it carefully and placed it in my jacket pocket. A souvenir of our very first face-to-face meeting that I knew I would always treasure no matter how our futures played.

The lights dimmed, and all the other patrons had vacated the premises.

"Where's your car?" Mac inquired lightly. "I think they want us to go."

I glanced around, the place was deserted. "Outside the bank, not far." There was a slow realization that the time had come to say goodbye which caused a dreadful sinking feeling in my stomach.

"Can I walk you?" he asked.

"I would like that very much."

Mac picked up my jacket and held it out for me to slip my arms into the sleeves. Together we said good-night to the last remaining waitress and stepped out into the cool night air.

He took my hand and walked me slowly up the street. I could see the car waiting silently under the streetlight. I should have parked further away.

"This is me," I said quietly. "Thank you for a wonderful day."

"No, Ellie. Thank you." He took both my hands in his and looked into my eyes. "I have wondered for a long time what this would be like."

"Me too," I replied. "For weeks I have wanted to ask

you to meet me for coffee."

He smiled; his eyes sparkled under the streetlight. "Why didn't you?"

"Too scared," I said. "I would have been devastated if you'd said no."

There was something else too. What if he'd turned out to be a frog not a prince after all? I was more afraid of having my dream shattered than having Mac say no. The unnatural disasters I called relationships in my past warned that there was a high possibility of Mac being a frog. If that were so, my only option would be to renounce men completely and fulfill my mother's prophecy.

"Babe, I wouldn't have said no." He hugged me tightly; it was so easy being in his arms and hugging him back. So far so good, he was looking like a prince not a frog.

"I still can't believe it's you," I whispered. "...Before you go, take this." I pulled back from him a little and reached into my jacket pocket. From my wallet I removed a business card and passed it to him, "It's my card, so we can do this again."

"Definitely," he said and looked at the card in his hand. "Special Agent Gabrielle Conway."

"Yep, that's me," I replied leaning on the car door. I didn't trust my legs they seemed a little unsure at holding my weight.

"How many phone numbers does one person need?"

"Apparently I need four." A direct dial, a cell phone, a fax, and the division phone number; Just the regular amount. "Oh and my home number." I held my hand out for his pen which he pulled from his pocket and handed to me along with the card. I wrote my home number on the back and gave them both back to him. He smiled; a melt your heart type fantastic smile.

I watched Mac take out his wallet and put my card in it then remove a yellow card which he handed to me.

"I'll be home in four days. If I don't get lost." He chuckled. "Call me anytime, I mean that Ellie, anytime. We'll get together soon."

"Anytime?"

"Yes!"

"Okay. You might be sorry you said that."

"Never, I would never be sorry." He shook his head.

I studied the card in my hand just three-phone

numbers, home, work, and cell phone, "Cormac Connelly-technical analyst." I stopped and looked at him, "I remember the graphs you showed me one night, stocks, right?"

"Yep." He was still smiling but I detected something new in his eyes. "You know what?"

"What?" I asked, the look in his eye seemed sad, his smile began to fade.

"You know how some nights it's really difficult to say goodnight?"

I nodded.

"Never mind," he said quietly. "You should get on, you have a long drive, and it's after midnight."

I knew what he was going to say, he was going to say what I felt, neither of us was ready to say goodnight.

"Your drive is about the same, except I know where I am going!" I said.

Mac raised an eyebrow. "Always the fuc'n smartass."

He leaned forward and kissed me affectionately on the cheek. It took much self-control not to turn my head toward his kiss.

We stood looking at each other, our smiles dissolved as we both realized it was time to say good-night.

And that was how Ellie met Mac IRL.

All I Wanted Was You

(As told by Mac Connelly)

"Mac!" Caine hollered from the darkest of the shadows in the parking lot. "Mac!"

I cracked the window a few inches and called back, "What?"

Ellie's SAC, Caine Grafton, hurried over to my car, and leaned down by my window. "Keep your cell phones on." He sounded tightly wound but it wasn't without reason.

"Okay," I replied.

"Be alert. Watch for a tail," he said, his voice vibrating low in his throat. "Do I have to remind you how to drive?"

"No, sir," I replied, and could see why Ellie said he growled when he spoke.

"I hope you know what you're doing, boy." Caine looked past me to Ellie. "I want that report tomorrow. I want to know what other freaks from that chat room of yours could be lurking out here."

She replied tiredly, "You'll have my report first

thing. I'll email it."

"Mind how you go." He pulled back a bit and spoke to me, "Mac, I want to know what you know about this chat room too."

Caine slapped the roof of the car.

I nodded. Zapped the window closed.

And waved over my shoulder as I drove out of the lot and the hell away from the Interscape Café.

I didn't care if I ever saw another internet café; in fact, I hoped I never did.

Ellie's head was bobbing almost as soon as we left Lexington. I glanced at her but fell short when it came to saying anything. She rested her head on the passenger window; with eyes closed, she seemed almost peaceful. I left her to sleep and concentrated on the long drive back up to Fairfax.

A light misty rain had been falling for some time; the roads were slick. The headlights played across the wet surface. Streaks of light illuminated the centerline.

We weren't in any particular hurry and night driving wasn't something I enjoyed. I found myself a little more mindful of the conditions and the speed limit than normal.

Even so, my mind wandered into the tediousness of the journey. Ellie slept. A yawn escaped.

I switched the radio on, setting the volume low. I'd hit upon an eighties segment and recognized the opening of Bon Jovi's I Want You. It struck me as peculiarly fitting. Strange thoughts flowed from the darkness. Would we ever talk together in the chat room again? Or would we just pick up the phone and call? We did a lot of that anyway, but it was still fun chatting online during the late nights. Everything had changed. For the next week at least, we were going to be in the same house. Something unexpected tugged at me as I realized I would miss seeing Otherwisecat has signed in on my messenger – it was an odd sense of loss that I hadn't prepared for.

I checked my mirrors.

We were almost alone on the road, two cars away back behind us and one about forty yards ahead. In my mind, I could clearly see the little messenger pop-up. Consoling myself with the idea that we could still do that once things returned to normal, telephone or not, even if it was just for old time's sake and fun, took the edge off slightly. Four months ago, all we had was the internet, and then a bolt from the blue pulled us to the same place at the same moment in time. She was wearing a white tee shirt, dark blue jeans that day, had a gun on her hip, and an FBI badge hung around her neck on a black lanyard. White suited her well. She swept her blonde hair back behind her shoulders; it shone as it tumbled down her back, ending in soft waves an inch or above her waist. Her blue eyes danced with amusement under bangs that just grazed her eyebrows.

She laughed at me.

She laughed with me.

The day drifted into evening, flowed into night, and I hated knowing we had to say goodbye.

I sighed to myself. Dragging my mind back to the road as I fumbled one-handed for my cigarettes and lighter.

They were still in my pocket, because their usual place on the seat beside me was occupied.

I freed the pack, lit a smoke, and opened the window a little to stop the air becoming too foul.

My mind wasn't giving up on the bolt from the blue. The entire meeting was etched as firmly into my brain as the day I first said hello to her in a chat room two years previously.

There were times when my steel-trap memory served me well, and this was one of them. I sucked smoke into my lungs, adjusted the wiper blades to cope with the steadily increasing rain, and let myself drift back in time.

Whatever it was that drew us together that first evening was surprisingly strong. We had so much in common; it was if I were talking to myself at times. Who'd have thought I'd come across someone so like me in a poetry chat room?

My stomach growled loudly, reminding me how damn hungry I was. I felt Ellie stir slightly and figured she'd probably heard the noise.

"It's raining a little harder," I commented, to see if she really was awake. Rain bucketed down; I flicked the wipers to high.

"Yeah," she said, sitting up a little more and looking out the window. "Everything okay out there?"

"Quiet out tonight."

"Good."

"You hungry?" I looked over at her; she looked a little paler than normal. It struck me how cool it was that I could make that observation in person.

"Nope," she replied.

"Well, I am; we're gonna eat at the very next place we see." On second thoughts, I had a condition. "As long as it's not a cyber café."

"Good call."

She was uncharacteristically subdued in her responses. I looked over; her head was again resting against the window, with her face turned slightly toward me.

Her eyes closed.

I watched a for a familiar road sign. We'd been on the road a while and couldn't be far from home.

A cell phone rang. I grabbed the offending piece of technology from its holder on the dash and immediately recognized the phone number displayed.

Mom!

I took a nicotine-filled breath hoping to stop trace of annoyance from creeping into my voice as I answered the call.

"Your father is an idiot!" she spewed venomously into my ear.

"Hi, Mom." I sucked the life out of my cigarette, flicked the smoke butt out the window, and readied myself for whatever the problem was this time.

"This printer is a piece of shit! It keeps printing out

pages and pages of the same thing and your father says it's my fault!" She was furious and I knew it was going to be a difficult phone call.

"Mom, I'm not home right now. I can't look up the printer manual for you."

"Can't you just fix it?"

I moved the phone away from my ear and sighed. Yep, I'll just teleport myself right on over to their place and sort it all out.

"How many times did you click the print icon?"

"The stupid thing wouldn't print! It took several clicks before anything happened! I need a new printer!"

I wanted to yell, No, Mom, you need to stop clicking the goddamn print icon a hundred times and just wait for a minute, but I didn't. The worse thing was I knew she wouldn't listen to my simple instructions to remedy the problem.

I could still hear her clicking the buttons.

Dammit!

"Let it run, Mom, and stop clicking on things. I'm driving, I gotta go."

"You have to help me, you know about this stuff!"

What am I, a techie working for Hewlett-Packard?

No, I'm...

My thoughts paused as I considered the implications of disclosure.

Don't.

I'm a stock trader.

It was enough that Caine Grafton knew who I was. I figured he'd come up with a way to give me a badge and a gun without me having to break cover. He needed to hurry along with that. I didn't like how the situation with Carter had progressed over the last twenty-four hours.

"Mom, I have to go." I adopted a firm but patient tone. "I'll call you when I get home." I hung up the phone and turned it off. I knew she'd call right back; she always did.

I briefly considered how much shit I was going to get from my handler for getting involved with Ellie and the potential media circus that was bound to follow an FBI agent with a body in the trunk of her car. It wasn't the first time I had to ask the hard question: Was she worth it?

Again my answer was yes.

The other big one was if should I remain "Mac the stock trader" or tell her the truth and let the chips fall where they may. I was acutely aware that my decision would shape any possible future for us.

From the corner of my eye, I saw Ellie slump forward in the seat belt.

I pulled off the road and stopped the car.

"Ellie!" I called loudly but she didn't respond. "Ellie?" I undid my seat belt and slid across the seat, flicking the interior light on as I went. She wasn't just pale; she was ghostly white. I touched her face. She didn't move. I gulped as I placed two fingers under her jaw feeling for a pulse. I exhaled, realizing I had been holding my breath. At least she still had a pulse. I leaned closer and could feel her breath on my cheek.

"Ellie!" I called again. "Ellie! Wake up!"

Her eyelids flickered. I tapped on her collarbone.

"Ellie!"

A few seconds later, her eyes slowly opened. She lifted her head up and rested it on the window. Her hand covered her eyes. I figured the light was making them hurt.

"Hey. You feel okay?"

"No," she replied. "My headaches."

"What do you need?"

"Death," she muttered and almost smiled.

"Yep, that'll fix ya right on up." I was watching her closely. "How about food?"

"Maybe that would help."

"Maybe's ass." I turned the light out. "Better?"

"Yes, thank you."

Then I remembered I had a granola bar and a Dr. Pepper in the glove compartment. I grabbed them and opened the soda.

"Here, drink some of this, then eat this delectable and yet nutritious granola bar," I said, doing my best infomercial impersonation.

She took the soda and drank nearly half before handing it back.

"Mmmm, warm soda, delicious." She sounded more like her somewhat sarcastic herself.

I think my sales pitch was a little off on the bar. She opened it and looked none too thrilled at its contents.

"Eat the damn thing," I told her firmly. "We're only about half an hour from home."

Her hand flung out and smacked me on my arm. "I'll try and stay awake." She pulled a face and bit into the bar.

"Okay?"

She nodded. I made a mental note to keep a closer eye on her as we continued homeward. I knew she had vomited outside the café, and I knew we hadn't eaten much all day, but it still bothered me. Most people don't slump into near unconsciousness like that.

I pushed the thoughts back, determined that I would ask her later, and meanwhile would pay careful attention. Her hand touched my arm.

"You're frowning," she said with a small smile. "I'm just tired. Frowning isn't required. It was shitty twenty-four hours is all."

"I wasn't frowning, it's just how I look," I retorted with a grin. Her smile somehow made everything all right. "It's gonna be okay, Ellie."

She smiled as she checked her weapon. "Yeah, it's gonna be okay. Just another day at the office."

"They'll catch whoever killed Carter, and you have a week off."

She reached for my pack of cigarettes.

"I have a week off because Carter shot me and the bullet gashed my forehead," she replied lighting a cigarette and exhaling smoke.

She zapped her window down a couple of inches

and leaned her head on the cool glass. "His death doesn't figure highly on my give-a-shit-scale."

From the corner of my eye, I saw the look on her face; I knew his death didn't bother her half as much as how he died. I could tell she wanted to block out what had happened, but she couldn't, any more than I could. God I wanted to. I wanted to fix it, to erase the memory, and I didn't know where to start. That wasn't entirely true. Mac the stock trader was lost. Mac the special agent undercover knew exactly where to start and was powerless. It was a shit of a situation to be in. Controlling the urge to whack my head into the steering wheel wasn't easy.

She smoked a cigarette and watched quietly out the window. I readied myself for the impending shit-storm. I'd had two years and four months to figure it out and I'd spent most of it daydreaming. Now it was decision time.

I had forever wondered how her world revolved, where she walked, what her smile was like, her laughter and her tears.

I thought I would never know her like this. And now I'm taking her home.

Every Beat Of My Heart

I was humming but it wasn't long before the words popped out my mouth, "Ho ho fuc'n ho, what a crock of shit...we all work for Beatrice Claus and I'm sick of it."

"Not a fan of Christmas?" Mac asked with a wicked grin. "Or is it the lunacy of my mother that's riled you up?"

"I'm sure the day will be... interesting."

I stretched my arms above my head, and loosened my shoulders. I noticed a small twinge in my right shoulder blade. Nothing to write home about just an annoyance, a reminder of something I'd sooner forget. I dropped my arms and rotated the offending shoulder.

"Tired?" Mac asked cutting yet another piece of red paper adorned with Santa's and reindeer. His face suggested concentration on the task.

"Yeah. Looking forward to a break from work," I replied. "Seems like an extraordinarily tough year so far."

This was our first Christmas as a couple, an engaged couple at that.

Also, my first Christmas without Mom; which wasn't a bad thing, it was just different.

We had Mac's mom making a production out of Christmas.

Such a familiar pattern. Over the top decorating, everything has to be just right.

Too much food.

Color coordinated everything, including wrapping paper. I picked up another roll and cut a length off for the next gift. Best to get on with it. A fated resignation fell over me.

I dropped the roll of paper onto the thick carpet and commented, "Nice of your mother to supply the wrapping paper."

Mac grinned, wrapped another gift, and wrote on the tag. "And the tags."

Guess we were lucky to be able to choose our own gifts for the family. I wrote on another tag and stuck it to the parcel I'd wrapped.

"What time tomorrow?" I asked.

"Eight," Mac replied.

I didn't think he meant at night. "When's lunch?"

"About two."

I saw a long day in front of me. A long tortuous day.

I could tell Mac was enjoying the idea of having company in his tinseled hell. We both remembered the hideous wooden bows she was making earlier in the year. At my suggestion, she added everyone's names. Now the hideous things adorned the outside of their house – hanging on a large wooden Christmas tree she'd also made. We're talking ugly about fifteen feet tall – painted, lit with lights and hung with the God awful wooden bows which themselves were at least thirteen inches wide.

"A long long day," I whispered.

My trepidation escalated much like his mother's creation of Christmas. Beatrice Connelly loved Christmas. She loved it so much no one else had to.

"Don't suppose you wanna make coffee? Mac asked with a smile.

I raised an eyebrow. "Actually I do..."

"That'd be nice."

I held the bedroom door open to leave and his cat stalked in with her nose in the air. She eyed me with disdain.

"Won't she rip the paper?" I asked, kissing him as I

left.

"Yes, that's why she's not staying." Seconds later the cat and I stood staring at each other on the landing as the bedroom door closed. I shrugged. She skulked downstairs ahead of me. In the kitchen, I turned the coffee maker on then filled her bowl with cat biscuits.

I left the cat eating and hurried into the home office Mac and I shared. I pulled open a drawer in my desk – my hand sort out a small box hidden in the back. It didn't take long to find. I pulled it out and opened the lid. Nestled against the white satin lining sat a pair of citrine embedded silver cufflinks. They sparkled in the lamp light.

The coffee maker gurgled. The smell of fresh coffee made from one hundred percent Arabica beans wafted down the hallway. I found the small square of Christmas paper I had stashed days before in the office cupboard. Thick gold paper embossed with baubles of blue and silver. With care, I wrapped Mac's surprise gift and added a blue and gold gift card. I hid the present in my handbag that sat on the kitchen counter.

Under our tree in the living room sat large

wrapped boxes. In multi-colored paper – defying the orders that only one particular red paper be used this year. It was my tree in our home; I'd have what I liked. It was the rebel in me, or maybe the large dose of contrary I was born with.

There were presents for my father and brother, gifts for my best friend, Holly. Gifts for my colleagues slash trusted friends in Delta A, namely Sam, Lee and our boss SAC Caine Grafton.

The wall clock ticked.

I called up the stairs, "Dad and Aiden will be here soon." A car pulled into the driveway. "They're here ..."

The bedroom door opened then shut. Mac bounded downstairs three at a time and raced me to the front door. I won.

"You cheated!" he crowed.

"I did not," I replied turning the handle and trying to open the door. It stuck. I jiggled the door handle.

"Karma," Mac said. "You cheated and the door knows."

I tugged harder and it swung open.

"Did not."

Aiden was already unloading the bags from the

trunk. I spotted Dad fetching things from the back seat. My cell phone buzzed in my jeans pocket at the exact same moment as a black Ford Expedition pulled into the driveway behind dad's car. Lee leaned over the passenger seat and waved at me. I waved back and checked my phone. Sure enough, the text was from Lee. 'Not a social call - we have a case.'

Lee hauled from the car. "Howdy Colonel, Aiden," he said. My father strode over and shook Lee's hand. Aiden followed suit a reserved smile upon his lips. Mac's arm snaked around my shoulders as he whispered in my ear, "Lee's early."

I whispered back, "we've been called out."

"You're on leave," he reminded gently.

"It's not a job, it's a way of life." I kissed him. "I'll be back as soon as I can." A dark part of me hoped it was a messy involved case and I'd be busy until New Years.

"No problem. I'll hang out with the Colonel and your brother and hear all about young Ellie."

"There'll be a quiz later – take notes."

Lee coughed quietly, indicating he was close by. "All set?"

"One sec." I hurried back inside the house. I

grabbed my gun and holster, and snapped the holster firmly to my belt, then stuffed my ID wallet into my jeans pocket. Pulled on a jacket from the closet in the hallway, charged into the kitchen, and hooked my handbag over my shoulder. Ready I stepped out the front door into the cold afternoon air.

"Let's do it," I said.

Aiden glared at me. "It's Christmas."

"I know."

Lee held the car door for me. The three men waved from the doorstep. Half way down the street, I asked about Sam.

"He'll meet us," Lee replied flicking the window wipers on to swoosh snowflakes from the wind-screen.

"Snowing," I muttered watching more stick. "Why were we called?"

"Caine wants us in, that's all I know. He said you'd know why when we get there."

Oh, goodie a mystery. I held my sarcasm in check. "Where are we going?"

"DC."

No kidding Einstein. My phone buzzed, it was Sam.

"How long will you be?" he asked.

"On our way – trouble?"

"It's Christmas Eve, and this ain't good."

I hung up, leaned forward, and pressed a button on the dash. Our rolling lights sent beams of red and blue into the snowy air, the siren wailed. Cars began pulling off the road and out of our way. The drive took longer than it should have, with fresh snow falling and slippery conditions.

The radio station cranked out Christmas song after Christmas song, the temptation to sing along was high, but luckily for Lee I resisted.

Propelled through an open door by an unseen force, I found myself standing in the spacious foyer of a very expensive home. Two police officers stood inside the front door. They greeted us with nods and small smiles. In one corner of the room stood a huge tastefully decorated Christmas tree. Its lights twinkled and blinked, making the glass baubles seem alive. Presents wrapped in gold and silver with bows and iridescent ribbons piled high under the tree. I smiled to myself – someone else color coordinated Christmas. The strangled sobs of a young woman emanated from somewhere unseen to my right. They made me wish I were home. I'd even take my chances with Beatrice the mother-in-law from tinsel-hell. Sam seemed to emerge from an ornate wall, he hurried over to us.

We shook hands. He placed a large hand in the middle of my back, both to usher me forward and to keep me close so he could fill me in using suitably hushed tone. Lee stepped into place on the other side of me.

We walked slowly, listening to Sam.

"At one this afternoon Judge Meaghan Hartwell disappeared from her chambers. She was supposed to pick up her four-year-old son from daycare at one twenty. She never showed."

"Okay."

"There was no sign of a struggle. Her car is still in the parking garage, her phone, purse, and keys still in her desk drawer."

Even though we were further away from the sad sobbing, I could still hear it.

"Who is the crying woman?"

"The Nanny. There is a uniformed police officer with her."

"How likely that she's involved?"

"In my opinion, she's not."

Good enough for me.

"Anyone see anything? CCTV?"

"We have footage of the judge in the hallway out-side her office at five minutes past one with an unidentified male."

"That's something. Get an ID. Find him. Family?"

"Her husband, Peter Hartwell is..."

"...is a Special Agent." I thought the name Judge Hartwell was too much of a coincidence. There aren't too many agents married to judges. And with that in-formation in hand, I knew why we were called. "Has there been any contact? Any ransom demands. Is there any chance she could have walked away from her life, on purpose?" I was sure there hadn't, Sam would've told me that first.

"No, no, and no to the later."

I stopped and surveyed the distraught man holding a small boy on his knee.

They sat on a cream leather settee in front of us. I knew him. He knew me. This was no time for beating about the bush and taking it slowly.

"Peter –where is your wife?"

He held the boy tighter. "I don't know." He looked up at me, worry etched lines into his face.

"You're certain?"

"Conway, I have no idea where my wife is."

I wasn't about to ask if he'd killed her in front of the child. Peter's manner told me, he really had no idea. He wasn't lying. Good to know. Spouses are always the first suspect, whether I know them or not.

"Where were you between one this afternoon and... when the daycare called you to pick up your son?"

Sam interjected, "Two. They called at two."

"Working," Peter replied.

"Case?"

"I'm investigating a cold case. Someone came forward with information, a missing person's case from 1997."

"Where exactly were you?" I asked.

He placed the child on the ground. The little boy looked up at me and smiled. "My name is Alec. I'm four," he said holding up four fingers.

I smiled at him. "I'm Ellie and I'm too many to count," I replied wiggling a hand full of fingers at him. He laughed and ran off.

Peter handed me his notebook. "I was interviewing a witness."

"Great." He had an alibi and I really wanted him to

have one.

I hauled up information from a case I'd studied once.

It was an amazing blueprint of how scary stalkers can be.

"Peter I hate to ask this, but how long ago was the stalker situation resolved. I remember you were placed under the protection of the US Marshalls and they put you both into WitSec, yes?"

WitSec is the witness protection program, witnesses to crime, people who testify in major cases, are given new lives. In this case, the judge, and her husband were placed in WitSec to keep them safe from a stalker who used to be a special agent. They spent three years being moved from place to place before being able to return to their former lives. One thing about us special agents, we make the best stalkers. We're very good at finding people and have astounding resources.

"Yes," he said. "We returned to our lives three and a half years ago. We picked up the pieces in Richmond then moved up here to D.C."

"Any chance this is related?"

"None," he replied.

"Do you think this is about Meaghan or you?"

"I have no idea. I've given it a lot of thought in the last hour and a half. Mostly my work is cold cases. Meaghan works for the family court."

"She's a superior court judge?" Lee asked.

"Yes."

"Has she reported or mentioned anything untoward in the last six months?" he questioned. His voice remained smooth and calming. I watched and listened to Peter's reactions and answers.

"No. She made the move to family court because it was less likely that anyone would come gunning for her over granting an adoption or a divorce."

"Less likely but not impossible," Lee said and turned to Sam. "Is someone going over recent cases and psych reports?"

"Yes, Chrissy is in Judge Hartwell's office now. She's about half way through the cases from the last six months," Sam replied. "She's paying special attention to any cases with court ordered psychiatric assessments."

Music built up slowly until I recognized the song. The title track of an album I loved. Jon Bon Jovi's Destination Anywhere. I scanned the room, just making sure it was in my head and not coming from a stereo somewhere. The movie came to mind then twisted and warped, taking the underlying tragedy of the loss of a child and re-formulating it. A light went on in my head. Everything it illuminated was ugly. I had a horrible feeling this was revenge. And it was about Alec but it went wrong.

My questions came with urgency. "Does Meaghan spend much time with Alec? How much responsibility does the nanny have –day to day?"

I watched him swallow hard and knew he was trying to remain patient and helpful.

"Meaghan spends time with him every afternoon. Nanny has him in the mornings; she usually drops him at Meaghan's office at lunchtime. Today –she had a dental appointment so took him to daycare at about eleven and Meaghan was to pick him up from there."

"She drops him off at the office every day, except today?"

"Yes."

A feeling of cold dread was building.

My mind ran scenarios as fast as it could - building blocks of possibilities on the songs I could hear.

I held onto the feeling of a lucky escape for Alec but it mingled with dread.

"Peter, you know how this goes, and I do understand how tough it is to be the case and not be working the case." God knows I've been there before. "Sit tight. Can I chat with Alec? He might just hold the key." The second reason we were called; Kids like me.

He nodded. "Alone?"

"Will that bother him?"

Peter shook his head. "I doubt it, he's a happy kid and out-going." He pointed to the hallway and told me how to find Alec's room.

I looked at Sam and Lee. "I think we're looking for someone who had access revoked recently, if that's the case there is probably a police report attached to the court file. Or maybe this is someone who was turned down as an adoptive parent. Whoever it is I have a feeling the person is constantly at his or her lawyers complaining about every little thing while making themselves out to be whiter than snow."

Sam smiled. "Must've been some song."

"Was almost an entire album," I replied. I was thankful I didn't have to explain how I garnered so much information from an album that became a movie about grieving parents. I hurried off to find the boy. His door was open. He lay on a large rug playing with cars. One of those cool rugs that had streets and buildings woven in. I knocked. He looked up and smiled.

"Can I play too?" I asked.

"Okay. You can be the police car."

I grinned and sat cross-legged on the floor. Alec gave me a car and pointed out the police station. I quickly learned just how bossy and imaginative four-year-olds could be. I let myself enjoy the game for a few minutes before asking questions. The game continued.

We chatted and played. With a loud sigh, Alec rolled over onto his back and stared at the ceiling.

"Yesterday at the park a man was playing with some kids in the sand pit."

"Were they his kids?"

"I don't know. They played with me on the swings."

"What about the man, was he nice?"

"No. He said something to mommy and it made her cross and we had to leave."

Bingo.

"Have you seen him before?"

He nodded and sat up. "He goes to the park a lot. By himself and he plays with kids."

"Can you tell me what he looked like?"

Alec thought for some time. I saw he was struggling and offered help. "As old as your daddy?"

He shook his head. "Older, he had not much hair and wrinkles."

"Like Sam out there?"

"Is he the black man with a shiny head?"

"Yes."

"Older than him but some hair."

I smiled Sam kept his head hair free and shiny. He was Mr. T without the Mohawk or a darker version of Kojak. Scenes from the A Team vied for position in my mind with Kojak, the battle of who was cooler began. I much preferred the Kojak opening scenes to the A team. Kojak won. Gimme a lollipop.

I pushed the intrusive lollipop thoughts away and asked Alec another question. "What shape was he?"

There was a struggle within Alec, visible in his eyes and his expression. "I'm not supposed to say things that can hurt someone's feelings."

"It's okay Alec. You're allowed to tell, it will help me." He was so cute. Just a little boy still learning about social filters and how not everything we think needs to be vocalized, it's not an easy thing to learn. I still find both feet in my mouth more often than not.

He whispered, "He was fat, and smelly."

I suppressed a smile. Fat and smelly.

"Tall like daddy and my friends out there?"

He shook his head. I could see his mind working. "When mummy stood up, she was taller than him."

"You're very helpful, Alec. Very helpful."

"I know." He smiled. "The little boy called him something, a name, but I don't know what it was. The little girl she called him Nonno."

"Nonno?"

"Yes."

"Can you remember what the boy said?" Interesting that the girl called him Nonno, Italian for grandfather.

He thought some more and shook his head. "No. I don't think the boy liked the man. When the man tried to hold his hand he pulled it away and went and sat further away."

"What about the girl, did she like him?"

He nodded. "I think so." Alec took a ragged breath. "He was a mean man. I accidentally broke the girl's sandcastle. I didn't mean too, I fell over. He was mean." Alec began to cry. "It's all my fault. Mommy didn't pick me up and it's all my fault."

I touched his shoulder. "No, it's not. Come and see your daddy. I'm going to go and find your mommy. You have been very helpful." I had my fingers crossed behind my back. I didn't want to promise his mother's safe return but I knew that's what he heard.

I took his hand and led him back to Peter. Peter scooped him up into his arms. I told everyone about the park.

Lee, Sam, and I stepped away briefly. "We're looking for a fat smelly man with very little hair, probably Italian origin – one child with him called him Nonno."

Sam chuckled lightly. "Anything else?"

"Yeah – how tall is Judge Hartwell?"

Sam flipped some pages in his notebook. "Five foot six."

"In that case we're looking for a short, fat, smelly, balding man." I heard my voice crackle but ignored it. I could laugh later once the judge was safe.

I walked back to Peter and Alec. "Alec was amazingly helpful."

Sam and Lee joined me. It's as if they knew I was in danger of bursting out laughing.

"I'm waiting for a call back have alerted Chrissy – and given the description," Sam said with deadpan delivery. I couldn't look at his face. I knew I'd see the glimmers of humor behind his eyes that no one else saw.

My phone rang. It was Chrissy. She had a name and an address for us. Cyril Maletta was the man we wanted to speak to. Judge Hartwell revoked all his access to his five-year-old grandson the morning before. The order was effective from December 24th.

Chrissy also sent me a picture our technicians had retrieved from the CCTV. I showed the picture to Peter and Alec. "Do you know him?"

Peter shook his head. Alec nodded his voice crumbled as he whispered, "That's the mean fat smelly man."

I looked at Peter. "I'd ask you to come, but Alec needs you. We'll be back."

Tears ran down Alec's face. I shoved my hand in my jacket pocket and pulled out my orange iPod. I adjusted the volume for little ears and handed the ear buds to him. "Do you like Christmas songs Alec?"

He smiled. "Yes."

I hit play on the movie screen and passed him the iPod. Moments later, his head was bobbing to Bon Jovi singing Run Rudolph Run.

"I'll grab it when we get back. There's nothing unsuitable on there – just Bon Jovi, Grange, Elvis, and some Michael Bublè."

"All things his mother listens to. Bring her home, Ellie."

We both watched the boy for a second. Peter leaned closer and whispered, "You think he was going to take Alec?"

"I do."

Sam, Lee, and I lit out like scolded cats. Lee was on the phone as I snatched the keys from his hand and jumped into the driver's seat. In my rearview mirror, I saw Sam slide into his car. We pulled out of the driveway with full lights and sirens. Lee snapped his phone shut and fastened his seatbelt. Good call.

"SWAT is on their way. I expect them to get there at least fifteen minutes before us."

"In this weather on Christmas Eve – we'll be lucky if we get there within half an hour." Snow flurries made visibility tricky.

From the corner of my eye, I saw Lee's hand reach for the radio on the dash. I knew what he was doing before he spoke. My focus was the road and the traffic – I listened to him speaking.

"This is Special Agent Lee Davenport. Requesting backup at Lindenbrook Street, Fairfax."

The radio crackled then a voice erupted. "Fairfax police. We have two cars in the area, what do you need?"

"A road block, no one in or out of Lindenbrook except SWAT, FBI and police."

"Message understood."

Another crackle preceded a question, "All noise?"

"Negative. Stealth approach."

"Message understood."

As I drove, the radio buzzed and crackled. Police cruisers were responding from all over Fairfax County. We let comms field the rest of the calls. Ask and you shall receive. A song drifted then settled in my mind. Please come home for Christmas. I felt a weight on my shoulders that came from knowing I had to return a mom to her little boy, alive.

We approached Lindenbrook Street and a police cordon. The SWAT truck was already inside and standing by. They had control of the scene; more exactly Special Agent Danny Godwin was scene commander.

I zipped my jacket up against the freezing wind and the blowing snow.

Lee, Sam, and I clambered into the mobile SWAT command center.

It was cozy bordering on close.

"Hey Danny, seen any movement?" I asked.

"Hey Ellie - not yet. My team is trying to get cameras into the house now. How sure are you that your man is in there?"

"I'm not, but I'm hoping he's home and has our missing judge with him."

I saw his shoulders slump. "Ah crap doodle, I hoped it wasn't really a hostage situation on Christmas Eve."

"I think this Cyril Maletta man wanted to grab the judge's kid but picked the wrong day." I watched the computer screens. A picture popped up on one. It looked like a living room. There was a man pacing back and forth and someone sitting in a chair. We could only see the top of a head. "That could be her. Don't suppose we can get a camera in on the other side of the room so we can see?"

Agent Godwin smiled. "We may be able to." He spoke quietly into the headset he was wearing. Giving directions to get a camera where we could see the person in the chair. "They'll do their best; it's a matter of getting it in silently. Not easy if they have to drill a special hole. That camera there is utilizing a hole made by the phone company for a telephone line, under the house."

Five minutes later another picture popped up on the screen. A clear picture of Meaghan Hartwell. Her hands taped to the chair arms. Her feet taped together at the ankles. Beyond her, a Christmas tree all lit up.

"Is he smoking?" I asked peering closer at the screen.

"Yes," Lee replied. "He's also got a gun in his back pocket."

Danny pressed a few buttons on the keyboard in front of him. He gave us sound. Cyril was ranting at Meaghan. Going on and on about how he was the best role model for his grandson and how he should be allowed to see him whenever he wanted to. He waved in the direction of what we assumed was the Christmas tree and spoke of all the gifts he'd brought him. Meaghan remained silent, even when he yelled in her face. The man's right hand strayed to his back pocket. Then relaxed.

"Let's call him and get a dialogue going," Lee suggested as we watched his hand reach for the gun again. "What's his freaking name again?"

"Cyril Maletta. Screw that - take him out. Anyone got a shot?" I said looking at Danny. "He's getting too worked up. I'm not risking the judge's life."

He spoke into his headset again. Seconds later word came back that two snipers had clear shots. 'We have a non-fatal resolution.'

Danny looked at me and gave the order, "Take him."

I watched the screen as the man toppled to the ground. Meaghan slowly looked up at the window but never made a sound.

"Let's go," I said pushing the command center door open. Wind pushed back. Ice stung my face.

"He's down, wounded but not dead," Danny called after us followed by, "He's in custody and being removed."

When we reached the living room, an agent was

cutting the tape from Meaghan's wrists and ankles.

We waited.

The room stunk of cigarette smoke, both fresh and stale. The furnishings were ingrained with years of tobacco smoke. It was unpleasant especially as I'd only given up myself less than a month ago. The stench strengthened my resolve to never smoke again. A new song played. I wish every day could be like Christmas. Sometimes it's a shame no one else can hear my music.

Freed at last the woman stood and smiled as us. "I know you, don't I?" she asked me.

"You do. We were all at Director O'Hare's barbeque last summer. Are you all right?"

She nodded. "Alec?"

"Safe with Peter."

She smiled. "He wanted Alec. He wanted to teach me what it was like to have someone take a child away."

"I see he didn't take your ruling well," I replied. "Come this way..." I led her from the house. Outside in the fresh snowy air we could breathe without choking.

"He didn't take it at all well. Pedophiles rarely do."

A paramedic wrapped a thick grey blanket around her shoulders. "Before you arrived he'd spent an hour telling me how much he loved his grandson and how the boy enjoyed his demonstrations of affection." She wore a grim expression. "I just wish someone had listened to the child earlier. That depraved man's lawyer had everyone believing he was a saint. It took a kindergarten teacher to uncover the truth and get the boy to talk."

I shuddered.

No one told me the guy was a pedophile, but then we didn't have a lot of time.

Priority was to bring the judge home safely.

I looked at Lee; he shook his head in disgust.

Guess he hadn't heard either. I looked over at the gurney where the man lay. Alec was right. He was short, fat, balding, and smelly. There's a winning combination in a man.

"Sam – can you follow the ambulance and get a statement from Maletta, then arrest him for kidnapping a superior court judge and post a guard. Lee and I will take Judge Hartwell back to her family," I said.

Sam grinned. "My pleasure." He checked his watch. "Your dad still making eggnog?"

"Hell yes. Get moving – can't guarantee it will last long once Lee and I get home."

I said goodbye and thank you to Danny and then to the police officers who answered our call for help. I extended an invitation to each member of SWAT and each police officer to come home for eggnog.

It was the least I could do.

***

I had a feeling Christmas wouldn't be so bad after all. My feelings aren't always right. There was no song warning me of impending doom when Eddie rolled in the back door of the Connelly's house drunk at eight-thirty in the morning. His short chubby wife, wearing four-inch-stilettos, what appeared to be stage makeup and the smallest dress I'd ever seen, followed him. I didn't know fabric could stretch that far without ripping. A wardrobe malfunction was imminent and vowed to be the hell out of the way when it happened. Their two fat almost teenage kids barreled in behind them and headed right for the Christmas tree.

Bob Connelly grabbed them before they could rip

into the presents and sent them off to sit on one of the large couches with a candy cane each.

Like they needed more sugar.

It was going to be a day to forget. Eddie and Angie sat on opposite chairs. Eddie slurped a beer. Angie batted her long fake eyelashes at Mac. My father and brother talked to Bob. Beatrice banged about in the kitchen refusing all offers of help. The kids fought over presents they hadn't seen yet.

Mac pulled me closer so I was leaning against him. He whispered in my ear, "What's under your sweater?"

I giggled, "Shouldn't you know?"

"Smart ass. You're carrying." He tapped my side with his fingers.

"Maybe ..."

"Maybe's ass. You wore a gun to Christmas dinner ..."

"Eddie is here, hello. You think I want to be unarmed with that drunken octopus in the room?"

I settled back and watched the chaos unfold in front of me. Beatrice came in yelling about the ham not being right. Eddie fell off his chair. The kids punched each other. Bob separated them. The fat boy snatched a present, opened it, and threw the contents at his father. Angie spent the whole morning trying to attract Mac's attention. Every now and then, my hand strayed to my hip and rested on the butt of my Glock.

Christmas wasn't so bad after all.

Next year it'll be at our house with a strictly limited guest list. Us

I Just Want To Be Your Man

"Ellie!"

I ignored the insistently whiny voice behind me and kept walking.

"Ellie!" he whined louder. Several people turned around. I did not.

"Wait up!" he hollered, as I ducked into the nearest big store hoping to disappear into the New Year's Eve crowds. There I stood in a desolate store. Four hungry sales assistants bore down upon me from various points. I glanced over my shoulder. He'd be running in any minute. I scanned the displays of television sets, computer gear, and stereos and realized I was doomed. Or not.

The first assistant stopped abruptly in front of me, pertly announcing herself, "Hello, I'm Casey. I'm here to help you today. Is there anything in particular I can show you?"

I wanted to tell her to take a breath and button off the enthusiasm. Instead, I smiled, flashed my badge, and asked, "Is there another way out?"

Casey's bright smile faded slightly. "Follow me," she said. The other three assistants all vanished, and I imagined them tidying the pristine displays and frantically trying to look busy. Casey led me across the store to a door marked 'staff only'.

"Thanks I appreciate it."

I looked into the store as I closed the door and observed Eddie.

He'd just huffed and puffed his fat self into the store. This time my future brother-in-law's excessive weight worked in my favor.

Before long, I was back in my office, smiling to myself.

"This came while you were out," Sam said and threw a file onto my desk. It was a precision throw, and the file stopped right in front of my keyboard.

I dropped my bag on the floor beside my desk, sat down, and opened the manila folder bearing the FBI seal.

"Thanks Sam," I muttered as I picked up the pages within the folder.

I read the information contained in the file, twice. Took careful note of the photographs included and the request from local police for help.

"Did Chrissy pass this on?" I asked looking at the photographs again. They didn't get any better with subsequent viewings.

"Yes, and Caine approved our involvement."

Serial crime. That was usually what we dealt with. Although Christmas Eve we worked a kidnapping, as a special request. Now here we were again, being asked for help. An appeal from a police department to investigate a spate of dead Santas. Christmas was over. Three Santas were found shoved up chimneys, in three different houses over three days. No one wanted there to be a fourth Santa. For the life of me, I could not figure out how anyone shoved a grown man up a chimney like that.

"Lee?" My eyes would not leave the pictures.

"On a coffee run. Figured you'd need some when you read that file," Sam replied.

I finally dragged my eyes up from my reading to be met by his customary wide grin. I turned the pictures over, so I could no longer see the black boots and white fur trimmed red trousers hanging from within fireplaces.

"This is why team A is the best of Delta," I said picking up the phone from my desk and pressing four numbers. Chrissy answered on the second ring. "Hey Chrissy. Can you call the police chief who wants us to lend a hand? Tell him we'll be there this afternoon."

"Sure Ellie, what will you need?"

"Access to all the police files pertaining to this case and officers involved, forensics reports, somewhere to work and lots of coffee."

She laughed. "I'll pass it on. Travel plans?"

"We'll drive."

"ETA?"

I glanced at the clock on the wall. "Two hours. Depends on traffic volumes of course and road conditions. Is it still snowing?"

"I think so."

Chrissy said goodbye. A shadow fell from the doorway, a shadow that smelled of one hundred percent Arabica beans in Styrofoam cups. "Great timing," I said as Lee handed me a cup of steaming black coffee.

"I ran into Eddie," he said.

"With your car?" I knew it was too much to hope for but still I hoped for a post-Christmas miracle.

"Sadly no. He was in the coffee shop and whining about how you ignored him this morning and then ditched him in an electronics store."

I shrugged.

"Sorry you didn't run into him with two tons of steel."

Lee perched on my desk. "What is that guy's problem anyway?"

"You mean besides being fat and stupid? Is that not enough?"

Lee laughed. "For a normal person it would be, but I don't think there's much normal about that man."

"He's been hounding me ever since Christmas day," I replied. "Did I tell you about that?"

Sam shuffled his chair closer. Lee leaned in and said, "Nope."

I took a sip of the coffee and filled them in on how Eddie had attempted to grope me in the kitchen while his horrendous wife was hitting on Mac in the living room. What a family. The only blessing was they weren't blood relatives of mine. Eddie was Mac's brother. So in theory not my problem. Should I accidentally shoot one of them I could probably scream 'just cause'. If only theory translated into cold, hard reality like it did in my head. I sipped more coffee and listened to Sam and Lee discuss how best to shorten

Eddie's life. It warmed my heart.

After a few joyful minutes of listening to the delightful sounding tortures they devised, I threw my empty cup into the trash bin by the door and scooped the file folder and contents into my bag. By the time I scooted around my desk with my bag over my shoulder both men were out the door and waiting in the hallway.

We traveled in one car. I spent more time with the photographs of the unfortunate Santas.

"What the hell does this town have against Santas?" I mused aloud. "And why is someone stuffing them up chimneys post-Christmas?"

I read the information regarding the homes where the Santas were found. The families were all away for the holidays. Neighbors bringing in the mail, watering plants, and feeding cats discovered the bodies. Police found sacks with each Santa, filled with items possibly from the houses: jewelry, small electronic items, and money. They were waiting on families to return from vacation to identify property. None of the houses had alarms or security cameras.

So there was a plague of burglarizing Santas and a possible vigilante hunting them down and shoving them up chimneys. Or maybe a super hero. Bam! The theme song to The Greatest American Hero blasted in my head. I frantically searched for volume control as the 1980's television series hijacked my brain. Clear as day I saw Agent Bill Maxwell ask the reluctant superhero Ralph Hinkley if he'd been using his 'magic jammies' to shove naughty Santas up chimneys. I struggled with the bizarre interlude until it became apparent that Ralph Hinkley and his 'magic jammies' were probably responsible for the whole Santa fiasco and we may as well go home.

"Ellie, you're singing," Lee said swiveling in his seat to look at me.

"Singing?" I replied.

"Uh huh," Lee said. A grin spread across his face as he belted out, "Believe it or not, it's just me..." Reaffirming my feeling that an American Idol he was not. Sam laughed.

"Oh, sorry," I replied.

"Any reason?" Lee asked.

"Was just trying to figure how anyone could shove a grown man up a chimney...," I said.

"... and it made sense that a super hero did it," Lee added matter-of-factly.

"Seems plausible." I glanced out the window at the traffic. "A super hero or someone with superhuman strength. And not just any super hero – The Greatest American hero. The reports state that some of those Santas weighed close to two hundred pounds."

My cell phone buzzed on my belt. I answered it and heard Mac's voice. "Will you be home for dinner?"

"Don't think so. We've been asked to consult on a case."

"Okay. Just checking. I'll save you some then."

"Thanks. What time is the party?" I knew. I just wanted Mac to know I hadn't forgotten we were going to a New Year's Eve party. This was his first Delta party and he was looking forward to it.

"We'll leave about nine," he replied. "Should get us to the pickup point in time."

"I'll see you then."

"Stay safe Ellie."

I hung up. Sam spoke, "You both are coming to the party? Now that's going to make the night more fun."

I smiled. New Year's Eve Delta parties were legendary. Held in a secure location and organized by Director O'Hare. It was our chance to let our hair down and let loose big time, with no repercussions.

"We're here," Sam said pulling into a car park. Snow fell in fat lazy flakes. A police officer bundled inside a thick jacket hurried through the falling snow to meet us. We walked into the building introducing ourselves.

"We have a room set up for you," Officer James Johansen said leading the way behind a desk and through a glass door. We stood in the warm interior of the police department; five officers greeted us from various areas of the large room. They were friendly and welcoming. A Christmas tree in a corner twinkled with silver tinsel, lit by blue and red flashing lights. Christmas cards hung all over the walls. It was quaint. Officer Johansen reminded me a little of Robert Culp, when he played FBI agent Bill Maxwell on The Greatest American Hero.

Johansen opened a door and ushered us into a room with a large conference table in the middle. On the table sat a small fiber optic Christmas tree, also flashing blue, and red. Four places were marked with file folders and coffee cups waiting to be filled.

"I appreciate the trouble you've gone to, Officer," I said sitting on one of the chairs.

"Thank you for coming, Agent Conway. Your SAC

seemed to think you'd be able to offer some insight."

I smiled. My SAC did, did he? Well he was right. I knew something. Sam and Lee would catch on fast. James Johansen and his police force seemed clueless. What if we really were looking for Ralph Hinkley? Stood to reason. Only a super hero could do this, or maybe a cop. I was surprised that Maxwell hadn't already figured that out.

I checked the smile before it became an insane giggle. Pulled back a notch on the nutty thinking and flipped the file in front of me open.

"Max... sorry, Johansen – if you could rustle up some coffee for these cups I'd be truly grateful," I said.

"Coming right up, Agent."

"Smooth Ellie," Lee commented as Johansen hurried away shutting the door behind him. "Wasn't the agent in that American hero show called Maxwell?" I knew he didn't really want me to answer that.

"What do you know?" Sam asked leaning across the table at me.

"Every household is away on vacation - none stopped mail or newspapers but they did all notify the police department they would be away. What's sadder is it's even more obvious than that." I pulled a list from the file I'd brought with me and laid it on the table. "This is what Chrissy turned up. They're being burgled in the order in which they notified the department."

Lee whistled through his teeth. "Where's the cop connection? Santas are cops or the killer is a cop? Or someone who works here, maybe a civilian?"

I grinned. "Don't ya think if the Santas were cops that we'd know? Someone would be screaming cop killer from the roof tops."

"You think a cop is the killer?"

Sam rocked back in his chair. "Someone gave the list to a local pack of thieving Santas, set them up, and then killed them off. Nice."

"Why the Santa suits? I can understand that before Christmas but after Christmas..." I was more thinking aloud than wanting an answer. My fingers tapped on the desk. The door opened and coffee wafted in. "Someone walking around a neighborhood dressed as Santa after Christmas is going to draw attention."

Johansen and the coffee pot paused over my cup. "I'll ask around and see if any Santa suits were stolen, I'd know if suits were stolen in my town. Maybe neighboring towns or even out of the county."

"Good idea, Johansen," I replied. "Can we get a look at the last crime scene?"

He nodded. "Y'all wanna go now?"

"Sooner the better," Lee said, standing up.

A sigh escaped my lips as the delicious aroma of coffee teased me. It'd have to wait. I wanted to catch the Santa killer and go home. There was a party to attend. We drove to the scene, following a police car all the way, while I wondered if The Greatest American Hero lived in a small town in Virginia and got his jollies by stuffing Santas up chimneys. But they weren't Santas, they were just burglars. Burglars dressed as Santas. Burglars who hadn't actually removed anything from the houses. There was no actual theft. So they were just men. Men dressed as Santa.

I called Johansen on his cell phone. "Did your medical examiner find anything unusual on the clothing or bodies?"

"Unusual how, Agent?"

Oh God. He was going to make me say the words.

"Was there any sexual activity recorded. Anything to suggest recent sexual activity?"

"They. Were. Men. Agent," Officer Johansen replied

76

with slow precision.

"I know that, Johansen. Was there any evidence of sex?"

"You think the killer was a woman?"

I groaned internally. It was like pulling teeth but not as much fun. He announced we were almost at the house. I opted to leave my questions until I was face to face with him, or maybe just go straight to the medical examiner myself.

We examined the scene, the tool marks on the back door suggested someone broke in. No way of telling if that was the deceased or the killer. I walked from the back door to the living room, taking careful note of everything I saw. Then I spotted something. Nothing huge, nothing extraordinary. Just two long stemmed glasses seemingly missing from a set in a glass-fronted cabinet.

I walked back to the kitchen and opened the dishwasher. Two glasses. But nothing else.

"Sam, see if you can find any prints these. There are no water drops in here; it may not have been turned on." In the trash, I found a wine bottle. "There's a bottle too, Sam. Could be something on that." I turned to Johansen. "The other scenes, were they the same?"

"Yes."

"Can we go and look at them?"

"Sure." He looked slightly uncomfortable. Gas maybe. He shuffled from foot to foot then rocked back on his heels, looked out the window and said, "What was it you were saying on the phone about sex?"

"Was there any evidence to suggest sexual activity on the bodies?"

"No," he shook his head. "No woman could have stuffed them up the chimneys."

"I'm not suggesting a woman did this." But I reckon one could, given the right motivation –let's not test that theory today.

He peered out the window while he spoke, "You saying there was some sort of funny business going on?"

"I'm asking if it was possible," I replied in a soothing manner.

Funny business obviously didn't sit well with Officer Johansen.

He shrugged. "Sure, I guess it was possible. There's all manner of freaks in the world. You want me to call the medical examiner for you?"

"Please," I said with a nod.

After a quick phone call to the ME, I had him checking all the bodies for semen. I also had him confirm that there was wine in the stomach contents of all the dead Santas. There was no evidence of drugs. Death was by asphyxiation. No soot was found in the mouths, throats or lungs suggesting the Santas were not breathing when inserted in the chimneys. The team moved on and visited each crime scene, finding two long stemmed glasses at each, either in a dishwasher or draining on a dish rack, and an empty wine bottle in the trash, the same wine a Nobile de Montelpulciano. He certainly didn't have cheap drinking habits.

Back at the police department in our little room, we finally got our coffee and it was worth waiting for. I pulled all the pieces we had together. Sam ran the one partial print he lifted from a wine glass. The ME confirmed there had indeed been sexual activity, he found semen. That was great news for us. It meant DNA, but it would take a few weeks to get those results back. Meanwhile we needed to have something to compare to that DNA.

A suspect would be awesome.

"You think the Santas were lured to the houses, don't you?" Lee asked as I drank my second coffee.

"Yes."

"They're not burglars then?"

"Nope."

"How would someone meet another person willing to dress up as Santa?" Sam said, watching the screen on his laptop and waiting for a fingerprint match.

"Online, my pretty," I replied and typed 'Santa fetish' into Google. "Man that was a mistake, who knew I'd get so many results. Over four million." I began narrowing the search parameters until I came across some chat rooms that looked likely meeting places. "This is just downright unpleasant."

Within minutes, I was chatting with several people, all who wanted me to dress like Santa so they could play out some Santa fantasies. I was asking as many questions as I could without tipping my hand. From what I could gather none of them had ever meet anyone. One knew of someone who had regular offline meetings and gave me the URL for the chat that he hung out in and his screen name, Blitzen. They said he was pushy and slightly scary. Neither of them was tempted to take him up on his offers, they preferred the safety of the cyber world. I thanked them and followed the link to the chat room. It didn't take long for Blitzen to start private messaging me. Guess he smelled the new blood. I chatted, flirted, drank more coffee, and waited for him to make his move.

Sam's laptop bleeped. He got a hit on the fingerprint. I scurried around to his side of the table, leaving Lee to chat to Blitzen while running a ping and trace. "Ellie, the print came back as Nathan Johansen. His address is the same as James Johansen's."

"Is he a cop?" I asked the coffee in my stomach was bouncing about like it was on a trampoline; I hated the thought of a cop going bad like this.

"No. He works for a marketing company but he was a cop, hence the prints on the system."

"What's the relationship between him and Officer Johansen?"

Sam pulled up James Johansen's personnel records. "They're brothers."

I looked over at Lee. "Set him up, Lee. It'll take too long to get DNA results. Let's catch him."

Lee grinned. "Ping and trace comes back to Johansen's address. The computer he's using is registered to Nathan Johansen." A few minutes later Lee announced he had a meeting with Blitzen at an address. Blitzen told Lee it was his house. The address didn't match the address on record for Nathan Johansen.

"Get this... he wants me to bring my own Santa suit. We don't need to look for stolen suits. These guys must've all had their own. Guess you would if you got your jollies dressing like Santa."

We checked the address with the list we had of empty houses. It was the next one after the last crime scene.

"Let's roll, we need to be in place within the house before Johansen shows up," I said grabbing my jacket, and bag. "Sam, bring Officer Johansen don't tell him what we're doing and don't let him make any calls. It's doubtful he's involved but I don't want our man tipped off even by accident. If you could ride with him, then Lee and I can go on ahead."

"You want local law enforcement involved at all?" Lee asked.

I shook my head.

"This guy was a cop, this is a small town. Let's do it ourselves, then there's no backlash for the police here. Let's get wired for sound before we leave."

Sam opened his attaché case and took out a small box. From the box, we each took an earpiece and a small microphone that could be clipped anywhere and not noticed. Most often, we clipped the microphones under the lapel on our shirts. Moments later, we were all on the same frequency and could hear each other even if we whispered. The days of talking to our cuffs and obvious wires were over.

I left with Lee, while Sam was looking for Johansen and asking him for a ride to meet us.

Lee and I parked down the street from the house and cautiously made our way on foot. The plan was to install some bugs, both audio and video, in the house and for me to find somewhere to wait. The plan was not for Lee to be in a dangerous situation without backup.

It didn't take me more than a few seconds to tumble the lock on the backdoor of the very pretty Folk Victorian style house. I walked through the entire house, as quickly as I could, and made sure there was no one lurking in the basement or ready to pounce from the attic. It was a nice house, and felt like a happy home. Photos hanging on the walls suggested a nice normal family. Mom, Dad, and three teenage kids. I hoped we could catch the Santa killing freak before he sullied this home with his nastiness.

"Lee, I'm going to wait in the laundry room. There's enough room for me to hide and I can still get to the living areas quickly."

"Okay, Ellie. I'll head off and wait down the street."

I looked at my watch. "He didn't give us a lot of time; guess he can't wait for Santa to come." Lee shuddered. "I'm gone; see you in about twenty minutes. Holler if something happens, meanwhile."

Lee let himself out the backdoor, and it locked automatically. I disappeared into the laundry room and fired my laptop up; it was time to tune into the bugs in the house and watch. I loved to bask in the joy of Satellite internet. On my screen, I could see the backdoor, kitchen, living room, front hallway, and front door. Lee knew not to deviate from those rooms no matter what. Listening to Sam talking to James Johansen in his patrol car made the time pass quicker. They were close. I heard Sam tell Johansen to pull over and wait, at the same time I heard the sound of wood crunching and giving way. The backdoor swung open and a man entered the house carrying a bottle of wine and a crowbar. He closed the door firmly and left the crowbar by the back door. In the kitchen, he placed the wine on the counter. I watched as he searched cabinets, and then placed two wine glasses on the counter with the wine bottle. He opened the wine, and took a small vial from his pocket, tipping the contents into one glass. Nothing had shown in the medical examiners toxicity screen.

It could be something already in the body naturally. Gamma-hydroxybutyric acid sprung to my mind first.

I whispered, "Do not drink anything, Lee. He tipped something in the glass. Maybe GHB."

Lee replied, "That'd sure make it easier to kill someone. I'm coming up the front path."

I settled down to watch Lee's arrival on the screen.

The front door opened.

The man we assumed was Nathan greeted Lee with a hug and a smile. He was certainly big enough to insert a man in a chimney. Lee stood six foot six that gave me a good height comparison. I picked Nathan to be six foot four. He was well built, looked like he worked out a lot. His eyes rested on the black bag Lee carried. It was supposed to contain a Santa suit but it was just spare clothes, since we didn't have a Santa suit on hand.

They went through to the living room. I watched my screen, the camera planted in the living room gave me a clear view as Nathan produced two glasses of wine and handed one to Lee.

Lee put it down and began asking questions about some photographs he saw on a side table. Nathan steered him back to the wine. Lee broke off on another tangent. Nathan picked up Lee's bag and handed it to him. "I've a naughty boy, Santa," he said in a grating whisper.

"Yes, you have, Blitzen. Your name is on the top of my list." Lee held the bag up and appeared confused. "Where do I change?"

"Down the hall," Nathan replied, taking a swig from his glass. "You haven't touched your wine," he admonished gently.

I whispered to Lee, "Take it with you."

Lee took the glass and the bag down the hall. Over his shoulder he said, "You better think about how naughty you've been, Blitzen." Lee would need a lot of bourbon later to erase today's activities.

Lee found his way to the laundry room and we

watched the screen together.

Nathan relaxed on a sofa, drinking his wine.

"We done here?" Lee asked me, his voice full of hope.

"Let's see what happens when you go back out there without the Santa suit?"

Lee grimaced and did as I suggested. Nathan was not happy to see him in street clothes.

"Where's your suit?" he demanded, leaping to his feet.

"I must've picked up the wrong bag," Lee said apologetically, crossing the room and giving a good impression of someone slightly intoxicated.

"Where's your glass?" Nathan asked. The hard edge to his voice melted as Lee staggered slightly.

"I don't know, I left it somewhere, I guess." Lee plonked down rather heavily on the sofa, making sure Nathan couldn't see the earpiece he wore. Nathan crawled up beside him, his hands working their way under Lee's shirt.

"You ever been strangled, you know just a little?" Nathan whispered into Lee's ear. He deftly unbuttoned Lee's shirt.

"No I haven't," Lee replied, slurring his words.

"I think you'd like it." His fingers ran down Lee's chest and paused on his stomach.

"No," Lee replied, trying to stand up. Nathan was on him, using his weight to hold him against the sofa. "Get off me," Lee said, pushing him.

"Don't be like that, it's fun, you'll like it," Nathan said, his hands slid up over his chest, reaching out to Lee's neck. I wanted to burst in and save him, but I knew Lee could handle himself. At that point it seemed better to let Lee try for some kid of confession.

Lee jumped to his feet, hauling Nathan with him.

He held the man at arm's length. I don't want to play with you anymore."

"Maybe you should have another glass of wine," Nathan replied smoothly.

"No," Lee said.

I left the laptop, moved silently to the backdoor, and carefully dusted the crowbar for fingerprints, finding several. I lifted them and scurried back to the laundry room. It only took a few seconds to photograph the prints and upload them to my laptop, then compare them to the prints we knew belonged to Nathan Johansen. They were a match. I went back to the kitchen, and waited ready to enter the living room. I heard Sam telling Johansen we were about to catch the Santa killer.

Nathan complained that Lee was no fun. He should've had the Santa suit. "Have another glass of wine. Relax a little. You're a big man, no doubt you can handle quite a few glasses."

I felt a disruption in the force as Lee controlled the urge to squash Nathan like a blowfly.

Lee spoke, "One of my friends met someone the other day that was into Santas, and no one has seen him since. It wasn't you was it?"

"I shouldn't think so; you know how many of us are out there. You've been in the chat rooms." Nathan's voice took on a suspicious edge. "Were you just looking for your friend?"

"No, never mind, fill my glass. We don't need Santa suits..."

Nathan appeared delighted by the news. "Come snuggle with me, we'll forget all about the world."

I whispered in Lee's ear. "Here I come. He's not going to talk, and we have a match with his prints."

I walked into the living room.

Nathan jumped.

Lee joined me on the other side of the room, leaving Nathan looking quite confused.

"As much fun as this was, Nathan Johansen, you are under arrest for murder," Lee said. I handed him my handcuffs to use. He moved in on Nathan, twisted one arm behind his back, closed the cuffs around his wrist, and repeated with the other arm.

Sam and Johansen appeared in the doorway. The shocked look on Johansen's face said it all. He had no idea what his brother had been up to.

"Why?" Johansen asked, as Lee marched Nathan toward to the door.

"Because I could," Nathan replied with a sick grin. "As long as everyone happily denied who I really was I could do anything."

I looked at the brothers; I saw the crumbling of lives as the decades spent living in denial collapsed in front of them.

Sam's huge hand rested on my shoulder he spoke quietly to me. "Let's wrap this up, quick. There's a party waiting."

Officer Johansen looked back at me from the doorway. "Thank you," he said with caustic correctness.

I didn't reply. I had nothing to say that could make the man feel any better about what had happened in his small town.

We headed back to DC pushing the Santa case out of our minds.

There was a New Year to welcome.

It was time to party.

Every Rose Has Its Thorn

My office walls provided a safe zone as I sat at my desk flicking aimlessly through a pile of case files. Lee and Sam were out on an investigation. Caine was in his office. A buzz of voices and phones ringing from the bullpen penetrated the walls as muffled sounds of life.

With a sigh I leaned back in my chair. Tiredness washed over me. It wouldn't hurt to close my eyes for a minute.

Staring at the ceiling I found myself counting glow in the dark stars as a small voice whispered, "You're not in D.C. now, Ellie."

The room was the same as when I was young. Nothing had changed. Except me. My laptop sat on my star-covered bedside table.

Grey light squeezed through a gap in the curtains. It was barely morning.

I dragged the covers back up off the floor where they'd fallen during the night and then picked up the laptop. With a sense of coming home, I logged into my own little world. I wasn't expecting anyone to be around at the crack of dawn; my checking in was more about missing the comfort of my virtual home than wanting to interact with others.

The screen changed to the familiar blues of Cobwebs' chat room.

My name sat at the top right-hand side of the screen with a golden hammer next to it.

The gold hammer meant I owned the room, and I bestowed hammers upon people I trusted to moderate in my absence. With the help of friends we'd created it as a place where poets could share their work.

Already there were several good mornings typed into the main chat box. The list of names below mine surprised me. Obviously no one slept much last night. I scanned the list twice looking for Galileo, while replying to those who had said hello. He wouldn't be there, not that time of day and not on the day he was heading to Virginia Beach on vacation. A private message from Stormy lit up bright red at the bottom of my screen. I clicked it open.

Stormy: You seen Carter lately?

An odd question for such an early hour. I found myself muttering at the screen, "Nope and I don't wanna see him either."

I typed a more pleasant reply.

Otherwisecat: No. You do mean in here, huh?

Stormy: Yeah. We may have a problem with him. He's been a little spooky and freaked Bitter out a few hours ago.

That's not so odd for Carter.

Otherwisecat: I'll change the room code. Recreate the room so he isn't a gold hammer anymore. Tell the other gold's not to hammer him.

It's no real surprise that he's gone freaky. I'd come across him in life and odd is the nicest thing I could say about him.

Otherwisecat: Stormy, you seen Galileo in the last few hours?

A whoosh of air escaped my lips and I realized I was holding my breath waiting for her reply.

I really need to get some guts here and just ask him to meet me for coffee someday. It's hardly inconceivable. I heard it then, the loud clucking inside my head.

Stormy had replied while the clucking occupied me.

Stormy: Nope. Why don't you two just get together?'

Because I'm chicken, but why hasn't he asked me? Hmmm? Maybe he doesn't feel like I do. I gave myself a good hard mental thwack; no sense thinking stupid thoughts when I know otherwise. The clucking got louder.

Otherwisecat: I'm chicken.

Stormy: LOL you scared? I don't believe it.

Thank God, our relationship medium was a computer and she couldn't see the rising color in my cheeks. I bet she was really laughing too.

The main chat window captured my attention; a girl was posting a poem. It was beautiful, well-crafted, and full of delicate imagery. When she'd finished I commented on the imagery and heart that went into the creation of such a poem and thanked her for sharing with us. Stormy lit the bottom of my screen up.

Stormy: Wow, that kid is amazing.

Otherwisecat: Sure is.

We could do with more like her, and then maybe I wouldn't be the most hated host in the chat system. I don't think I am the most hated, Stormy, Bitter, and I probably share that honor. Our zero tolerance policy gets us a lot of flak. We don't tolerate rudeness, bright-colored fonts, gore, or graphic sex and violence.

Galileo has the same zero tolerance but doesn't tend to get people's backs up as we do.

Guess he's just a nicer person.

I watched the room respond to the new poet, ready to privately admonish anyone who overstepped the line. We all agreed on disciplinary actions: two private reminders to be nice, one public, and then I kick them out.

If they come back and behave badly again they face a twenty-four-hour ban, and after that it can easily become permanent. People should be safe in our room to share their work without harassment by others. I yawned and stretched. Everyone was playing nice.

Morning noises in the house reminded me I had to get moving.

I'd been in Richmond working for weeks on a particularly nasty serial rape case. Yesterday Delta A arrested a suspect. Last night we finished up the paperwork. The case was closed. Confession made and corroborated. Suspect my ass. He was guilty as sin and twice as ugly.

Best of all, instead of rejoining Delta A back in Washington, D.C., right away, I was going home to Mauryville in Rockbridge County.

I typed my goodbyes into the main room.

Then typed a private goodbye to Stormy.

Otherwisecat: Tell Bitter blocking Carter from her messengers would be a smart idea.

Stormy: Okay. Why don't you email Galileo and ask him out for coffee. Which she followed with a smiley face.

Otherwisecat: I can't.

Stormy: You will and get back to me tomorrow telling me you did.

I poked my tongue out at the screen and then sent her a cheeky smiley face.

Stormy: Do I have to do this for you?

Pure panic rose as I answered: No!

Stormy: Then do it.

Otherwisecat: Bye Stormy, I gotta go do the breakfast thing with the family.

And get the hell out of Dodge.

An hour later I walked into the kitchen. Dad was nowhere to be seen.

Sun streamed in the window, bathing my mother

in a golden glow as she busied herself at the counter. Light reflected off the loose fitting scarlet silk shirt she wore, her long golden blonde hair clipped back into a low ponytail, her expensive jeans pressed to a sharp crease.

My mother was immaculately groomed as always no matter what the time of day. She seemed so normal, like everyone else's mother, as she made breakfast.

Deception of appearances.

A large cloud meandered across the sun, casting odd-shaped shadows in the room. I sat at the kitchen table. Dad had already eaten. His coffee cup sat almost empty and his plate bore the remnants of scrambled eggs.

"Where's Dad?" I asked, hoping he was coming right back.

"He had errands to run."

Damn looked like I was eating with Mom and without a buffer zone.

"I'll call him later from home then." Home resonated in my head. Home. Alone. Miles away from people. If I closed my eyes I felt like I was already there.

"Do you want eggs, Gabrielle?"

"Sure," I replied.

The spell was broken; my shoulder muscles tensed.

For a moment, it felt like I was staring down a gun barrel.

I recognized Mom's interrogation opening and could barely begin to imagine what she'd come up with this time.

A plate appeared in front of me. Obviously, there had been no question in her mind about breakfast. My eggs were accompanied by a glass of orange juice.

I forced my shoulders to relax but could do nothing to alleviate the tightening ball in my chest.

She sat across from me at the kitchen table. Mom's slender fingers toyed with the edge of a napkin, repeatedly smoothing the same section of fringe. I reached out for a bread roll, willing my hand not to shake.

Buttering the roll to within an inch of its life helped a little. I managed two mouthfuls before Mom spoke again.

"Do you have an eating disorder?"

I put down the roll and started on my eggs. With a death grip on my fork, I forced myself to eat a mouthful knowing she was watching me with abnormal interest.

Had I not been subject to the same accusation on a regular basis since early childhood, it may have been funny. But I had and any amusement factor had long since worn off. My internal voice made a frantic attempt to pacify my rising temper, "Come on Ellie, just one meal, surely you are adult enough to get through one meal in a civilized manner, then you can go home?"

The attempt was thwarted with a resounding, 'Hell no!'

"Gabrielle, do you? I'm sure you've lost weight."

My eyes met hers, my stomach churned, and I hoped my voice was calm as I replied, "No, Mom."

"You look skin and bone. There's nothing to you." She scrutinized me. "Your face is drawn and sharper than I recalled."

Oh God! I wanted to scream, "This is how I look this is how I have always looked!"

Compared to the internal screaming and stamping I was doing, my actual response was almost civil.

"Can't you let me be how I am?" I shoveled another load of eggs into my mouth to stop myself saying anything more and watched her from under my bangs.

"You're too skinny."

I swallowed my mouthful – she wasn't going to let it go.

"I'm really sorry I'm too skinny for you, Mom," I said quietly. "What is it you want from me?"

"Eat more! For God's sake, Gabrielle, you are wasting away. Perhaps we should be looking at some sort of help."

My fingers tightened on the fork. My mind chirped, Here we go again.

"Luckily you don't need to concern yourself, Mom. As a Special Agent I have regular psychological exams," I replied, then hissed under my breath, "So I don't end up like you."

"What do you mean by that?" her eyes narrowed as she found an opening she could use.

What a way to find out her hearing was as sharp as ever.

I sighed.

"Don't push me. Mom."

"I think I deserve an explanation."

I felt powerless to prevent my outburst.

"I'm having trouble with your sudden interest and

concern. Let's face it your track record lacks in that department."

"You ungrateful little witch!"

"That's right, Mom, I'm ungrateful, and you gave me so much to be grateful for. The times you'd disappear for days on end while Dad was at sea and came back wearing the same clothes you left in and stinking of booze. Those times you took off and left Aidan shut in a fuc'n cupboard until I came home from school to free him. The sudden concern you displayed when you wrote notes to excuse me from gym class... why was that again, Mom?"

Mom fidgeted with the fringe and focused on the sugar bowl.

I continued, "Oh, I remember, so no one would see the bruises you left on my body."

Her voice faltered as she whispered, "You were a clumsy child."

"No, Mom, I wasn't."

"What is it Gabrielle, anorexia or bulimia?"

"Neither, Mom, I'm not ill." Then something occurred to me; maybe she needed me to be ill to make her feel better. "Do I need a mental illness to make me interesting, Mom?"

She snapped, "Don't be ridiculous, Gabrielle." Mom raised her chin slightly. "Bangs at your age? What are you hiding from?"

I groaned internally. She wasn't done yet.

"Let me eat my breakfast, please Mom."

She said, "Are you gay?"

Scrambled eggs lodged in the back of my throat. I grabbed the glass of juice and took a big swallow.

"What?"

"Are you gay?" she repeated, her piercing blue eyes narrowed as she stared at me. "Because it's okay to be gay. Your father and I just want you to be happy."

"No."

She was determined to make me much more interesting than I was.

"Gabrielle, you're nearly thirty and you have never even mentioned a man."

"I don't want to discuss this with you." I picked up my fork and tried to continue with my breakfast, quietly hoping the eggs would choke me. My hand shook as I lifted the fork to my mouth.

I don't want to discuss anything with you!

"Look at you, you're a wreck. You need a man."

Lowering my fork and raising my eyes to Mom's, I

spoke with calmness that took me by surprise, "I'm tired, Mom. I'm very tired."

"Perhaps you should consider a different career with more civilized hours."

"I like my job."

"You should eat more."

All hope evaporated with her last comment. My jaw muscles tensed and head started to ache. My right hand slid to my hip, bringing a moment of relief followed by a deep sigh. My gun and badge were useless against my mother; time to invest in silver bullets.

"When did you last have sex?"

"I said. I. Do not. Want. To. Discuss. This."

Pulling my gun and decorating the walls of my parents' kitchen with my brains would've been more enjoyable than her questions, but choking to death on eggs seemed like a more reasonable option.

"Have you ever had sex?"

I desperately attempted to relax my taut muscles. Pressing my fingers to my temples, I massaged gently, hoping to ease the headache before it became thunderous. "Have you, Gabrielle?"

I let my arms rest lightly on the table and tried for a reasonable tone, "I'm not ten years old anymore. I don't have to answer to you."

"No, you were much more respectful when you were ten."

I pushed my plate away and stood slowly, making deliberate eye contact with her. Biting my tongue didn't work and there was no way to keep the truth in now, "That wasn't respect Mom. That was fear."

I stepped back from the table.

She never missed a beat, "That's right, Gabrielle, run off and vomit."

"Actually, Mom, I am going to vomit then have sex with the first woman I can find and the next man I come across – just in case I swing both ways, and maybe if I'm very lucky I'll develop some totally fascinating mental illness so you can feel good about yourself. I'd hate for you to think I was a regular normal person, lord knows you can't cope with normal!"

Her lip trembled. I had to get out before she started crying.

She watched me close the car door from the kitchen window. In my mind, she appeared like an ogre but in reality, she was simply a sad human being. It was hard to see the insanity as tears trickled down her beautifully made-up face.

If only she could disguise the mental illness as well as she could her advancing age.

Sheer stupidity on my part coupled with extreme tiredness – never a good mix around Mommy dearest. I didn't wave as I drove away.

It was hard to know what made me relive the last meal I'd shared with Mom, three years after her death. I had a brewing theory that everything hinged on my actions that day. My inability to deal with my mother led me to a coffee shop in Richmond instead of going directly home. There I met Mac for the first time in the flesh. Two months later Mac and I were an item; the Son of Shakespeare was on a killing spree and killed my mother along with a long list of people I knew. A while later Mac and I were married. He joined the FBI and a year later while working with me in Delta A was killed. That breakfast with Mom started a chain of events that left me feeling gutted.

Maybe it was mortality. Maybe it all hinged on the fragility of life. Maybe nothing lasts forever, not even scars. Maybe if I'd handled Mom better, Mac would still be alive.

Mac's voice drifted from the car radio. "Maybe's

ass."

My smile was fleeting. "Maybe's ass."

A song buried his voice under the recognizable opening bars of Poison's Every Rose Has Its Thorn. I listened hoping the song would make me feel better somehow. It didn't. All it did was remind me that his voice was fading and one day I wouldn't be able to remember what he sounded like.

My focus turned to the road. I wasn't driving from Richmond to Rockbridge.

I sat in my car outside a house in Georgetown with absolutely no idea how long I'd been there. House lights twinkled up and down the street. The song finished.

I grabbed my bag from the passenger seat and got out of the car. The door opened as I raised my hand to knock.

Special Agent Noel Gerrard of NCIS smiled a little as he said, "You're on the wrong side of the river."

"It's been a long day." It's been a long few weeks.

"Wanna drink?"

I stepped inside and let the door close behind me. Bathed in the warm glow of electric light, I followed Noel through the house to the kitchen and dropped my bag on the floor by a chair. He placed two tumblers on the table and produced a bottle of whiskey from a cabinet. I liked his kitchen. The wood felt cozy.

We sat at the table with the bottle between us.

"I was wondering if you were ever going to come in," Noel said, pouring three fingers of whiskey into my glass. His eyes flicked to mine.

"Me, too."

"Thought you were on leave."

"Didn't wanna rattle around an empty house, so I went into the office to catch up on paperwork."

"I heard you were asleep at your desk."

Guess the not sleeping at night is catching up with me.

I raised my glass. "To Mac."

"To Mac."

Glasses clinked. The amber liquid slid easily down my throat.

"To hindsight."

Noel put his glass down. "I'm not drinking to second-guessing and twenty-twenty retro vision. Gimme something else."

"I got nothing." I drained the glass. Noel filled it again.

He held his glass in the air. "To those that made us who we are today."

"To Mom."

If Tomorrow Never Comes

The stereo lights flickered and music filled the room. I closed my eyes as Garth Brooks sang. It took me a moment but I recognized the song. 'If Tomorrow Never Comes.'

Mac used to love Garth Brooks. I listened for a little bit but the lyrics broke my heart all over again. Sometimes tomorrow never comes. I turned the stereo off and sat in silence. It wasn't long before my own thoughts created a commotion.

Words rolled around in my mind. They'd been taunting me for over a year, the poem became muddled and disjointed. I wasn't even sure if it was the beginning and I didn't want to open our poetry book to check.

I whispered, "When the world has done, lost in time too tired to run, a safe place came to be..."

My engagement ring slipped on my finger. I straightened it, pausing as the princess cut diamond sparkled in candle light. It still captivated me, even now that our life together is nothing but memories stolen by the night. Time sliding dividing light, jumbled thoughts trapped inside, who I was suddenly died.

I remembered the day he pushed the ring onto my finger. A smile reflected back at me from the television screen.

My smile.

Candles flickered.

My wedding ring sent tiny pools of iridescent light across the ceiling. They almost looked like butterflies. I poured another glass of wine.

A voice I knew too well and missed too much spoke, "Wine? We out of bourbon?"

Words fell from my mouth as my eyes searched the room, "Bourbon holds too many memories."

"How about tequila? You always loved te-kill-ya." His voice flowed warm and smooth, like he was right there.

Feeling his words surround me I shook my head. "Mac..." Again, my eyes flicked around the room but I never moved.

Seemed I was always looking for a ghost and he was always finding me. A faded reality trapped in my head.

I looked down to find the TV remote in my hand, my fingers pressed buttons, and the screen changed. Flashing pictures on the screen. Jingle bells flooded from the set of a cheesy sitcom Christmas party.

Christmas party.

Shit!

I jumped to my feet knocking the coffee table and spilling wine on the rug. I hurried to the kitchen and grabbed a fist full of paper towel. Moments later the rug was dry and the paper towels sodden. I tossed them in the trash. The house would smell like a winery later.

My keys and cell phone were on the kitchen counter, I took them.

I blew out the candles in the living room and switched off the television.

The room plunged the room into darkness.

No more glittering lights to play upon the ceiling as I moved my hand. Darkness folding images like cloth. Out in the hallway I put on a long woolen coat and hat, then wrapped a scarf around my neck and tugged on soft purple leather gloves. The threat of snow hung heavy in the air when I arrived home an hour earlier. I didn't expect it to have changed much between then and now. Unsure reality dripping through a dream.

On the way into the city, I tried to raise some Christmas cheer. It wasn't a happening thing. I found an unexpected car park right outside the venue and even that didn't change things. I knew I'd have to fake it. So fake it I would. At least I didn't have to walk miles in the freezing air. Snowflakes drifted down and stuck to the windshield.

Happy fuc'n Christmas.

Cassie was waiting by the door. She smiled warmly and hooked her arm through mine.

"It's starting to snow. Come on, the kids are waiting," she said squeezing my arm.

"How'd you know I'd come?"

"You wouldn't miss this." She looked quite smug when she added, "Carla is waiting for you."

And suddenly the fake smile was replaced by the real thing. So I wouldn't miss it on purpose for Carla's sake. Touching a heart giving hope.

"Did Sam and Lee make it?"

"You think they'd miss the Butterfly Christmas party? Are you mad?"

Free food and kid's games.

"Nope."

And maybe yes, yes I am mad.

Stark raving bonkers.

Silver and gold butterflies hung from tinsel, high up on the ceiling. I didn't know if the butterflies were real or imagined. The room sparkled. A deep breath revealed an undertone of teen spirit with top notes of Christmas. Pine trees and eggnog.

The noise level within the conference room settled at dull roar. One end of the room boasted an enormous Christmas tree. It took up the entire corner of the stage.

"Stage?" I questioned Cassie.

"We thought a stage would be a fitting platform for that huge tree, and make it easier for the talent to perform."

"Talent?"

Now we have talent. A neon flashing light went off in my mind and Mac floated just out of reach waving his arms yelling, "Warning, warning."

Cassie laughed.

Lost in Space? Oh no, not Lost in Space. Oh, crap. Talent. Stage. Mac warning me. This is not boding well for a pleasant evening with friends, family, and kids.

"No. Not me. No way." I looked over my shoulder for an exit. No exit just Sam and Lee closing in fast. Long legs, long strides. I had nowhere to go. Sam's smile shone. Panic set in. A hand clamped down on my shoulder and another gripped my other shoulder. Cassie released my arm.

"Traitor," I hissed as she moved toward the stage.

"Chicky Babe," Sam crooned. "Looks like the kids want to hear some poetry."

"Uh huh," I replied. That ain't gonna happen.

"Come on Ellie, Cassie wants you up there," Lee said steering me by the shoulder. "You're up, you'll be great."

The three of them laughed as I grew nearer to the stage and the horror. Cassie scooted ahead. I watched her climb the steps.

There was a parting of the sea. Children lined the way, clapping, laughing, and being kids. I felt sick.

Cassie was talking into the microphone. Words became airborne; they flew on little silver tinsel wings all over the room. A few dive bombed me. I ducked involuntarily. Sam's hand gripped my shoulder a little tighter. He leaned in and whispered in my ear, "You all right?"

"I'm okay," I replied wishing it were so. If I wished hard, there could be a Christmas miracle and I might not make a complete dick of myself on the stage. Then it dawned on me. They were taking the mickey. There was no way my friends would let me spout dark morbid poetry at innocent kids. I relaxed just a little but I still had to venture onto that terrifying stage.

The crazy enthusiastic clapping was punctuated by squealing. I turned and there was Carla Torres, squealing with joy along with the other hundred and fifty or so young people in the room. She waved frantically at me. I waved back. My eyes scanned the area beyond the seething mass in my wake. Obviously, someone cool just walked in. I expected to see Rowan Grange, Lorenza Ponce, or maybe even Jon Bon Jovi. No one was behind me just Lee and Sam.

Man kids are excitable.

The clapping continued as I climbed up to the stage.

There I stood – dwarfed by a giant tree (I'm not short) and in front of a microphone.

Behind me was an impressive drum kit.

There were also guitars and other equipment,

mostly hidden by the tree. I guessed there was a surprise in store for the kids. The real talent. My mouth was dry. Sand dry. I imagined trying to speak and the sand falling from my mouth all over the stage. The sand became glitter sprinkling magic.

An older deeper male voice spoke and came closer. Then another joined in. Mac's father and mine materialized from the tree and introduced me to the kids.

There was no escape. Instead of Lee and Sam, I had the fathers flanking me. With no clue if my voice would be heard through the sparkling sand, I spoke into the microphone. A little voice inside told me I could do this.

Do it for the kids. Show no fear.

Part of me couldn't believe we'd come this far. The kids who looked up at me from the floor had better lives because of a vision Mac and I had. Mixed emotions confusion reigns. Holding love in shaking hands.

A golden butterfly tumbled from above and landed on the microphone. I wanted Mac. I wanted him to know that I'd never missed anyone the way I missed him. The butterfly whispered, "I miss you too." I wrapped my heart around his words and cradled the fragile sound. They held strength and I needed to capture every ounce.

I waved to Carla and took a breath before injecting as much joy into my voice as I could. "Thank y'all for coming down here tonight. I'm truly delighted to see so many of your smiling faces."

You could've heard a pin drop. Such focus. And all of it on me. I swallowed hard and pushed the panic aside.

"I'm happy I could be here. I can see some familiar faces out there, are y'all looking forward to Christmas?" A cheer went up. "I guess that's a big fat yes! When I came in, it'd just started snowing..." Noise reverberated off the walls around me as they all yelled some more. I held up a hand, silence fell. "I'm going to turn this here microphone over to my Dad. I think he has a few things to say to y'all." I stepped aside as Dad took my place. He took the microphone and walked to the edge of the stage with it in his hand. Dad spoke to the kids about the Butterfly Foundation and our goal for the coming year. I stood with Mac's father. We watched the kids respond to my dad and the joy in their faces as he wished them all a merry Christmas. From the back of the room, I heard bells.

The kids turned. Double doors opened and Santa waddled through dragging an enormous sack.

Dad put the microphone back in the stand as Cassie whispered in my ear. "We have a surprise for the kids. Every one of them is getting a gift."

Mac's Dad grinned. "We're not talking girl or boy age-12 type gifts here Ellie."

Santa dragged his humongous sack ever closer, chatting to kids as he made his way to the stage.

Cassie continued, "We went through every one of the online profiles and we shopped for each and every kid."

So that was what the family had been doing while I was hiding from the world and burying myself in work. A lid banged shut. Dust rose. The picture in front of me was that of a coffin wearing a badge.

"That's impressive," I replied, blinking to clear the dust and remove the image of death. Santa reached the bottom step. I went to help him with the sack. Under the bushy white beard, I detected a facial twitch. "Caine?"

"No, it's Saint Nick. Who'd you think?" he growled.

"A night of surprises. I hope someone has a camera."

He grumbled under his breath and twitched so hard the beard jumped. A large padded chair appeared on the stage. Caine settled in it. The microphone was adjusted and moved closer. From his bag, he pulled a scroll and unrolled about ten inches. A smaller chair was placed on the other side of him. I figured that was for the kids. We don't do the sit-on-the-fat-man-in-reds knee thing. It's just wrong. The whole Santa thing irked me. Here we spend years teaching kids not to accept things from strangers ... but an old fat man who says 'ho ho ho' is okay? I put my feelings regarding Christmas aside.

This Santa was my SAC not some semi-toasted mall Santa or some sick bastard who had a Santa fetish.

Sam and Lee appeared in the wings, they carried a large sack each. The sacks were placed beside Caine. I really hoped there was some kind of order to this, reading out a hundred and fifty names and finding the matching gift was going to take all night.

Cassie pulled my arm gently. "Come on."

I was happy to escape the stage. Caine began calling out names. Lee and Sam, and both fathers had the job of finding the gifts. I'd escaped without having to spout poetry. Thank God! The only Christmas poem I knew by heart was one I wrote years ago and it really wasn't for children.

Angels on the Christmas tree.

Christmas time is here again
Pick up the knife and count to ten
There's no light in my eyes,
Hold the knife until the pain subsides
Sparkling lights and twinkling stars
Tinsel, streamers, and emotional scars
All mix and mingle on Christmas day
The angels of death watch me play
Christmas time is here again
Pick up the knife and count to ten
Candy canes and mirrored balls
Blood drips down the painted walls
Santa Claus and reindeer shit
Elves, toys, and their little bits
Gather around the Yuletide log
I wish that I had become a frog
Christmas time is hear again
Pick up the knife and count to ten
Popcorn threaded on pieces of string
Stabbing people is my thing.

I looked at my hand. No knife.

Cassie noticed. "Problem?"

"Nope."

"Good, figured you and I could have a drink while the men folk do the Santa/gift thing." She led the way through a door into a smaller room with a bar that housed decidedly adult beverages. "Eggnog?"

"If it's not the non-alcoholic one you have out there for the kids." I nodded my head to the outer room. I could hear Caine's gruff voice call out the first name.

"Pretty sure this stuff is made with Irish whiskey."

"Then, yes please!"

I perched on a stool and took the offered cup.

"Merry Christmas," Cassie said taking a sip.

I followed suit. It was hard to remember a time when I actually meant those words. All was quiet where we were, apart from the occasional squeal of delight as gifts were received and the wrapping subsequently torn to pieces. Sounds of life that filtered through the wall.

"The kids are having fun," she commented.

"That is the point." I took another hefty swig of eggnog. "How'd you get Caine to do the Santa thing?"

"That wasn't me, he volunteered."

Ah, there we have it, the Christmas miracle.

"Christmas makes people do weird things," I replied.

"It brings out the best in people," Cassie said.

Not necessarily. Christmas's when we were growing up were interesting. Ones when dad was deployed off shore were horrible. At least when he was home we had Christmas. Mom didn't always attend. Some years she was in hospital, others she was off her meds and gone both were preferable to the Christmas's she came too.

"You're such a Pollyanna." My drink was gone.

"It's not a bad thing to see rainbows, you know." Cassie's voice held promise and even joy.

She saw rainbows where ever she went and it astounded me.

A social worker who still believed in her ability to change the world one kid at a time, after everything she'd seen. She still believed people could change and she still believed in happy ever after.

"I see rainbows. I just don't let them color my world."

"And I do?"

"Oh yeah, you are fully rose tinted." I smiled. "It's

what we love about you the most."

"I see the good." She started to defend herself then realized I wasn't picking. I was just stating what I saw. "You see the bad… we're two halves."

I poured another drink for us both. Mine disappeared a little too fast.

"Two halves make a whole," I replied. "Ying and Yang."

She gave me a hug and refilled my drink. "You and I need to talk about Carla."

"Is she all right?"

Cassie smiled. "She's wonderful, as you know." Her serious face replaced the smile. "I want to discuss her future. Your future."

Oh here we go. The hard sell for Christmas. Maybe if I mentioned the butterflies that have become part of my life she'd re-think her plans to create a family of Carla and me. I watched as a silver butterfly floated near the ceiling. It soared effortlessly. One by one more joined in and as I watched enthralled, they spelled out, 'What do you got?' I got fuc'n nothing, that's what I've got. Just like that, the magic butterflies filled my head with the name I'd been looking for all year. Unsure reality becomes a crazy glued dream.

"Ellie?"

"What?"

"Did you hear me?"

"I don't think so."

"How much did you have to drink tonight?"

I grinned. "I'm not drunk, I was thinking about something." From the other room I heard music. Recognizable. I looked around for an exit.

Recognizable and familiar the music wrapped the past in a silvery glow. It pulled at me and made me want to stay but there was something I needed to do.

"How do I get out without going through there?" I asked pointing at the source of the music. I could barely believe I was going to walk away without so much as poking my nose in to see the talent.

"You can't leave!" Cassie was horrified. "Carla was looking forward to spending time with you tonight."

"She'll be fine with Sam and Lee. I have to do something."

She pointed to a long curtain. "There is a door behind that; it goes to a hallway that leads to either the stage or the front lobby."

"Thanks. I'll be back. You'll see."

I took off at a fast walk, as I hit the lobby I checked my hip. Relief stormed me as I realized I was still wearing my gun. Always good to be prepared. I left the building and ran to my car. The cold air and the eggnog combined to form a potent mixture. Probably the two wines I had at home didn't help. I wasn't driving anywhere. Mac's voice repeated some lines from an old poem in my head, "We sometimes start over, a new life begun. Nothing is permanent, everything changes, it's the way that it is as life rearranges."

It didn't make a lot of sense. I slid into the passenger seat and made a call.

"Lee?"

"Chicky, problem? You don't seem to be in here. Thought you liked this band?"

"I do, wanna stall them for me, so I get to use my badge to meet cool people for a change?"

"Sure I'll get Sam to sit on that lead singer."

"Thanks, I appreciate it. Now – the problem."

"What do you need?"

"You to drive for me, I've had a few drinks. I'm in my car – out on the street."

"On my way."

We hung up. Twenty seconds later Lee climbed behind the wheel and shoved the seat right back.

"Where we going?"

"Work, we're going to work. I need to use the computer."

"Now? Christmas party. Caine doing his Santa thing. One of your favorite bands playing, and you wanna go to work. This isn't meshing. What's up?"

"I got a name. I think I can find Carla's uncle. I'm looking for Jonathon Francis Torres."

"You pulled his name out of thin air?"

"Yeah – I did."

It was a quiet drive.

Lee didn't pursue how I came by the name. He was well used to me pulling answers out of the air.

I sat behind my desk and started running every known search program hoping to locate Jonathon Francis Torres.

Carla never knew her father's family.

There was no record of any relatives but I had a feeling there was at least one. I'd been looking ever since that night that changed our lives. With all the resources I had at my disposal I still came up empty on a relative until the music, the talent, and another butterfly visit. Ironic or just weird?

Lee perched on the edge of my desk. We were both watching the screen as numbers, faces and names flashed by at a rapid rate.

"You sure it's him?"

"Yep."

With that something flashed and beeped on the screen. I clicked on the image. A photograph opened. A picture of a young man. Possibly in his late twenties. He looked like Carla. Same eyes and mouth. Information began to fill the screen. A death certificate. Jonathon Francis Torres was deceased. He died fifteen years ago. Two years before Carla was born.

"He's dead?" Lee muttered pointing to the screen in front of us.

"I don't think so." We sometimes start over, a new life begun.

"He doesn't want to be found?" Lee asked.

"Feels that way."

I started opening files from a list at the bottom of the page.

They lead to a rabbit warren of more files. Every alias I touched was fascinating.

Several had long rap sheets. His choice of employment swung from CEO to nightclub bouncer.

This guy was clever.

None of the aliases overlapped.

 Some of them were active for years, indicating he lived for extended periods as certain people. There were gaps between 'lives'. In some cases there were months between them. Months of nothingness. I am an enigma that doesn't exist. A name in the realm of swirling mist. There's nothing to say I was even here.

None of the aliases matched up in any way, even the identity photos were different. He changed his appearance. The name that popped into my head at the party. That was the key. His life was like a Chinese puzzle box. No wonder none of the reports led to his real name, he was well protected. He even had multiple social security numbers to match his multiple identities.

"He's been a busy boy for a dead man," Lee commented.

"How did finger prints fail to link him? He can't change those, surely." I skimmed police reports.

The screen went blank. A white square popped up. One word.

Classified.

"Shit!" Lee said, leaning closer. "You've been locked

out."

We stared at the white square for a few beats and then each other. My desk phone rang.

"This should be good," I said, my eyes rolled as I picked up the receiver. "SSA Conway."

"SSA, stay on the line for another party." Interesting. I shrugged at Lee and waited. A few moments later, I heard a quiet click and a male voice spoke, "This is Jonathon Torres. You were looking for me?"

Hells bells that was unexpected.

"Yes."

"Why?"

"You have a niece that is orphaned. Thought she could do with some family."

Silence filled the air space between us.

"I don't exist. I've been deep so many years I can't even tell you if I ever met her."

That explained why finger prints didn't lead to anyone other identities. Classified.

"You haven't, not as you anyway and she has no memory of an uncle. Can we meet?"

"No."

"Which agency?"

"Doesn't matter." His voice softened, "It's above

your pay grade."

"You're her only relative."

"I don't know how to take care of a kid."

"You're in the mist?"

"I am the mist and this never happened."

"Now what?"

"Take care of her. You obviously care a great deal to track me down. No one has ever managed that."

I care.

"I'll see she's happy and well taken care of."

"How'd you find me?"

"A Christmas miracle." I can't explain my mind to a stranger any more than I can to myself.

"Look after the kid."

He hung up. The line went dead. I called the switchboard and asked them to give the last number that called my line. No number registered. I asked them to re-check and list all numbers that had called my line over the last four hours.

None.

I hung up. My computer was back to normal.

"I just received a call, how can there be no number registered?" I leaned back in my chair and tapped the keys. "Check this out! There is no record of any computer activity."

"You've been wiped," Lee muttered.

I smiled. Was hard not to. This kinda spooky shit was usually confined to movies and books.

"Yeah, I was wiped. Guess that means he's a spook." I had what I needed. If Jonathon wasn't going to step up and he was the only relative, then someone had too. Maybe Cassie was right. I needed to think. Best place to think was in a room full of happy kids and awesome music.

"Now what?" Lee asked. "And you're smiling."

My eye brows rose. "Let's go back to the party."

Glittering Ice.

It became and so it was
All that was known now lost
Time ticking slowly away
A silent cry rings out for you
Heart breaking
Mind wandering, recreating.
Past frozen in an icy tomb
Your image dissolving
Voice fading into the dark
Taking with it my heart
Looking back at you
Time distorting my view.
Sparkling diamond on my finger
Glittering ice in shining moonlight
Time ticking slowly away
A silent cry rings out for you
You were mine, you were true.
Heart breaking
Mind wandering, recreating
All we were and all we had
It became and so it was

All that was known now lost.

One Way Or Another

A light knock on my office door was followed by Sam's entrance.

"Chicky Babe - you need to see this..." Sam drawled, sliding his kindle into my hands.

I glanced at the screen. For the life of me I couldn't imagine why I needed to see whatever he was reading. My eyes roamed the e-ink on the screen looking for Reed Farrell Coleman's name, hoping Sam had stumbled upon another Moe Prager mystery for me to enjoy.

No such luck.

"Unless this is the latest Moe Prager mystery I'm not interested."

"Nope...," he replied.

I started to hand the Kindle back. "I don't have time..."

"It's not even close to being as cool as a Moe Prager mystery, but it is a mystery," Sam replied holding both hands up, to indicate he wasn't about to take the Kindle back off me.

The only thing for it was to play along.

"Fill me in?" I asked looking up at him. The instant I looked at him I noted an expression I'd seen before. Amusement mixed with concern. The concern was normal. If I was being completely honest with myself, so was the amusement.

"Read, we'll talk," he said.

"I'm not going to read an entire book ...," I protested with a feeble gesture at my laptop. "Working here."

"You won't need too," he replied ignoring my work comment.

I settled back in my chair and began to read. Two paragraphs later I looked at Sam. His coffee colored eyes danced with glee.

"Punctuation would help." As would better dialogue, plot, and characters. Sam's request that I read the story had me perplexed.

"Good ain't it?" Sam asked.

"Yeah, no!"

"Keep reading, it gets worse." He paused. "And you might recognize someone."

"Can I skip?" My eyes not so subtly checked the time on the clock above the door.

"Some where you'd sooner be?" Sam crooned.

"There is a messy crime scene.... somewhere." I can feel it in my bones.

Sam chuckled. "Read."

I skipped pages and skimmed as much as I could then all of a sudden I saw my name.

My name.

Well, that got my attention.

"Who is this idiot?" I growled at the screen, not expecting Sam to answer. I read another few pages. "And why am I a character in this God awful story?"

Sam laughed. "See told you this was interesting."

"Who wrote this?"

"Clarvell Bruyere."

"We have background on Mr. Bruyere?"

Sam handed me a file and pulled up a chair.

It seemed Bruyere was a professor.

I read on. Or that's what he told people. His online bio's implied he had degrees in human resources, accounting, and management. I made a note to check that. The more I read the more I knew we'd be paying Bruyere a visit.

Canadian. His residence was listed as Montreal. That made it tricky but not impossible.

Lee poked his head around the door.

"What's going on?" he asked.

Yeah right, like he didn't know.

"We're going to locate this lunatic. A-sap," I replied. "He's obviously addled." I circled my finger in the air by my ear.

Lee swung the door wide open and ambled in.

"Does Kurt know?" he asked.

I rocked back in my chair and shook my head. "Unless either of you told him." I looked from one to the other, neither flinched. "So, no, then?"

I watched the affirmative head nods and went back to my thought train.

"Apart from appalling fiction, what is this guy guilty of?" I needed something more than my name in a crappy novel that no one in their right mind would read.

Sam coughed. My eyes landed on him. He fidgeted.

"Problem?"

"You didn't get to the best bit yet."

I groaned. "There's more?"

"Oh hell yeah."

I picked the Kindle up and read more. If it weren't for the men in my office I would've tossed the entire thing in the trash.

"Help me out Sam, how far?"

"Three quarters through."

I skipped page upon page, eventually finding more mentions of me. According to Bruyere I was a helicopter pilot with Special Forces training, who did a stint with CIA in the Middle East before returning to the FBI. He bandied about words like extraordinary rendition and black sites.

I wasn't a chopper pilot.

Carefully, I placed the Kindle on my desk and leaned forward, resting on my elbows. Sam and Lee waited.

"We need to know if he's taking a stab in the dark, or he has access to classified information..." I sighed. "Dammit let's find him."

Lee tapped the desk, his eyes glazed over. He was thinking. I let him think and turned to Sam.

"How did you find this?"

"Twitter. He's been blowing his own trumpet all over Twitter." He smiled. "Maybe you should use your Twitter account."

I shrugged. "I don't need too, as long as you use it for me. I much prefer the mental image of people thinking they're talking too little ol' me, but in fact they're talking to a big black dude like you."

"Whatever floats your boat."

"My boat's floating right out of the harbor," I replied. "All right people, let's get this fucktard."

Lee pulled his phone from his pocket and made a call. He walked out of the room and paced the hallway. I could hear him. Sam could hear him. Sandra popped into my office, alerted to some fun by Lee's pacing and talking.

"What's going on?" She asked slipping into the spare chair next to Sam.

"Is that the new phrase for this team?" I asked, smiling.

She shrugged. "What do you need?"

"Intel on a Clarvell Bruyere from Montreal," I said.

"And he is?" she asked writing his name into her notebook.

"A wannabe author."

"And he did?"

"He used me as a character in a very very bad novel."

She grinned. "I always thought bad writing should be a crime. Can we arrest him for that?"

"I wish," I replied. "He appears to have access to

classified information."

A ping sounded from my laptop. I glanced at the screen. "Oh, hello. Check this out."

I motioned to Sandra and Sam. They joined me around my side of the desk.

"Moron," Sam hissed.

"You still want me to use my Twitter account?" I asked as I 'unfollowed' Clarvell Bruyere.

Sam shook his head. "Nope. I'll take care of it."

I read the message again. "@EllieConwaySA, you should read my book. I use you as a character. You rock."

I could feel my blood freezing in my veins.

Sandra excused herself. "I'm going to start pulling files on that man."

"We have a back ground check," I said.

She smiled sweetly. "But you don't have - what I can do. Let me take my fingers to my computer and I'll get you everything there is on Clarvell Bruyere."

"We await your brilliance," I replied as she left the room.

Faith.

Sam sat rocking on two legs of the chair. His phone was in his hand. He was texting. I checked my email, and answered two work related emails then one from Carla. She wanted Joey to come for dinner. She always wanted Joey to come for dinner. I had no problem with that. Joey was the product of a super dysfunctional family, but he had potential. The more time he spent in our home, the safer I knew he was. I called my father and let him know there was an extra for dinner again. Like me, Dad was not surprised. He too liked Joey. Carla had good taste in best friends. Although part of me waited for the day that one of them said or did something that would test that friendship. Boys and girls. It's the nature of the beasts.

A chime alerted me to yet another @ message on Twitter.

An open message from Clarvell Bruyere. @EllieConwaySA You seem to have unfollowed me. :) #JustSaying

"Sam, how could he know this?" I asked spinning the laptop to face him.

"Now that's creepy," Sam replied. He tapped a few times on my keyboard and let out a long sigh. "He has one hundred and fifty five thousand seven hundred and fifty four followers. No way could he know you 'unfollowed' him so quickly, unless..."

143

"Unless he was watching for activity from me, specifically or he has an app."

"Yep. I'd say he's running an application that tells him when people unfollow him."

"Well fuck me, that's still creepy."

"You've got a fan."

"Nope, I've got a potential stalker. Let's shut him down before he gets any closer to home."

A beep sounded.

The cold clawed.

"Sam ... @EllieConwaySA You have a daughter but no husband. Who will raise her with you?"

"Not good, Chicky Babe."

"Incoming, we have more. @EllieConwaySA She's beautiful, like her mother."

Sam growled, "This guy is pushing it."

"I'm ignoring him but he's persistent. And we have another, @EllieConwaySA Is she home alone today? I'll sit with her and wait for you."

I felt sick. Part of me wanted to whip out a smart-assed reply about how we don't live in Montreal and my daughter is trained to kill.

Sam shut my laptop, severing any connection to Twitter. If only it were so easy to get rid of lunatics.

"Lee!" I called through the half open door. "Get in here!"

He swung the door open and shoved his phone into his pocket. "Here!"

"I want a protection detail on Carla, now."

His eyes widened. "Done." He picked up the phone on my desk and pressed three numbers. "Special request, protection for an active agent's family. Credible threat."

It seemed stupid that I couldn't just do it myself. But I was about to be the subject of a protection detail along with my teenage daughter. Ordering it for one's self just seemed panicky. I don't do panicky. I do death. A smile settled on my face. Lee saw it.

"And what's the smile?" he asked.

"Nothing." I shrugged.

Yeah, like I was going to tell the team I was thinking 'I do death', nope. Not happening.

"We have a problem," Sam said.

No fuc'n kidding Einstein.

"A new one?" Instead of being wise-assed I encouraged him to share. It wasn't easy for me. "Give."

"A protection detail... and you. You don't see a problem?"

I shrugged. "Nope."

Lee intervened. "I do."

"How's that?" It was my best attempt at innocence.

"Yeah, whiter than white. It's not washing with me."

I tried another innocent look.

Fail.

"Give it up Chicky, you know damn well..."

"I know jack."

I smiled. I do know Jack. But we're not talking about Jack we're talking about jack shit.

Sam grimaced. Guess he'd seen this mood before. Well, crap, me too.

"We want you to cooperate with the protection detail."

"Sure, I'll cooperate." I changed the subject and gestured the Kindle in front of me. I've got a brand new stalker who is writing bullshit and including me in his sordid tale. That is just about as un-cool as anything could get. "Is anyone reading this crap?"

He grinned so wide his white teeth glowed.

"From what I can tell he's not exactly making the top 1000 list," Sam said.

"Well that's comforting." It wasn't. The thought of

anyone reading that shite and coming across my name made me ill. "How about we spread some rumors through social media about how awful his writing is, or throw around a few truthful reviews. He might just crawl back under the rock he came from."

"A smear campaign. I like it. But I doubt it'll work."

"Me too, but it'd be fun."

"Not like you to be so quick to condemn." He arched an eyebrow at me. "I'm not buying. What do you want?"

"His head on a pike." The more I thought about it the more pissed off I became. "We're going to Canada. Get me whomever I fuc'n need to talk to at Homeland. If he knows then we have national security breech."

"You want to involve them?"

"Hell yes. I'm seeing Guantanamo Bay in this moron's future."

Sam laughed. "I hope he likes water sports."

I smiled. "Show me his picture again?"

Sam held out the photo in the file.

"Looks like he needs a good wash," I commented. "What happens in Gitmo stays in Gitmo."

"Wow, you're not pulling any punches."

"He mentioned Carla, gloves are off."

"Let's find out where he really is," Sam replied cracking his knuckles. "And go get him."

"Not without me."

We stood up and headed for the door together, it instantly became apparent we weren't going to fit. Sam stepped back. I walked through the bullpen and called out to Lee and Sandra. "I need a location."

Sandra smiled and called me over to her desk. "We're getting interest expressed by several agencies. He must've pissed a few people off. Kurt is in Reston. Do you need him?"

"I wondered where he was," I said. "We're good at the moment."

I called Carla. "Hey sweet pea, get Grandpa to save me dinner. I might be late home."

"How late Mom?"

"I don't know, sweetie. Could be late late."

With a sigh Carla deflated. "Oh."

I knew she hated it when I was late home. In all fairness, I was often late home. I sucked at nine-to-five.

"There will be uniformed officers outside the house soon. Don't give them a hard time."

"Why?"

"A precaution, that's all. Just be nice."

"Okay, but Joey can still hang here, right?"

"Yes, but stay inside."

"Okay Mom, bye."

I hung up. Lee's phone rang, my phone rang, and Sam's phone rang. Sandra called out from her desk. "He's not in Canada." Bruyere arrived at Dulles two and a half hours earlier. Security cameras had him leaving the airport with only hand luggage. That would certainly speed up his exit. No taking escalators and a train to find the luggage carousal, for him. I walked over to her desk and leaned down. "Erase his trail."

She looked at me for a beat.

"Starting the process."

I smiled as I walked away. My phone rang again.

Kurt.

"So he's here, do we know where he's heading?"

"Nope, but he's been online. So where ever he is, he has internet access." Which wasn't exactly helpful.

The sigh Kurt blew out was audible. "Yeah well this is Virginia; you can be online in coffee bars, malls, hotels, McDonalds ..."

I hung up and shoved my phone in my pocket. "Lee, can we get a fix on him?" I asked. Lee had planted himself in a chair by my desk and was using his laptop.

"Sure, sooner or later I'll find him," he replied. "I'm checking out your Twitter feed. Your little friend is insisting that you follow him."

"Can you get him a chat room?"

"I like how you think Chicky."

Yeah, me too. We have chat rooms that we activate occasionally. Over the years they've come in handy.

"You need to be me, Lee. @ reply him and send him a link to our chat room."

"We might get some others following along," he replied as he typed.

"That's okay."

"Yeah, makes it seem more legit, if there are other people in there."

"You okay there Chicky?" Sam asked nudging me.

"Freaking wonderful," I growled.

"I got your man in our chat room, pinging him now," Lee said. "Standby."

"Let's hope he's not clever," Sam grumbled. He had car keys in his hand, they jangled impatiently. "Got him, he's not clever," Lee replied. He read out an address. "He's twenty-five minutes away."

Sam held up the keys. "Okay kids, let's go."

I said a silent prayer. Don't let it take forever to get out of the city today.

I called Kurt and gave him the address. He would hopefully arrive at the address within a few minutes of us.

"We'll wait for you, half a block east of the address."

"See you soon."

I hung up and watched traffic while Lee carried on a ridiculous conversation with Bruyere in the chat room. Maybe I wasn't watching, maybe I was zoned completely out because it didn't seem like twenty-five minutes before I heard Sam's voice.

"Chicky – we're cruising by now." Sam He drove past the address. I scanned the front yard for signs of kids. I hate when retards do dumb shit with kids around. No toys in sight. Sam pulled over and parked.

"Honey, we're home," he said grinning at me.

"Kurt will be here in a minute or two. We'll go in together."

Tapping keys from the backseat meant Lee was

still working on getting information. "The house is owned by Richard and Mary Arwood, they're in their seventies," Lee said. "He's using their broadband."

"And they are?"

"Mary Arwood is his aunt."

"Let's get the Arwood's out." My words were followed by more tapping.

"Currently on a cruise in the Bahamas and not due back for another eight days."

Convenient.

"Excellent."

Kurt pulled in in front of us. He walked back to our car and opened my door.

"Conway, all good?"

"Yep." I indicated to the house down the block. "Owners are away on a cruise. He is still online, chatting to Lee."

"He knows he's talking to Lee?" Kurt asked. Amusement danced in his eyes.

I shook my head.

"He thinks he's talking to Ellie...," Lee said. "Gimme a minute."

I climbed out of the car.

"Lee stay with the car and keep Bruyere talking.

We'll go say hello while he's distracted."

Sam, Kurt, and I walked up the path. I peered in the nearest window to the door. Bruyere was sitting on the sofa, his back to the window and us.

Sam slipped around the side of the house. We waited for a few seconds. Then I knocked. Kurt smiled. "He's standing up."

I glanced at Kurt and saw his Glock 22 in his hand.

I pulled my gun from the holster on my hip and adjusted my grip. A shadow moved over the frosted glass panel at the side of the door.

Breathe.

The handle turned and door swung inward.

There he stood blinking rapidly as our weapons trained on him.

"Clarvell Bruyere?" I asked.

He nodded dumbly.

"FBI." With my left hand I flashed ID. He never had a chance to see the name. "We would like to talk to you about your work." I was quietly impressed with myself for saying work and not something rude or derogatory. Despite the nasty thoughts that flowed unchecked through my mind.

"Why?"

Because you are a retard and you wrote about me, dick!

He found his balls and stopped blinking like a demented owl. His shoulders squared.

Here we go.

"I don't know what you're talking about," he said. One hand moved, as if to steady himself on the door frame.

"Keep your hands where I can see them." I sensed he'd summoned calm he didn't really feel and that was my cue. "We'd like to talk to you about your work." Again I felt pleased with myself for saying work.

"I don't know what you are talking about."

"Yeah you do. You wrote a book and used me as a main character."

His face blanched.

"You got it now?" Kurt asked. "Let me introduce, SSA Ellie Conway."

Fear oozed from his pores. He wiped his face with one hand. The other hand grasped the door frame. Knuckles white. He wasn't calm. He wasn't collected. He was beginning to panic.

There was a small smile on my lips, as he focused

on the Glock 17 in my hand.

"I didn't, didn't... I didn't mean any harm."

"Really," I replied. "It was all a misunderstanding?"

Sam came up behind him. Bruyere had no idea. Sam was two feet away, how could Bruyere not know there was an armed walking wall behind him?

"It was a misunderstanding."

I nodded. Sam winked at me.

"We require you to accompany us to our office."

Panic flashed. He spun round and ran into Sam.

"Wrong way buddy," Sam cooed. He turned him back to face me.

"Going somewhere?"

"I didn't do anything... I didn't..."

"Yeah, we'll see, we need to ask you some questions about the things you didn't do." I beckoned to him. "We've got a car waiting."

He stepped through the doorway then stopped.

"You must have a warrant?"

Stepping back I asked Bruyere to put his hands on his head. His eyes moved. I asked again.

His hand moved.

"Hands on your head," I said.

Sam spoke from behind him. "You better do as she

says."

He resisted, and then slowly raised his hands to his head.

Sam's voice bellowed, "Gun!"

Sam was on him so fast I had to jump back to get out of the way. He had him by one wrist and seconds later Bruyere was spread eagled on the ground, over the doorstep. Sam reached back and took a gun from the back of Bruyere's trousers. He passed it to me.

"You have a permit for this?" I asked, trying not to smirk. It'd have been better if he'd tried to use it. The inside of his head splattered all over the living room amused me. So clear was the image that I smelled blood.

"It's my uncles," he muttered.

"Great," I replied. "Do you have a permit?"

"No."

"Why are you carrying it?"

"I didn't do anything ... I didn't ..."

"Yeah, and we still need to ask you some questions about the things you didn't do." I moved back so Sam could lift the man to his feet. "There is a car waiting."

Bruyere staggered trying to find his footing then stopped and leant on the door frame.

"You must have a warrant?"

Kurt waved folded papers at Bruyere.

"Right here."

Sam took the paperwork and thrust it into Bruyere's hands which were cuffed behind his back.

The warrant rustled as it waved behind him.

"I can't read it!" he squawked.

"It's okay, someone will read it to you. Later."

Sam pushed Bruyere ahead of him out the door and down the path. I watched as Lee greeted him and then helped him into the car. Bruyere toppled sideways across the seat. He'd wake in about eighteen hours in a secure location completely unaware of our involvement.

Kurt waited until they were in the car, and then slipped inside wearing gloves. Moments later he had Bruyere's laptop packed into its case and his carry-on luggage, he dropped everything into the trunk of Lee's car and smacked the roof, letting him know they could go.

Kurt then hurried back into the house and erased all evidence of Clarvell Bruyere ever being there.

Bruyere was done – Sam and Lee would take him to a secure facility before another team picked him up for a long flight.

I wondered how often he fixated on women online and how often he'd taken his infatuation into life.

As much fun as it was seeing Bruyere sweat, it would've been more fun to introduce him to some water sports.

I called Dad, "Change of plans, I'll be home in time for dinner."

The Battle Field

"You ready?" Kurt called into the house.

"Yeah," I called back. "Hold ya horses."

From the kitchen door I could see him as he leaned on the front door jam, one hand shoved into his jeans pocket, the other swinging his sunglasses. A smile crept over his face as he looked down the hallway at me. I think I was smiling back. Maybe I wasn't but I felt like I was.

"We've got all day, no hurry." The inflection in his voice alerted me to something else as I walked toward him.

"Uh huh? So what's up?"

"Nothing."

"Liar," I ducked under his arm and headed down the path. "Lock the door on your way out."

I heard the door shut and his footsteps following me. "Wait up," he said as his fingers wrapped around my upper arm. "Can we talk?"

Forward momentum ceased.

"So talk," I replied turning to face him.

"You can't ignore this Ellie," he said with a smile.

"This?" And he was so wrong, because I could. If it meant preserving what was left of my sanity I could.

"This," he replied. Like I was supposed to know what he meant. Except that didn't work, because I did know. I. Knew.

"Kurt, what do you want from me?"

"The truth," he stated. His arm dropped to his side.

And so many wise-assed comments circulated in my head that I nearly exploded trying to simply look innocent.

He grinned. "Nice try, not buying. We need to talk about what happened in Lexington?"

Air rushed from my lungs so fast it made me gasp.

"I lost the plot," I replied. "You know why. What's to talk about?"

"My jaw still aches," he responded, rubbing the side of his face.

"I thought you said I hit like a girl?"

"I may have misspoken."

I saw it in his eyes, there was no way I was going to get out of this conversation. And I knew damn well he wasn't talking about his sore jaw.

"Don't we have to be somewhere?" I reached for the car door but wasn't quite close enough.

"There's no hurry. Unless you want to have this conversation on the way." His fingers encircled my wrist. Guess he really wanted to talk.

I thought about it, I really did. A distracted Kurt driving in rush hour traffic. Didn't seem like the smartest option. I turned to face him.

"You can let go my arm. I'm not going anywhere. And I'm not going to hit you."

He nodded, his fingers released, and his hand was once again thrust into his pocket.

"Do you remember what I told you?"

Of course I did. But did he remember how I repeated it and that the entire team knew? I had a feeling it wasn't such a surprise to Lee and Sam. He was right there in front of me, his eyes never left mine. Not even a little bit unnerving. Should it have been? Probably not. Kurt wasn't just my partner, he was also a doctor. He often watched, but usually with a mixture of professional concern and amusement – this was something else entirely.

"Ellie?"

Oh right, I have to answer.

"Yes, I remember."

"So where to from here?"

Ah, crap. Do we end our partnership? Do I leave Delta? Do I insist he leaves Delta? What about Rowan? Rowan. Jesus. There's a complication. What about my no LEO rule? It'd been my rule since Mac's murder. I took a few steps back, and leaned on the car. How do I feel about Kurt? How do I feel about Rowan? What's with all the extra attention from Noel Gerrard.

Men.

Stupid.

They think with the wrong head.

But in front of me I saw a man who was far from stupid. I saw a man who knew exactly what he was getting into. And I saw a level of physical and emotional security that few could offer.

"Ellie? You with me here?"

I blinked. Everything I saw stayed right in front of me.

"Of course," I replied. "We need to work this out. Can we maintain a relationship within the same team?"

A light twinkled in his blue eyes. His shoulders relaxed slightly.

"Yes."

Well, that was the quickest answer I've ever gotten.

"It changes the dynamic. Are you sure?"

He laughed. "It changes nothing. You know how I feel, have felt, and for how long." His voice drifted. "It changes nothing."

Kurt had a point.

"I have some things to work out first. I cannot and will not move forward with you until that's taken care of."

"Rowan?"

"Uh huh."

"Answer me one question?"

"Sure, if I can."

"How do you feel about me?"

Can I do that?

I took a breath. "I like you."

He smiled. "You're hard work sometimes, ya know that?"

"So I've been told."

"That's it?"

"That's it. Right here, right now."

He grinned. Leaned very close and kissed my cheek. "That's it until you green light me."

Bastard.

Backdoor Santa

Oh, man this sucks.

I heard the announcement again. Un-freaking-cool people. Five fuc'n hours in the air and now this?

There is no way – carousel three, my ass.

Kurt waved and walked over to meet me.

"Did you hear that? Carousel freaking three?"

"I did."

I looked at Kurt. His head shook vehemently. "No way."

"Please?"

"No."

"But if I have to walk for ten minutes over there, go down the fuc'n huge escalator twice and get on a fuc'n train then go up another fuc'n escalator and walk for ten minutes just to get my bag someone is going to get hurt."

Kurt's head tipped back, his laughter bounced across the floor in front of me then suddenly stopped, absorbed by the seething array of people all walking toward the escalator.

"Come on, we'll go together."

My head was shaking but my feet were walking. Traitors.

"This is not going to end well," I muttered at Kurt as he stepped upside me. "Already these 'tards are getting in my way."

"Those 'tards as you so delightfully put it, are the people who shared your flight, the very people we are supposed to protect."

"I tried to protect them, but you insist I walk for freaking miles..."

"As long as it's my fault, I'm sure we can live with it."

"Didn't my bag and I arrive on the same plane at the same gate?"

"Yes."

"Then why do I get off here." I gesticulate wildly back toward the gate I'd emerged from. "And my bag end up six miles away?"

He had no answer. I watched him flounder as the first escalator ride ended. "Bit of an exaggeration don't you think?"

That was the best he could do?

"Nope. We arrived at the same gate – and yet I

have to travel down escalators, on a train, up escalators and walk forever just to pick up my bag..."

"Okay, point made. But Dulles is an attractive airport, and if you didn't have to go so far you'd miss the experience that is Dulles."

My eyes rolled so far back in my head I couldn't see to walk for a few seconds. Travel documentary much?

"Maybe someone should open the thing up to the public as an art gallery and put the baggage carrousels in a more passenger friendly place."

Kurt stepped off the escalator two steps ahead of me and waited.

I spotted a cop about ten feet away. Kurt turned but it was too late I was already heading for the cop while pulling my badge over my head.

"Ma'am," the police officer exclaimed as I showed him my badge. "How can I help?"

"Find a way of getting my bag from carousal three to me here within the next two minutes."

His jaw dropped. He stepped back. His mouth snapped closed then fell open again. "Ma'am?"

"Yes?"

"Why?"

I sighed. "Because I don't want to walk all the way

down there when both my bag and I were on the same flight that arrived at the same gate and I have a job to do – it's not to see the sights of Dulles airport for the fifteenth time this year."

Its Christmas Eve eve. I promised Carla I'd be home for Christmas. Guess being trapped in the airport counts as almost home.

"I can't do that ma'am."

Yes, I know that you dork. That's why we're still walking. But why are you still walking? I had a thought, it was uncharitable, mean spirited even.

"Do you know Eddie Connelly?" My ex-brother-in-law was a deputy once, before being ousted for nearly killing someone on a crosswalk. True to form, he was drunk, in uniform and driving a marked car at the time.

Kurt leaned close to my ear and murmured, "Stop playing with him. It's not his fault."

I smiled at the cop and ignored Kurt.

"You do know Eddie don't you?"

"Yes ma'am, he's a friend of mine."

I knew in that instance that nothing I said to the officer was going to make any difference. He classed Eddie as a friend. Stupid was probably his middle name.

"As you were officer."

I glanced at Kurt. His shoulders shook as he struggled to compose himself.

The cop carried on walking with us. Kurt intervened, "No need to escort us officer. We can handle it from here."

He faltered, his jaw dropped again. I reached out and tapped his chin thus closing his mouth.

"Tell Eddie I said Merry Christmas," I called as he turned and walked in the opposite direction. I couldn't believe I offered a Merry Christmas to Eddie. Must be the holiday season softening my brain or maybe it was the five-hour flight.

Kurt tried not to laugh.

"You are impossible," he said with a grin.

"And yet you love me," I whispered under my breath.

"Let's get the bags and get on with the holidays," Kurt said. He gave no indication of having heard my comment.

An hour later Kurt entered the gate code and pulled up my driveway. In the dull late winter afternoon, Christmas lights twinkled from the trees that lined the path to the house.

"You coming in?" I asked as I opened the car door.

"No, you go spend time with Carla. I've got some things to do this afternoon." We said goodbye.

An hour later I'd unpacked, and was on my second coffee. I wrote a last minute list of Christmas things I still needed to get. I then promptly lost the list while trying to get ready to leave the house.

I checked the living rooms expecting it to be on a coffee table somewhere. It wasn't.

"Honey, have you seen my list?"

"On the kitchen counter, Mom," Carla called from down the hall.

I tripped over the cat almost spilling the precious black liquid in my mug.

"Shrek, keep out of the way," I growled hurrying into the kitchen. Sure enough, the notepad with list still attached was on the counter. Bite marks and needle like punctures decorated the bottom of the list.

Shrek.

Carla bounced into the room.

"You ready?" I asked checking the list. Twice.

"Yes, Mom."

I glanced at her.

"Let's try that again. Jacket, hat, scarf, gloves?"

"It's too hot in the mall," she complained.

"Jacket then." I'm all about compromise if it means we can get going.

She smiled. "Okay." My phone rang.

Carla squawked. "Don't answer it!" Tempting.

"I must, you know that."

The screen flashed with Sam's name. I almost crossed myself. Please don't let it be a case, not this close to Christmas. Not again.

"Hey Sam."

"Hey..." He paused, cleared his throat, and continued, "Glad you're home Chicky babe." "Uh huh." It didn't sound good.

"How was San Francisco?"

"Good." Okay as good as it can ever be when someone asks for my help with a case. We won; even so several innocent people lost their lives. "Did you call to ask me about San Fran?"

"No." He paused. "Are you taking Carla shopping?"

"Yes."

"Fair Oaks Mall?"

"Yes."

"Me and Lee will meet you for coffee at Starbucks

in an hour. That's downstairs by the Apple store?"

"Yes it is." I heard no stressors in his voice. Nothing in the background noises indicated trouble. "Everything okay?"

"Yeah, we'll see you at the mall. Talk then." Curious.

"An hour?"

"Yes."

I hung up and pocketed my phone. The odd phone call stayed with me as Carla twirled around the kitchen.

"Can we go?" she asked.

"Yep."

I grabbed my keys, list, and handbag. I mulled over Sam's call. A potential problem. My hand slid to my hip. Reassured by the feel of my gun I pressed thoughts of the phone call aside.

Alone at the front door I turned and called out, "Waiting on you kiddo." She hurried toward me from the kitchen with a sandwich in her hand.

Hungry as always.

Snowflakes tumbled from the sky. I hoped they would stop. Driving in snow is not as much fun as it used to be. Back when I was ten foot tall and bullet proof, pre-Carla. Kids change you.

I parked in the Seers parking lot.

"Remember which entrance we used Carla or we'll be trapped here all day."

Carla laughed. "Yeah because the parking lot is full of federal cars."

"Smarty pants."

The mall was over warm as usual. Outside the jewelers, Carla asked for cash.

I am now an ATM for a teenager. Not only did she ask for cash but she also disappeared with it. I used the opportunity to shop in peace and find a few extra things for Carla's stocking and get Sam and Lee their gifts. Ticking things off. I grabbed a coffee from Caribou while I was upstairs shopping. When I strolled to the Apple store shopping bags dangling from one hand and my delicious Caribou coffee in the other. I found Sam and Lee at the Starbucks across from Apple, drinking coffee and seated at a table.

"Okay so what's going on," I said slipping into the empty chair.

"What are you getting Kurt for Christmas?" Sam asked pushing his cup in circles.

"Seriously?"

This is the problem?

Lee nodded.

"What do we get Kurt?" Sam asked tapping his cup.

"He's not that difficult." I pulled my list out. Kurt's name sat there ringed in red with a big question mark after it. "Okay he is."

"Come on Chicky, you know him better than us. He's your partner."

"You'd think but I just spend more time with him than either of you. He doesn't share much." "Crap," Lee groaned.

"We're investigators. So we investigate," I said. How hard can it be?

Lee's eye lit up.

"Anyone ever been to his house?" Lee asked.

Sam and I stared at him. My mind tumbled over the events of the last few years.

He always comes to us.

"Hang on. We do Sunday dinners every two weeks... are you telling me we've never done Sunday dinner at Kurt's place?" I asked.

"Can you remember going to his house for Sunday dinner?" Lee turned it back on me.

I shook my head. How the hell he managed to

weasel out of having us all at his place was anyone's guess.

"What music does he like?" I asked.

"No, no, no, that's your department Chicky," Sam replied.

"We're screwed," I said finishing my coffee. "Field trip," Lee announced. "We're going to Kurt's." "Ballsy," I replied.

"Where's Carla?" Lee asked scanning the mall near us.

"I'll call her."

She answered her cell quickly with a question. "Mom what do I get Kurt?" The million-dollar question.

"Ah, the question of the hour. Are you done?"

"Yeah, apart from Kurt."

"Meet me at Starbucks, ground floor by the information center and Apple."

"Coming."

I hung up.

When Carla arrived, a fiendish plan hatched.

Carla, Sam, Lee, and I piled into my car. I pulled over a block away from Kurt's home and called Kurt's house.

No answer.

I called his direct dial at work. Not his cell, you can answer a cell anywhere. I wanted to know where he was.

He answered on the third ring. He was at his desk.

"Ellie? You need something?"

"Nah, not really. Just wondered if you'd like to come over for dinner tonight?" My fingers crossed all by themselves.

He paused, I knew he digesting my invitation. "Sure, what time? I'm just finishing up some paper work."

I checked my watch. It was just after four.

"Seven?"

"Should be done by then, but I'll probably come straight from work. Shall I pick up a bottle of wine?"

"Sounds great. See you then."

"He's not home, so we can't visit," Carla sounded disappointed. I smiled.

So young, so innocent.

"Now what?" Sam asked.

"You and Carla stay here. Lee and I will do some recon." "Here?" Carla asked.

"Yep."

With a wave, Lee and I headed off up the street. We walked casually up the path to Kurt's front door. His porch was in full view of the neighbors. No trees, shrubs or even a fence to provide cover. Nowhere to hide. I wondered if there was an alarm system.

Lee peered into the window beside the door.

"Can't see an alarm panel," Lee said.

"Good."

There was no outward advertising if there was an alarm. I glanced around the street was quiet.

No curtains moved. It was possible that all his neighbors worked.

"Keep watch," I said to Lee. He turned and faced the street, blocking me from view of anyone looking. From my pocket, I pulled a small leather case and took two thin pieces of metal, never leave home without a lock pick, gun, and clean underwear.

I tumbled the lock and swung the door open.

"After you," I said standing aside and letting Lee through the door.

"Let's hope there is no alarm."

"Or camera," I replied following him in and closing the door.

We stood in a surprisingly spacious entranceway.

Doors opened off the almost octagonal area. By the front door was a table. On the table, a bowl and a letter rack. No mail waited. I looked closely at the bowl noting tiny chips and cracks.

"He keeps his keys here," I aid indicating to the bowl. In my mind, I saw Kurt walk in the front door and drop his keys into the bowl then check his mail or set it in the letter rack for later.

"This is a really nice place," Lee commented. "Let's get snooping."

I should've felt bad but I didn't. I was breaking laws and several friendship codes yet I didn't feel guilt. Maybe I didn't feel guilt because being a lapsed catholic I was so used to guilt it no longer registered?

I found the living room. Tasteful, comfortable and tidy. It was as I expected. Photographs lined the walls, some old, some recent, all interesting. Some candid shots of Delta team members and what I thought may have been family shots mingled with amazing scenery in black and white.

He was quite the photographer.

My eyes fell on a stack of CD's. It looked like something from my place. Lorenza Ponce, Grange, Bon Jovi, Aerosmith, Rolling Stones, the Eagles, and some

Queen. The order intrigued me. I knew that order. It was my preferred order when listening to those particular albums.

Okay he had good taste in music. Moving on.

Lee called me from another room. I followed the sound of his voice to another room. Books lined two walls, floor to ceiling, there was a fireplace and a comfortable looking leather sofa and an old oak desk. A library.

"He reads a lot," Lee commented.

"He does." I scanned titles on the walls. "Lot of crime fiction and thrillers here. He likes

Jeffrey Deaver, a lot."

Also many medical texts. There were a pile of medical journals on the corner of the desk.

I looked around the room no sign of an eReader anywhere.

"Let's see what he reads at night...," Lee said.

"Bedroom," I replied. A little bit of guilt edged in.

His bed was unmade. The closet open. His many suits hung in color order. From left to right, starting with a platinum pinstripe and ending with a black tuxedo. I wouldn't mind seeing him in that again. I peered into the bottom of the closet and saw a large shopping bag. Red and gold gift paper peeked out from inside the bag. Gifts. For whom I did not know. But I did know they weren't for family. Kurt was an only child and lost his elderly parents some time ago. It comforted me that I knew something about his life. Kurt delivered that nugget of information while we were on a case in Lexington not so long ago.

On his nightstand, there were three books in a pile. No eReader.

"All right. An eReader. That's what we're getting him." "Maybe he likes the feel of books," Lee replied.

"But he's also out of shelf space," I countered.

"Clever." He nodded his head. "Liking this plan."

"Let's get out of here." My phone rang.

Kurt.

"Hey," I said while following Lee to the front door.

"I'm done just heading home to change. Might be a little early, that okay?"

"Sure." I hung up.

"Let's go. He's on his way."

We hurried out and relocked the door. On the way to the car, I had some observations.

"No Christmas tree," I said.

"No decking the halls," Lee replied.

"Apart from his bedroom it didn't look like anyone lived there."

"He reads, takes photographs, and listens to music. That's all we know," Lee said.

"Not all. He's a good photographer and he reads a lot." I decided the music thing bordered on creepy and left it alone.

We climbed back into the car.

"We're going to Best Buy. Carla and I will buy him a Kindle you two can buy him a case and light," I said pulling away from the curb.

Christmas solved.

I decided on the scenic route from Kurt's to Fair Lakes Shopping Center. Didn't want to risk seeing Kurt on his way home.

"I'll drop you back at your car when we're done here," I said as I pulled into a car park across from Best Buy.

"He does celebrate Christmas, doesn't he?" Lee asked. "Nothing indicated Christmas in his apart-ment."

"Did you look inside his closet?"

He shook his head. The four of us stood in the icy cold outside the car.

"There were gifts wrapped in red and gold paper at the bottom of his closet."

"Let's go get his presents before we freeze to death." Lee shoved his hands into his jacket pockets and hunched his shoulders against the cold air.

"And I have to get home and cook dinner - can't very well have nothing to offer Kurt when he arrives."

Carla linked her arm with mine. "What are you going to make?" "Roast beef," I replied.

"We're coming for dinner," Sam said nudging Lee. "Unless you want to be alone?"

"You're not as funny as you think you are," I said walking in the door of Best Buy. The greeter smiled at me. "Where do you keep your kindles?" I asked.

He pointed to the left of the store and spoke into his headset then to me. "Someone will meet you by the display stand, ma'am."

Fifteen minutes later, we had a kindle, a cover, and a light, all gift-wrapped.

"Market for beef then home," I said to Carla.

Presents wrapped in shiny paper lay piled under the tree. Carla curled into the sofa and flicked channels until she found a Christmas special on the television.

In the kitchen, Sam and Lee peeled vegetables.

The roast beef was cooking in the oven and the aroma from the meat was just beginning to waft through the room.

My stomach growled.

An open bottle of tequila sat on the counter.

Kurt called out from the front door as he let himself in, "Where is everyone?"

I walked down the hall to meet him. "Kitchen."

He smiled, lifted a bag up and said, "I'll put these under the tree and then join you." Red and gold gift-wrap peeked out of the top of the bag.

"Okay."

I headed back to the kitchen and the sound of liquid pouring into shot glasses.

Four shots were waiting when Kurt appeared and placed a bottle of wine on the countertop. He sat next to me on a barstool. Sam and Lee finished off the last of the vegetables. Kurt lifted a shot-glass.

"Funny thing," Kurt said. "Got home and found this on one of my jackets in the closet." He retrieved something from the inside pocket of his suit jacket. When he opened his hand, I saw a small plastic bag.

"What is it?" I asked. Sam and Lee turned to look.

Kurt held the bag up so we could all see. I saw all right, I saw a strand of blonde hair.

"Yours?" I asked Kurt.

"No. The strand is over a foot long." I swallowed.

Lee dropped the peeler into the sink; it clattered against the stainless steel.

"Looks like one of Ellie's," he said. "You two have something you want to share?"

Sam leaned over and took the small bag from Kurt's hand. "You two been snuggling up all cozy?"

Kurt smiled. "It was on a new jacket."

Without missing a beat Sam replied, "Transfer from another jacket." I downed the shot in front of me.

"That's what I thought," Kurt said. "It's not like Ellie was in my closet." I watched Sam pour me another shot.

"Exactly, it's not like I was in your closet," I replied, swallowing the second tequila shot. Maybe a hairnet would be a good idea before I go snooping again.

Mac's voice bounced around inside my head, "Maybe's ass."

A very Delta Christmas Eve eve stretched into the

night.

Merry Christmas to all and to all a goodnight.

Room at the End of the World.

Places that should be safe and we think are safe aren't always.

Lee waved over his shoulder.

Doc handed me a cup. "Don't look so suspicious. Coffee at this hour is not going to do you any good. You need sleep."

"Yes, Doc, and this is?" I sniffed the hot washed out looking liquid. Tea, he'd made me herbal tea.

"Chamomile tea."

"Chocolate would've been better."

Regular sweet tea would've been better.

"There was only one chocolate sachet and you had it earlier."

"Thought that woman filled up the beverage containers," I said.

"Me too."

My nose wrinkled. Doc watched as I took a sip. It wasn't horrible. In fact it was quite nice, hot but nice. "Chamomile tea? Who knew?"

Doc smiled. "I'll be back. I'm going to go rescue our

clothes."

"Oh, yeah, the drier." I'd taken our saturated clothing to the laundry room, washed it then put it in the drier.

Good thing Doc remembered, I probably would've forgotten.

Was that kind of night?

I was tired beyond belief.

We were no closer to finding answers to a series of horrendous rapes cases that had us traipsing all over Virginia.

The door shut behind Doc. The tea was a little too hot to drink. My head felt heavy, like my skull was thick. I could see the coffee table. My hand stretched out to put the cup down and missed. The cup hit the floor, hot tea splashed up onto my right shin.

It was wet but didn't hurt.

My head was so heavy that if I leaned down to get my cup I knew I'd fall off the sofa. I watched my fingers open and close. I watched, but couldn't feel them. Was there pain? Not that I could determine. Heaviness, fog, stars swimming in front of my eyes. They needed to stay still.

I knew I was alone. That wasn't good. Things that

used to make sense seemed like hard work.

Slow motion. Sweaty, clammy, dizzy, sick. My left hand pulled my phone from my pocket. Who you gonna call?

It took forever to find Doc's number. Would've been easier if I looked under K for Kurt not D for Doc. My slowness frustrated me. I knew what I had to do but couldn't seem to do it.

Forever became nothing. Time stood still. My thumb pressed the call icon on the screen. The phone rang. I couldn't count the rings. I was trying but the numbers spiraled out of sight, hiding behind the stars.

Then there was a voice spilling words. They weaved between the stars but couldn't catch the numbers.

"I need you."

His words jumped a tall building and swooped around me. "I'm coming. Don't move."

Two words hovered right above the coffee table.

"Don't move."

Fascinating. Sparkly.

I don't know how long they were there or how long I watched them.

Maybe I closed my eyes.

Words came back. Clearer but not sharp enough for me to understand them.

More words.

The voice.

I knew it meant I was okay, I could hear him talking to me, but was clueless as to what he was saying, and if I was answering.

There was something very wrong.

Something was on my face.

The room came back.

"Ellie?"

"Kurt."

"Welcome back," Kurt said with a small smile. "Can you tell me what happened?"

"I don't know."

The walls undulated, picking up pace and gathering the rest of the room into a writhing mass. So much saliva I couldn't swallow fast enough to get rid of it.

I knew what came next. I struggled to my feet with my hand over my mouth.

Kurt was right beside me. He knew too. I leaned on him, I had no choice, walking was difficult.

He opened the bathroom door. A quick flash of this being funny one day was all I got.

We'd been here before, but last time he held my hair for me, it was self-inflicted.

I did not do this to myself by drinking too much champagne.

No, I did not.

The only thing I ate different to everyone else was a candy bar. But no one but me drank a hot chocolate or chamomile tea either.

What the hell?

A cold towel was waiting when I stopped talking to the porcelain. I sat on the floor and hit the flush button feeling sorry for short people without a decent reach.

"Feel better?" Kurt said.

"I think so." I took a breath. Black spots danced in front of my eyes. Saliva built up.

Oh God.

I leaned over the toilet bowl and hurled again.

Rinse and repeat.

Eventually even the gagging stopped.

"How about now?" Kurt said.

"Yeah, no. Jesus, Kurt …"

He helped me stand. Shaky didn't begin to describe how I felt. Swirling grey-edged fog wafted in and over me. The floor wobbled away from my feet. Stumbling is so attractive. Way up there with vomiting and drooling. Suddenly I knew. This was not a stomach bug.

"Drugged," I mumbled and tried to get the wrapper from my pocket.

Sleep came too fast. As I drifted into dreamland, I wondered if Kurt slipped Ketamine into my tea. No, it was before the tea, dumb ass. And everything was gone. Gone crazy. I had no idea what was happening or if any of it was real. A dream, perhaps.

The world shimmered like a heat wave in the sand.

A kitchen door came into view.

I could see Kurt as he leaned on the door jam, one hand shoved into his jeans pocket, the other swinging his sunglasses.

Sunlight shone from his sandy hair. It seemed a little longer than usual. It suited him. A smile crept over his face as he looked down the hallway at me. I think I was smiling back.

He was happy. I ducked under his arm and headed down the path to the edge of the driveway. I heard the door shut and his footsteps following me. His fingers wrapped around my upper arm.

I turned to face him.

A giant soap bubble appeared over his head; as he spoke words appeared in the bubble written in black Comic Sans script. "You can't ignore this, Ellie."

"This?" I had a word bubble of my own. It was fascinating.

"This," he replied. Mesmerized by the advent of the soapy speech bubbles I watched as a new bubble attached to his first one. "We need to talk about what happened in Lexington."

Air rushed from my lungs so fast it made me gasp.

Without any effort on my part, a new speech bubble grew. "I lost the plot," I replied. "You know why. What's to talk about?"

"My jaw still aches every now and then," he responded, rubbing the side of his face.

His bubble popped. Soapy suds flew in all directions.

My words filled a new bubble. "I thought you said I hit like a girl?"

As I watched, Kurt grew a shiny new speech bubble from his mouth. "I may have misspoken."

It was hard to maintain eye contact with a giant bubble anchored to his mouth.

That was when I noticed the color and texture of the world had changed.

There were only four colors; everything was flat and framed by black lines. We'd become a comic strip. I reached for the car door but wasn't close enough.

His fingers encircled my wrist. The word bubble in front of me filled again. "You can let go my arm. I'm not going anywhere. And I'm not going to hit you."

He nodded, his fingers released. He thrust his hand into his pocket.

Kurt's bubble reformed; the words appeared and flashed. "Do you remember what I told you in Lexington?"

I stretched out my finger and poked the bubble. It wobbled. He was right there in front of me, paying no attention to the bubbles. "Ellie?"

Oh right, I have to answer. Movement on the roof of a nearby house drew my attention. Spiderman crouched on the edge of the roof, watching. A thought bubble emerged from his head. It said, I can't help her with this.

And he calls himself a superhero.

"Yes, I remember."

"This isn't going away. We need to face this and deal with it."

I saw his words before he said them. Cool. They shimmered inside the bubble. It was so clear. All I needed to do was pop the bubble to destroy the words. I stretched out my index finger and pressed on the surface of the bubble. Words jumbled then straightened out.

"Ellie? You with me here?"

I blinked. Everything I saw stayed right in front of me. Enough. I pulled back my hand and jabbed my index finger into the bubble. It wobbled like Jell-O. I jabbed again. It popped.

Soapsuds soaked into the page. The ink smeared.

One last bubble floated from Kurt as he smudged across the wet page. "Don't ever change."

When I next opened my eyes, the room was dark apart from a lamp on the far side of the beds. There was no heat shimmer or sunlight.

No movement. No voices. Parts of a strange dream floated across my internal screen. Glimpses of Kurt and the conversation we shared. Thirst.

There was a glass of water on the nightstand. Sitting up enough to drink it was okay. I figured sips were smarter than gulping the whole thing. After three I stopped. Not keen on tempting fate I put down the glass.

"Hey."

I jumped.

"Sorry," Kurt said. He wasn't. I heard him laughing. "How you doing?"

"Not sure." My mind seemed clearer. I'd held down water. "Better?"

"Good." He crawled over his bed and onto mine, his fingers resting on the inside of my wrist while he looked at his watch. Thirty seconds passed.

"Good," he said again.

"Anyone else sick?"

"No."

"This isn't a bug?"

"No."

"What is it?"

"A drug of some kind. I sent the vending machine contents to our lab. Could be a case of some nut job poisoning candy bars for kicks."

It's not like that hasn't happened before.

"And I ate one ... what are the chances?"

"Slim," he replied. "This is why Sam and Lee are interviewing all the hotel staff."

"Wasn't an accident was it?"

"I don't think so."

"How the hell did someone drug me? And what was it?"

"I'm picking Ketamine," he said.

"Didn't feel like Ketamine. Or maybe it did. Not like I can judge, last time I met Ketamine I also met its friends skull fracture, broken arm, and coma."

Kurt smiled. "I remember."

"What makes you think Ketamine?"

"Most common side effects are blurred vision, confusion, drowsiness, increased or decreased blood pressure or heart rate, mental or mood changes, nausea, nightmares, vomiting."

That seemed about right especially the nightmare thing. Yeah, that's what it was a nightmare. Not something I wanted at all. A twisted Ketamine dream.

"Is truth part of it?" I said, hoping to make the question sound casual.

"It does make people a little freer with observations."

What if it wasn't a dream? "Was I talking?"

"Yes."

Oh, man. "What'd I say?" I braced myself.

He smiled and stood up. "I'll make you a cup of tea, and then I'll tell you."

Again with the tea.

I watched him make the tea and talk on his phone, and pace the room while talking on his phone. I remembered bits and pieces of my dream. It wasn't a nightmare.

It was a possibility.

Tea. Hot, sweet, tea. Tea never tasted so good. I listened to Kurt tell me what I'd said. It could've been a lot worse. I'd remained noncommittal. It was what it was. I just didn't know what it was.

I finished the tea and slid back down under the covers.

"You had the perfect opportunity," I said, hoping I hid my smile.

"I prefer my dates to be awake," Kurt said, his voice quiet. "I need to take blood." Kurt opened his case.

"Tomorrow?"

"Depends what the drug was, could be gone by then. Let's do it now."

I extracted my left arm from under the blankets.

"Go on then."

I didn't even feel the needle but I did watch the vial fill with blood, then another, then another.

"You leaving me with any?"

"You've got plenty."

"Why so many vials?"

"Running bloods, may as well run everything."

Great.

Kurt made a phone call to a courier while he sat with me for a few minutes. "Sleep, you'll feel much better in the morning."

I don't think that's an assumption that can be made.

"Goodnight."

When I opened my eyes, it was daylight. Kurt sat in the chair by the window.

"Breakfast in the dining room when you're ready. How do you feel?" Kurt said.

"Okay, I think." Breakfast in the dining room. "Do we know how the drug got into me yet and what it was?"

"Yes, we do. Sam is good at getting information out of people."

Understatement of the century. "And?"

"The waitress we had last night spiked your hot chocolate with powdered Ketamine. She initially spiked your coffee but you didn't drink it. I think you only had about a third of your coffee after dinner."

Which could've been enough. So she doped me twice. I had a feeling I was lucky to see the morning.

"How did she know I'd drink the hot chocolate?"

"The waitress overheard a comment I made in the restaurant about you drinking hot chocolate."

"I'm pretty sure they call them servers now," I replied letting his words sink in. Ketamine in the hot chocolate powder. Ketamine in coffee has been done before but hot chocolate that was new. A step up from spitting in the coffee I guess. She's one sick bitch. Just glad I didn't see rainbow people and sing like Mac did. Because vomiting is so much better than singing? Keeping it classy.

"Did we talk about hot chocolate?" I asked Kurt.

"Yes, we were discussing how you should drink less coffee at night and you said you'd developed a taste for hot chocolate," Kurt replied. "There was also a discussion about who would pay for dinner, and you told the server to put it on your tab, that way the Bureau would pay. From that conversation the server leaped to the conclusion that you weren't sharing a room."

"Hang on, I don't remember drinking hot chocolate?" I realized my mouth was still moving too late and the rest of my thought tumbled from my lips, "Why would anyone do that? What the hell? I mean, really, what the hell?"

"That's how she gets her kicks. Last night the same server delivered tea, coffee, and a hot chocolate sachet to our room. I didn't notice until after I'd made you chocolate that there was only one. I suppose she noticed you didn't finish your coffee and figured you didn't get enough of a dose."

"You're fucking with me ..."

"Nope, she's a complete psycho and picks people at random to drug. She got the room number when you charged dinner to our room. While you were sleeping we found a camera in here."

"You what?"

"She chooses a woman from the restaurant. Someone who charges the meal back to their room, drugs the chosen woman, usually by adding the drug to the meal, sets up a camera, and sells views over the internet. Once the drug starts to take effect she sends in someone to ..."

I swallowed hard. "Oh, my God."

"Yeah, she's been doing this for about six months ... that's a lot of women who have been sexually assaulted and raped and have no fuc'n idea."

"You guys have been busy."

"We have. She's been charged by us and is being taken to the nearest field office by local police."

"You did take my blood, yes?" Considering the night, it was smart to ask.

"Yes. Results will be back tomorrow."

"Was I alone long enough for anything ...?"

"No, you called me. I came straight back and I never left you."

"We don't need to do a rape kit?"

"No. Nothing happened to you. I was there. I think her plan fell over when she realized we were sharing a room."

He cleared his throat. "It didn't fall over completely though. She was still selling views."

"That's not good ..."

"Well, no fun for the viewers – nothing was happening except for you vomiting." He smiled. "Although I guess some people like that kind of thing."

"Yuck."

I wasn't sure how to feel. Lucky. Relieved that I wasn't alone. Sad for the victims who'd lived happily unaware, because now they would know. Now someone had to find them and tell them what happened to them. Life has a way of being both sucky and lucky all at once.

There I go again being a human target. Albeit an unwitting one. Where the hell was Chance when I needed him? A small smile broke free.

Chance meet Kurt, and he's very very real.

"Give me half an hour." Then I had a thought. "Cameras are gone, yeah?"

Kurt's smile returned with added cheek. "Yeah. I'll be with Lee and Sam. We'll wait."

I'm With You

Sam ambled into my office carrying a pizza box.

"Yo, Chicky, hungry?" He grinned, set the box on the coffee table, and planted himself on the sofa. "Look who I'm asking. Is water wet?"

"What are you saying?" I closed the file on my desk. My chair slid back as I stood.

His smiled beamed at me. Sam opened the box and folded the lid back.

"Just an observation on your appetite ..." Sam's voice trailed off as his gaze settled on the contents.

"I burn a lot of calories," I muttered. "Active life."

"Chicky you need to see this," Sam said pushing the box to the middle of the table.

I joined him on the sofa and looked into the box.

Gross.

"What the hell is on that?" Sam didn't respond. His head shook from side to side. "On second thoughts, I'm not hungry."

"I'm with you, Chicky." Sam leaned back on the sofa. I knew the look on his face. He was trying to detach.

"What did you order?" I had my phone in my hand and a pen in the other. I flicked one of the lumps in the pizza with my pen. Nausea washed over me. Dropping the pen, I made a call.

"Kurt, my office, now." I hung up.

"Pepperoni," Sam said. "I ordered pepperoni." He hauled himself to his feet and walked across the room. I watched as he leaned on the edge of my desk. He didn't look good. His usual Denzel Washington meets LL Cool J look washed out.

"Not eyeball then?"

He shook his head.

"You okay?" That was new. I'd never seen Sam so shaken. "Get some air, Sam."

He nodded and headed for the door. I took pictures of the pizza with my phone. Kurt walked in as Sam left.

"Should I go after him?" Kurt asked motioning to the door. "He did not look good. We having pizza for lunch?"

"Sam needs some air. Pizza was for lunch. Check this out," I replied.

Kurt leaned down and peered into the box on the

table. He picked up my pen and pushed one of the lumps. Mozzarella strings stretched from the eyeball as Kurt rolled it over. He repeated the process with the second lump. Saliva welled in my mouth and not in a good way. I swallowed hard and tried not to think too much about what I saw.

"Interesting choice in topping," Kurt said putting the pen down. He folded the lid over and looked at the name on the box. "Field trip?"

"Yep." Anything to get away from what was in front of me.

I called the techs.

"It's SSA Conway. I need a crime scene tech in my office, please."

"I'll send someone, might be a few minutes ma'am."

"Okay."

I ended the call and stood up.

"You didn't ask," Kurt said pointing at the pizza box.

"I don't want to know?"

Kurt laughed. "You have a pizza with a matching pair of eyes nestled in the mozzarella and you don't want to know?"

I stood up and walked over to the window. Steading myself with a hand on the wall, I watched the street below. A minute ticked by in silence. One deep breath and turned to face Kurt.

"You don't look so great Conway."

I shrugged. "Are they human?"

"Probably."

"That's what I figured."

A noise at my open door attracted my attention. Sam and a tech. I beckoned them in.

Kurt called the tech over to him and the box. Sam and I stayed by the window. Seemed safest that way. We'd both developed sensitive stomachs all of a sudden.

I ignored Kurt and the tech, focusing instead on Sam.

"Where's Lee?"

"He's following a lead on a case that came in yesterday."

A case that came in yesterday? My mind stumbled about in the dark looking for a light switch. All it found was partially cooked eyeballs.

"Enlighten me ..."

"Metro wanted a hand with a missing person."

Nope, not ringing any bells.

"Was I even here when that came in?"

Sam regarded me for a moment. A smile spread across his face.

"You might have been out. The call came in about lunchtime. Lee said he'd look at the case and see if he could help."

Lunchtime. I was out. Running with Mitch.

"Okay." Another thought popped into my head. "Do you have the receipt for the pizza?"

"You going to get my money back?" Sam asked, only half a smile made it to his eyes, the rest fell away.

"Hell yes – they got your order wrong. It's the time and who served you that interests me most."

Sam pulled out his wallet and found the receipt. He pressed it into my hand.

Kurt approached us. "Ready?"

We nodded. I was happy to leave the tech to whatever the tech was going to do. It looked like he was taking the box and its contents back to the lab. Fine by me.

We walked in the door of the pizza place ten minutes after leaving my office. The girl on the counter had both eyes.

A shudder ran through my body leaving me cold. She might have but someone didn't. I looked at Sam, he shook his head indicating her didn't recognize her.

I showed my badge and ID.

"Point me to the manager."

The girl faltered then pointed behind her. "She's out back."

"Call her over here please."

The girl obliged and the manager appeared. I noted the name on her uniform. Caroline.

She had eyes. I showed her my ID and asked if there was somewhere we could talk. A quick glance at Sam told me he recognized her. Interesting.

"My office," she replied. "This way."

Caroline opened a gate in the counter and let us through. Sam and Kurt went into the work area. They would speak to other staff members and locate the person who took Sam's order, while I handled the manager. The smell of the cooking pizzas made me feel ill. I was done with pizza.

"Take a seat, Agent. How can I help?" Caroline sat behind her desk.

I opted to stand and handed her the pizza receipt.

"One of my agents ordered a pepperoni pizza."

A frown crossed her face. "Yes, I can see that."

"We found extra toppings that weren't ordered," I said. "Any idea how eyeballs got onto the pizza?"

"There was what on your pizza?"

"This ..." Scrolling through my phone I quickly located the pictures taken of the pizza and showed the manager.

She paled and leaned back in the chair. The same reaction that Sam and I experienced it. The need for distance.

"I have no idea," she said. "None. How would that even happen?"

"If I was to speculate I'd say eyes were removed from someone and added to the pizza. But it didn't happen at the beginning of the cooking process. The eyes were still quite soft. What sort of ovens do you use?"

"Wood fired traditional pizza ovens."

"So the pizza can be removed part way through cooking?"

She nodded. "Yes, it can."

"Who has access to the ovens?"

"All the staff."

"No one person in particular?"

"No, on the busiest shifts I have five people in the kitchen making the pizzas. Whoever is closest when the timer goes is who gets the pizza out, cuts it, boxes it, and passes it to the person in the counter. Then it's put in a warmer, or given to the waiting customer, or delivered by one of our delivery people." She looked at the receipt. "This was a pick up. Did your agent wait?"

"Yes, he did."

There was a knock on the door. The girl who'd been on the desk when we arrived entered.

She addressed me. "Ma'am there is another FBI agent here, he'd like to see you."

"Thank you." I turned to Caroline. "I'll be back. Meanwhile, I'd like a list of all your employees and shift rosters."

"Of course."

I followed the girl out. Lee was leaning on the counter looking out the door.

"Hey, how'd you know we were here?" I asked, joining him.

"I didn't. I followed a series of leads and ended up here. But your car is parked right out there, so I guessed."

"We need to talk, outside." At the door, I flipped the open sign over and called back to the girl on the counter. "You're closed."

She nodded. Fear settled on her face.

Lee held the door for me then followed me to the edge of the sidewalk. I wanted to remain visible from inside the store.

"This is the missing person case for Metro?"

"Yes. Male, twenty-two, attending George Mason. Didn't show up for classes for the last three days. No one's seen him or heard from him. Metro found his cell phone in his dorm room but not his wallet or car keys. No signs of a struggle or any misadventure in the room."

"And how did that lead you to here?"

"It was a convoluted trail," Lee said and went on to explain. "Timothy Claxton was last seen leaving the dorm four nights ago." Lee flipped his notebook open. "Metro had nothing apart from a sighting of his car and a credit card purchase on that night. His car was captured on a traffic camera on Pennsylvania Avenue at nine-forty-three that night, at ten-twenty he bought something at a bar."

"Bars often have cameras ..."

"They do, not this one. It's the kind of bar you go to when you don't want anyone to know where you are or what you're doing."

I knew bars like that. Conducted a few meetings in places just like that over the years. Dodgy establishments.

"So he's in a seedy bar drinking?"

"Rum."

"He's a pirate?" I could hear Christopher Chance so clearly I turned my head in case he was behind me. A modicum of disappointment surfaced no Chance. Just his disembodied voice-saying, pirate.

Pirates? They wear eye patches. What if the eyeballs weren't a matched set?

Lee grinned. "I don't think he's a pirate."

"Shame. Love a good pirate story."

"You like Mark Valley saying the word pirate."

I shrugged. That was true.

"Back to your rum drinking non-pirate ..."

"Timothy is in the bar drinking and that's the last record of him."

"And you turn up here?"

"The bartender was real helpful. He was less helpful to Metro."

I knew exactly what that meant. Lee has a way of charming information out of people, in contrast Sam scared information out of people.

"Okay and the bartender told you what?"

"He told me Timothy was with someone, an older man. The guy was in his late forties or maybe thirties and life had been tough. Not my words." Lee's eyes met mine. "I got a sketch of the guy. He apparently only used cash at the bar. No name. No distinguishing anything. This morning I ran the sketch through everything we've got. I found a few possibilities. Two bottomed out, the third led me here."

"A pizza place. Kids usually work in pizza places."

"They don't own the places though, do they?"

"No, they don't." I looked through the window and saw the manager at the counter. "Let's go back in and ask Caroline where the boss is," I said. "You got a name, right?"

"Yep."

Lee got the door for me.

"Caroline, who owns this business?" I knew before she said that it was her husband.

"My husband and I own the business together."

Lee referred to his notebook. "Is your husband's name Theodore Romano?"

She nodded.

Lee showed her a photo on his phone. "Is this him?"

She nodded.

"Where is he now?" I asked.

"He'll be here soon, he takes over from me at two."

"Does he come in the front door or the back?"

"Front."

I walked back to the door and flipped the sign to open. "We'll wait in your office."

Lee accompanied Caroline while I went to find Sam and Kurt.

They were finishing up the last interview with staff. I waited until the staff member returned to work.

"Lee's here, his missing person could be the owner of the eyes. He was last seen in the company of the owner of this store in a seedy bar across town."

"Fascinating," Kurt said. "We could be looking for a body."

"Or a blind man who needs medical urgent medical treatment."

"Yes, that's a possibility."

"You two need to be out here, Lee and I are in the office with the manager who is also the wife of our suspect. She says he usually uses the front door, but just in case ..."

Sam nodded. "We're on it Chicky."

He looked around. "They'd have big freezers somewhere, yeah?"

"Maybe," I said. "They'd at least have cold rooms for vegetables and meats. They make the pizzas with fresh ingredients." I remembered reading that on the wall by the counter.

"Over there," Sam said pointing to an alcove.

"Wait right there, I'll get the manager." I looked at Kurt. "On seconds thoughts, Kurt can you wait and Sam you come with me."

Sam and I hurried back to the office. "You and Lee wait for whatshisname, Theodore. I need Caroline to accompany me."

Worry lines creased her face. She followed into the kitchen area.

"What's going on?" she asked. "Why do you need me?"

"I either need you to give me access to your cold

rooms or to go get a warrant. It'd be simpler if you let us look."

She faltered. "What are you looking for?"

"Can we look?" I didn't want to tell her what we were looking for.

"We should wait for my husband?"

"I'd rather not."

Her thought process was evident on her face. Patiently I waited for her to come to a decision.

"Okay. You can look."

"Thank you."

Kurt was across the room and gone from sight almost immediately.

Caroline and I walked over to the far side of the room and waited.

"How many cold rooms?"

"Two," she replied. Her eyes fixed on the doors within the alcove.

Pacing would've worked for me but my nervous energy wasn't going to help her at all. The wait was tiresome.

Noises at the front of the building attracted my attention.

Sam's voice rang out. "SSA!"

That was my cue. "Stay here," I said to Caroline. I banged on the door. "Kurt!"

He emerged.

"Problem?"

"Maybe."

I drew my weapon as I moved with care through the kitchen to the sound of Sam's voice. Motioning to people to move back to where Caroline stood, frozen to the spot.

Breathing slowly settled my heart rate. Kurt next to me settle it more. I pointed. Kurt left, me right. I went in first. Lee was doubled over by the desk. Sam had a male in handcuffs. From the corner of my eye, I saw Kurt holster his weapon and go to Lee. My focus was Sam and the man.

"What happened?" I wanted to know why Lee was hurt and the male wasn't dead. He didn't look great but he was in better condition than Lee.

"He threw a knife from the door," Sam said.

"And he is?"

"Theodore Romano."

Kurt looked up. "Like knives do you Mr. Romano?"

The man said nothing.

Nothing at all. His face remained neutral. Kurt

called for an ambulance. Sam removed Romano from the room.

"You okay, Lee?"

"Yeah Ellie, it's a flesh wound." He didn't sound okay.

"Kurt, did you find anything out there?" I asked.

"I found the body of a male in a box. He had no eyes."

It would have to be a big box.

"Why would someone kill, store the body, and use the eyeballs, all at their place of work?" I said. They both looked at me but knew not to answer. Thinking out loud. "They wouldn't. Too easy to get caught. Makes no sense."

But something else made a lot of sense.

"How many police complaints have there been from or against the pizza place down the street, what's it called, Pisa Pizza or something?"

"Yeah it is Pisa Pizza," Kurt replied.

Lee winced and held out his notebook. Kurt handed it to me. I flipped through it looking for a contact number for the Metro detective following this case. I couldn't hide my joy at finding out who it was. Josh Konstram. He'd made detective. Well that explained why he asked for our help. Josh and Delta had a long history of working together.

I made the call.

"Josh, its Ellie Conway. We might have found your missing male, not good news though. Nothing is making sense. I need some background." I told him where we were and asked him to come down.

"What are you thinking?" Kurt asked.

"Pizza wars. I'm thinking someone else killed Timothy and one of the staff here added his eyeballs to the pizza. They wouldn't have known whose pizza it was."

I took my thought out to the kitchen and to Caroline.

"Who here was hired most recently and maybe worked for Pisa Pizza down the street?"

"Kristofer." She looked around. "The one washing vegetables over there."

"Thanks."

I figured the best way to approach him was outright. Sam was watching my back. His prisoner was on the floor, cuffed and out of harm's way.

"Kristofer, I'd like a word." He started to move away. "I wouldn't if I were you. I have questions and you are going to supply me with answers."

His shoulders sagged. He seemed to fold inward.

"Come on over here," I said, holding out my arm to direct him.

Ten minutes later, I had a confession from Kristofer. Sam has that effect on people. He had indeed doctored the pizza. He not only used to work for the other company but also was related to the owner. A tentative cousin connection. Apparently that's all you need in the pizza business. By the time Josh arrived, I had everything he needed to arrest the owner of Pisa Pizza for murder. Theodore would be arrested for assault on a federal officer. I'd be pushing for malicious wounding and the full ten-year jail term. No one throws knives at my team and walks away. No one.

The other pizza guy had followed Theodore to his rendezvous with Timothy. It wasn't the first time. Poor Caroline had no idea her husband batted for both teams. The owner of Pisa Pizza decided to frame Theodore and close his pizza shop in the process. Nasty. Sick. And not very bright.

And we wouldn't be eating pizza for a long time.

Subway is our fast food of choice from here on in.

Bullet

"Go left," I said, my words flew away on a sudden wind gust.

"How far?" Lee asked as he adjusted his hold on his assault rifle and used the scope to scan the tree line. The wind dropped. Stillness descended.

"Past the stand of three trees and into the clearing."

I used the scope on my rifle and swept it over the area to our right, looking for potential threats. Nothing noticeable. Didn't mean there wasn't anything. Our eyes are drawn to movement. Someone in a Ghillie suit could be lying among fallen tree branches and we wouldn't notice until they moved. We weren't after military linked Unsubs. We were looking for eleven missing young women. They'd disappeared over a four-week period from nine Christian Camps all across the state.

The last lead we found bought us to these woods. It was a long shot. A confidential informant thought he heard something after a meeting with someone we considered might be involved. Yeah we had nothing but conjecture. I opted to go in with Lee and do some recon. The rest of the team were following various angles thrown up by other agencies who were involved in the case.

"We're good," Lee said. He moved quickly and stayed low. Not easy for someone as powerfully built and tall as he is. I followed.

Remember to breathe.

Lee and I took cover behind the first of the three trees. Big old naked Oak trees had decent trunks and gave excellent cover.

"How far away is the cabin?" Lee asked.

I pulled out my cell phone and accessed the feed from the drone above us. Tapping the icon on the screen gave me control of the bird. Another icon allowed me to zoom in with the drone camera on the trees we hid behind. If it hadn't been early spring, we wouldn't have been able to use a drone. But the abundance of leaf buds not leaves on the trees and the lack of scrubby undergrowth meant air surveillance was possible. I thanked whatever Gods were out there for technology and early spring.

"Wave at the drone Lee," I muttered, moving my

finger across the screen to find the cabin. "One-click north east."

"See anything else?"

"Wait one ..." I swept my finger back across the screen highlighting the area between the cabin and us. No sign of movement. No sign of anything except woods. I gave it a minute and did another sweep. Taking careful note of anything that may have changed. Nothing.

I swung back to the cabin and zoomed in. Two cars. No signs of life. As I watched, a chicken pecked its way across the yard and joined several other chickens near the cabin.

"We got chickens," I said. "Two cars and a herd of chickens."

"I don't think they're called a herd, El," Lee replied, a smile bounced around his voice as he continued watching the area around us through his riflescope. "I think the collective noun you're looking for is brood, clutch, or peep."

"Herd sounds better," I said watching the screen. The light changed near one of the windows. A shadow maybe. "A possible shadow moved inside the cabin. I think they're inside."

Two cars. Possibly five people in each car. Two of us. Ten of them. That was fair? Moving the drone to the far side of the cabin, I saw a dumpster. A big orange Waste Management dumpster. Looked like a tarp was secured on the top.

"Look," I said handing Lee the phone.

"A dumpster in the woods. Now that's new."

"Isn't it. Wouldn't think there'd be enough crap in a little cabin for a dumpster."

"What's the road like into here?"

Fair question. We helicoptered in. Nothing like a little bit of fast roping to get the blood moving.

"Sealed, single lane in a lot of places."

"So maneuvering a truck the size required to carry a dumpster isn't the easiest thing ever?"

"Exactly."

"A dumpster in the woods," Lee whispered. "Why the hell would anyone need a dumpster in the woods?"

One last look at the cabin and the surrounding area. No movement except a few chickens. I tapped the screen in the upper right corner and gave control of the drone back to command central then pocketed my phone.

"I dunno, but I want a look," I said. Shame the drone wasn't capable of giving us a peek into the dumpster.

They're clever but short of using an armed drone and shooting the shit out of the tarp over the dumpster, we were out of luck. Ours was rigged with cameras and audio surveillance equipment not missiles.

"We going?" Lee asked.

"Yeah, let do this thing."

Single file. I stepped exactly where Lee had to minimize any noise from snapping twigs. Half a click out, we stopped, using some scrubby Dogwoods as cover. I accessed the drone again and checked the area. Two cars. Chickens. A big orange dumpster. Nothing but the chickens moving.

"Let's get in there," Lee said.

"Moving out," I said. "I'll take point."

Lee's jaw muscles tensed.

I smiled. He and Sam had this thing and they thought I didn't know about it. They always took point. Protective. Usually I let them. Not today. This was my call. We were here because of my decision. If anyone's walking into anything, it's not going to be Lee. I moved in front of him and quietly made my way through another wooded section to the edge of a glade. Snow still lay in the shadows of the surrounding trees from a late storm that hit the area a week ago.

From the other side of the glade a twig snapped. My finger slipped onto the trigger of my rifle, held snug against my body by a three-point sling. My left hand came up into a fist. I felt Lee freeze behind me.

I dropped my hand, using it instead to steady my rifle as I brought the scope up to my eye.

"Shit," I hissed. "They've put a patrol out."

Jesus! How did I miss that? I didn't look far enough? Or maybe long enough? I shook my head. It didn't matter how I missed it. What mattered was what I did next.

"I count two men carrying rifles," Lee whispered. "One each."

"We're going to bring shit storm down on us if we get into a fire fight."

That couldn't happen. Not here. Not without back-up. I tried settling the rising annoyance with a deep breath. The whole situation drove me crazy. What started out as fun now sent my blood pressure skyward. If there was nothing going on in the cabin except some old friends going hunting then there'd be no need for a patrol. My gut said our informant had good information.

"We're going to have to go hand-to-hand here El?"

"I know. We'll circle around and take them out." I let the rifle go, it settled quickly into place. Right there if I needed it. From my belt, I unsheathed a knife. Lee did the same.

The KA-BAR was our knife of choice. If I absolutely had to use a knife then I wanted one trusted by our SWAT teams and military alike. I really hate knives. Really freaking hate them.

I took a breath and held it.

"Left," I said on my exhale, calling direction and my target. "On three."

Lee gave me a nod and a half-smile.

"Three."

We separated. I came up behind my guy. He was heavier than me but I was two inches taller and had the advantage of surprise.

Surprise! I kicked him hard behind one knee. He tumbled forward, trying to turn as he did. Managing to almost get his rifle around before I kicked again. The rifle smacked him in the face. He hit the ground hard, rolled and came up swinging wildly. His movements felt exaggerated and slow. He struggled for breath and tried to call out. That wasn't going to happen. I ducked under his flailing fist, got in close, slipped behind him and wrapped my left arm around his head and tipped it back hard and fast. My right hand pressed the blade into his throat under his jaw and sliced ear to ear in one long swift movement. Blood gushed. Messy but effective. He gurgled as he slid to the ground his hands grabbing at his throat. Hopeless. I checked him for communication equipment and only found a cell phone. Easy. I turned it off and dropped it into a pocket on my tactical vest. Didn't want anyone calling it and giving our position away. There was a chance the phone might also contain useful Intel. Something to check into later. When I looked up Lee was walking toward me wiping his knife on his trouser leg.

Nice.

I stabbed mine into the hard earth twice. Then sheathed it. We carried on, moving with care. No more foot patrols. Ten minutes later, we crept up behind the dumpster. A faint but foul odor curled around me. Dumpsters often smell but this was several notches above unpleasant. I smelled death under a chemical blanket.

"Look?" I pointed to the ground under the dumpster. The dumpster was sitting over a pit on what looked like steel girders. The pit containing charcoaled remains of a fire. "Someone went to quite a bit of effort. Digging a fire pit, bringing in steel girders, and a dumpster." I tentatively touched the metal bin. It was quite warm.

Lee peeled back a section of the tarp and peered in.

"Holy shit," he muttered then turned away from the dumpster. His shoulders heaved as he retched several times.

Not a good sign.

"All right?"

"You know what sodium hydroxide and water does to a body?"

Yep, it turns it into a coffee colored oily liquid.

"Uh huh." I did not like where this was going but it explained the stench. "What's in there?"

"Goop," he replied, gagging again.

"That a technical term?"

"Fuck yes."

"And?"

"There is a lot of liquid in there." He tapped the side of the bin with his hand. "Smells like ..."

"Sodium hydroxide," I finished for him. "Caustic soda."

"Yes."

"Not acid?" I was pretty sure it wasn't acid. It took a lot more acid to dissolve a body than it did caustic soda. Caustic soda was easy to obtain. The purchase or theft of large quantities of acid would trigger an immediate law enforcement investigation.

"Not acid," Lee said. "They're dissolving bodies."

"Ah crap, that's why the pit and fire." A horrible feeling we weren't going to find the missing woman bounced around in my gut, making me feel ill.

Lee nodded. "Sodium hydroxide works best if heated to over 300 degrees. I doubt that was possible here, but, who knows?"

I stood on the edge of one of the girders and peered into the dumpster.

"Don't breathe in," Lee cautioned.

"Looks like they got it hot enough. How many bodies you think?"

"It's a big dumpster," Lee replied. He watched the cabin.

"So that's what they're doing out here, disposing of bodies."

"I'll call it in, El. We're going to need forensics out here and back up."

"You know what?"

"What?" Lee replied with his phone in his hand.

I lifted my rifle.

"Screw these assholes."

Lee fell in behind me. I heard him talking on his phone. I signaled left and moved. Trusting that Lee went right. Two doors and windows on three sides. I headed straight for what I deemed to be the front door. Because fuck this shit.

I stood four feet from the door. For a spilt second I considered announcing my presence and thought better of it.

Knocking seemed like a polite thing to do. So, I shot at the door. Wood splintered and flew into the air. A yell from inside made me smile. It shouldn't have. Sometimes I'm just not a nice person.

I called out, "FBI. Drop your weapons."

Scrambling, sliding, people stumbling around. Sounded like at least one person fell over furniture.

Lee called out from the back, "You're surrounded.

Drop your weapons and move out through the front door."

More falling, sliding, tripping, and then gunfire. I ducked behind one of the cars. Shadows flickered by the windows. I fired. Someone squealed. Another shadow. I fired again. This time no squeal but a sickening thud. That was a win. Lee called out again reminding the remaining people to exit via the front door.

A hand flapped something white out the trashed door.

"Come on out," I said, staying behind the car. A foot, then leg, then half a body appeared. The white cloth vanished. I fired as a hand holding a black object came into view. A scream filled the air. Blood spurted across the porch. The black object hit the ground. A pistol. Nice.

"Bitch!" the owner of the stump squawked, clutching what was left of his hand to his chest. He staggered out the door.

"You might wanna keep that elevated and use your belt as a tourniquet," I offered helpfully.

From behind him, I heard a familiar noise. A red mist sprayed across the ground in front of me as the stumpy guy fell, face first into the dirt. Killed by one of his own kind.

Twenty-five minutes after it began it was over.

We had two men in custody and six bodies, including the two in the woods. Turned out there were four people in each car.

I sat on the hood of one of the cars and watched the two men we had cuffed on the ground. We found female clothing in the cabin, a lot of it. That suggested there were women somewhere. My money was on the dumpster.

"How many bodies are in the dumpster?" I asked.

They smiled.

"You may as well tell me, it's not going to make a difference now. You can only be given one death sentence. The state can't kill you twice."

Neither responded.

Lee stepped in. "She's right. Death is a onetime event. Staying alive however, that requires you to talk."

And us not to shoot.

The smaller of the two men growled like a rabid dog then said, "What makes you think there are bodies in there?"

"The clothing we found in the cabin ... unless you all come out here and dress up like women?"

The smaller man smiled. "What if we do, it's not against the law to wear a dress."

He was really starting to piss me off.

"So which one of you liked to wear the pale pink dress with rosebuds on it?"

He tipped his head to the older man. "Rosebud there."

The other older man glared at his buddy.

"You lying sack of shit."

"Sorry, did you have something of value to add?" I asked the older man. "Like who you are, how many bodies make up the human soup in the dumpster, and a list of names?"

He shook his head. "I have nothing to say."

I shrugged.

"Don't you just hate when you can't find the right handbag to match your shoes?"

He glared at me.

"Really? Nothing to say?" I said.

He shook his head. The smaller man smirked.

Lee stepped closer to me, partially blocking their view so we could speak.

"We're not going to get anywhere. Back up is another hour away at least. It'll be dark in half an hour. What do you want to do?"

"Leave them out here. We'll go inside."

"The doors and windows are smashed, the place is splattered with blood and fresh meat. It's bear country. We're better off in one of the cars."

"Good thinking."

The car we were sitting on was unlocked.

The older man watched us.

"You can't leave us out here," he said.

"Ah, wrong," I replied. "It'll be dark soon and it's getting cold. We're going to wait for our back up in this car."

Lee took the driver's seat. I slid into the front passenger seat.

"The keys are here," Lee said.

"Good."

We watched the men. They weren't happy.

As darkness fell, I looked at Lee.

"Let's get some light on the subject."

He turned the key in the ignition and flicked the lights on just as an enormous black bear ambled out of the woods beside the cabin.

"Time we left," Lee replied as the bear homed in on the two men who were struggling against their cuffs and yelling.

Rolling In The Deep

Everyone needs a vacation, everyone, even SSA Ellie Conway. If the universe could just accept that life would be so much easier.

"Fourteen days of Saturday?" I asked leaning on the car door. No phone. No internet. No badge. No gun. Fourteen days of Saturday. And unreachable by normal means. It appealed.

His voice was clear over the cell phone I held to my ear, "Something like that. You up for it?"

"I've got four weeks off, so yeah, I'm up for it."

Four weeks off sounded better than being stood down for four weeks. On the plus side I still got to keep my badge and I was being paid. I'd skated a thin line and survived with nothing more than some enforced vacation time and a slap on the wrist from the Director.

"When do you want to leave?"

"Tonight," I replied. "I want to leave tonight."

"Just you?"

He sounded hopeful? Maybe he thought I'd bring

Delta. Nope. We're not joined at the hip despite what it looks like.

"Yes just me."

"Want me to go ahead and book the tickets?"

"Yep, I'll meet you at your place later this afternoon."

"We running today?"

"Absolutely."

"Then I'll come to you."

"Okay."

"See you soon."

I hung up and pocketed my phone. Kurt walked toward me carrying two coffees in take-out cups. The winter sun bounced off the edge of his sunglasses. I lifted mine from the top of my head and pushed them on.

"All good?" Kurt asked handing me a cup of coffee.

"Yep," I replied, taking the lid off the cup. Steam rushed out, fogging my glasses. It took a moment for the steam to clear. "Who's driving?"

"Me," Kurt said. "Scoot."

I walked around the car and slid into the passenger seat.

"We're done, yeah?"

"Yes," Kurt said checking the mirrors. "We're done. How long are you off for?"

"A month."

He glanced at me. "Going away?"

I smiled. "Yeah, I am."

"You going to make this hard?" he asked pulling out into the traffic.

I sighed. "I'm lucky I still have a job..." I wasn't feeling chatty.

"We all are," he replied. "We pushed Assistant Director Owen to the very edge." Kurt glanced at me. "And my question stands, are you going to make this hard?"

"I'm going to a place by the sea with a friend."

Not a lie. It is by the sea, just not a sea in this hemisphere. I smiled thinking about how far we were going. It was the sea at the end of the world.

I caught his interested glance and ignored it.

"Virginia Beach, Norfolk, Chesapeake Bay?"

"No, it's in the south."

It doesn't get much more southern and yet still remain warm enough for me to enjoy it. I'm not a penguin. I felt the smile on my lips. Not a penguin but sometimes Mitch referred to me as Penguin and I liked it. I couldn't remember a time in my life where anyone had given me a nickname. New. Nice.

"Gulf of Mexico?"

"More southern than that," I said and drained my coffee.

"Cotopaxi is not by the beach," Kurt mumbled.

"I never said Ecuador," I replied. "And how did you hear about Cotopaxi?"

"Iain Campbell mentioned you, him, and Mike Davenport were talking about climbing Cotopaxi in January."

Snowdrifts were piled by the roadside, melting in the winter sun. It was definitely January. I wasn't in a mountain climbing mood.

"They're going without me," I said. I felt like walking on a beach not struggling for oxygen at the top of a cold mountain, as much fun as that would be, it's not what I wanted or who I wanted to be with. "I'm going away, Kurt. I'm out of cell range and will have no internet for two weeks. Then I'll be back and I'll tell you all about it." Maybe.

He pulled up my driveway. The gates opened and then closed before the car got to the house.

"Be safe Conway," Kurt said as I opened the car

door. "Hope the mystery man is worthy."

"He is," I replied. "See you in a couple of weeks. Keep Delta ticking?"

"We'll be waiting."

I shut the door. Kurt waited for me to go inside before he drove off.

I walked into the empty house. It felt cold, I knew it wasn't cold, the heating was always on, but empty houses feel cold. They lack life. At the living room door I spoke. "Computer, listen. Bon Jovi."

Seconds later the opening bars of the first track on the latest Bon Jovi album filled the emptiness. The cat jumped off a chair by the window and stretched. He ambled over and purred around my legs.

"Come on, I'll feed you, then you're off to Aidan's for two weeks." Shrek was used to being bundled off to Aidan's. It happened so often I wondered why I bothered bringing him back home again. Pretty sure the cat liked Aidan better than he liked me.

By the time I'd fed the cat and packed. Mitch had arrived.

He looked good and I was feeling playful. I steadied the smile on my face, then swallowed it and replaced it with disappointment and took a breath.

"Bad news..."

"What?"

He leaned his hip against the kitchen counter.

"Work, I've got to go away," I said with the steadiest voice I could muster.

"You serious?"

"Yeah."

"But we..."

"I know, it sucks," I replied. "Sometimes shit happens. I don't like it much either."

Mitch sighed. I smiled.

"For how long?" he asked, a hint of resignation in his voice. I knew it wouldn't last long.

He bounced back faster and harder than anyone I'd ever met.

I was pretty sure that was a large part of his charm.

Upbeat optimism. Solution orientated. He was infectious.

"Dunno. A few days, a week, longer maybe..."

"Who am I going to run with if you're gone a week or longer?"

Already I heard his smile returning. I looked up and saw the sparkle in his eyes.

"You're good," he said with a grin. "And evil."

"I thought I was good. Occasionally a little evil."

He leaned over the counter and kissed my cheek.

Sweet. Affectionate.

He was driving me crazy and judging by the twinkle in his eyes, he knew it.

"Fire... you're playing with it," I cautioned.

His smiled widened. "Buddy, pal, best friend..."

All words I'd heard before.

"Having fun?"

The smile on his face said it all. Fun, he was having it in spades.

"Take it slow...," he said.

"Yeah, yeah. Pretty sure we both agreed..."

"Friends remember?"

"And again..."

I wanted to reach across, wrap my hands around his lapels, pull him over the counter and have my evil way with him, right there on the kitchen floor.

"El, you're hopeless."

"Me?"

"If you drag me over the counter there's no going back."

"Yeah, well." I stopped. Confused. "How'd you

know?"

"The look in your eye and the way you bit your lip."
Deflect.

"Time for a run?"

"Good idea."

I leaned over the counter and looked at what Mitch was wearing. Jeans. Really? Sliding back I straightened up before temptation got the best of me. Or Mitch did.

"You got your gear?"

"Yep," he replied bending and lifting up a bag from the floor.

"Let's get changed then." Not quite trusting myself to walk past him without touching I added, "Go on. Guest bedroom okay with you?"

Mitch looked over his shoulder and smiled. "That'll do me."

"Top of the stairs on the right," I said and followed Mitch down the hallway and up the stairs.

He pointed to an open door on the right. "Here?"

"Yes," I said and waited until he entered the room before I hurried to my room. I changed into academy sweats and running shoes. My gun and holster sat on the dresser next to my badge and phone. Tempting. I left them where they were. Running not working. At the door I changed my mind and went back. I scooped everything into my gym bag with my water bottle and towel. I wasn't on vacation yet.

Mitch waited at the bottom of the stairs. Water bottle and car keys in his hand.

"Ready?" I asked.

"Always."

I didn't doubt that for a second. As he opened the front door his car keys jangled. I dropped my bag on the floor in the back of his car and climbed into the front passenger seat. My door closed. Mitch smiled through the window as he walked around the hood and opened his door.

We ran at Rock Creek Cemetery. Running every path that wound through the undulating cemetery and avoiding the creepy circle of crypts.

Two hours later we were back at my place.

"Airport by six," Mitch said. "I've got everything with me. Mind if I use your shower?"

I froze. Mind if I join you was sitting there on the tip of my tongue. I nodded. Not safe to speak.

He laughed at me. He wasn't laughing with me.

My phone buzzed like a bumble bee trapped in a

paper bag. I freed it from my gym bag. The image on the screen caused an eye brow to rise.

Mike Davenport, the famous actor brother of Delta's Lee Davenport.

I read his text. 'Morning wifey, how are you?'

Funny man.

I replied: 'Great. How are you? Still enjoying being the tragic widower?'

'Beating them off with a stick. Smiley face.'

As I knew he would.

'And you wanted?'

'Come away with me.'

Vacation invitations in all directions. I'd never been so popular.

'Thanks for the offer but I have plans.'

'You don't know when I'm going.'

'It's January. Ecuador.'

'Smiley face. Be more fun with you.'

'Rules. Remember? We can't be seen together.'

He replied with a sad face. 'Take care Ellie.'

When I looked up Mitch was standing at the top of the stairs.

"All right?"

"Yeah." I waved my phone in the air. "Lee's brother

trying to get me to climb Cotopaxi with him."

"Do you want to?" He walked down the stairs and stopped two above me.

"No, I want to go to New Zealand with you."

"As long as you're sure." A smile filled his voice. It was infectious like him.

Seventeen hours of flight time was followed by another twenty minutes in a Cessna and an hour and change in a rental car. Mitch was surprisingly comfortable driving on the wrong side of the road. Me, not so much. The trip was fun. My cell went several times before reception dropped off. I smiled as I turned it off for the first time in my memory.

Goodbye world. I'm out.

The winding road afforded glimpses of the sea through the bush at irregular intervals. Promise of relaxation drifted on the tide.

"We're here," Mitch said turning down a steep driveway and parking in front of a garage.

"Nice," I replied, opening my door. Escaping the confines of the car felt good. I stretched. Standing on solid ground felt a little weird. Everything felt like it was still moving. Jetlag.

"You okay?" Mitch looked at me over the roof of the

car.

I smiled. "Yep." I stretched again, easing the knots out of my muscles. I wasn't designed to keep still for extended periods of time. "Where exactly is here?" I followed Mitch to the right of the garage to a staircase. At the bottom of the stairs I saw a house.

"This is where I come to fish."

"It's a long way to come for a few fish," I muttered.

He ran down the stairs, then another smaller set of stairs and unlocked the door. Mitch opened the door wide and said, "Welcome to paradise." He ushered me into a foyer. Stairs rose in front of me, another staircase descended to the right. The ascending stairs led to a mezzanine floor. French doors were visible from where I stood. I guessed there was a balcony up there.

I followed Mitch down the stairs; he opened a door at the bottom that led to the vast living area.

The house was a far cry from a fishing cabin. I wandered to the left and stood in front of large windows. The driveway came down the left of the garage and the house, curved around the front and then carried on down to the sea.

Noises behind me caught my attention. Mitch in

the kitchen, making coffee. I walked across the room, through the dining area and to the kitchen.

"Fishing?"

Mitch smiled. "Yes."

"You come all the way out here to this house and go fishing?" Incredulousness crept into my voice. I watched him as he moved about in the kitchen. "So who lives here when you're not around?"

"What makes you think someone lives here?"

"There's no dust." I walked around the kitchen table and opened the fridge. "The fridge is full." I picked up a bottle of milk and checked the date. "The food is fresh."

He laughed.

"The couple who live next door take care of this place."

"Uh huh. And?"

"No and, they take care of the house when I'm not here."

"Mind if I have a look around?"

"Go for it, I'll yell when the coffee is ready and bring our bags down."

"Want a hand?"

"No, you go explore."

I opened the door to the stairs again and decided to start with the room at the end of the hall. I walked past another stairwell. So many stairs. The room at the end was a master bedroom, walk-in-wardrobe, en-suite bathroom. Nice.

At the top of a much darker stair case I paused. I could feel cold rising from below but couldn't see anything. I followed the stairs to a landing. There was nothing on the landing, round the corner more stairs. At the bottom of those stairs the cold grew. A tiled floor, glass doors, on the right a solid door on the left another solid door. The door on the right had a key in it. I turned to the left and opened the other door. A wine cellar. Racks of wine bottles lay covered in dust. No one had been in there for a while.

The other door beckoned. I turned the key and swung the door open. Another garage. A double garage. There was a boat on a trailer on the far side. The side nearest me was empty. No car. Tools. Fishing rods. Life-jackets. Nothing remarkable just functional.

Mitch's voice rang out. "Coffee!"

I closed the door on the tidy garage and climbed back up the stairs. A loud crash of breaking glass echoed below me. I turned trying to determine where the noise came from. Garage? Cellar?

Cellars don't have windows but they are full of glass.

Garage.

Mitch's voice rang out from above. "All right down there?"

"Yeah, not sure what that was," I yelled back.

"I'm coming."

My right hand sought the grip of the Glock that was always on my hip and came up empty. I looked down. Nope no gun. No holster. Unarmed. Not good. I took a deep breath.

New Zealand not Virginia.

How bad could a crashing noise really be?

I heard Mitch running down the stairs. He slowed for the last few steps then stopped beside me.

"Garage," I said.

Mitch turned the key in the lock and swung the door wide. Light streamed from the window on the other side of the garage. It wasn't broken. Everything looked the same as it had except for a pile of boxes. They'd toppled over. Broken glass spilled from an over turned box onto the garage floor.

"Think we found the source," Mitch said.

"Why did it fall?"

I wasn't convinced. I scoured the garage looking for a reason. Another noise. Tapping. Mitch heard it too. He stopped and turned around. My heart pounded. There was something or someone in the garage.

I crouched down, peering across the floor I saw feet way over by the boat trailer.

"A bird?" I said pointing to the trailer.

Mitch pressed a button on the wall. The garage door slowly began to lift. We watched as a large brown bird strutted out of the garage and down the driveway. It was as big as a chicken but with much longer legs and a long pointy beak. Kinda like a taller bigger kiwi just going by the kiwi I'd seen at the zoo in Washington, D.C.

"What the hell was that?" I asked.

"A Weka," Mitch replied. "They're inquisitive. He must've got trapped in here."

"Guess I got him all excited when I opened the door earlier?"

"Yeah, he probably thought you were going to let him out."

Mystery solved. I smiled. "He was kinda cute."

Mitch closed the garage door. We locked the interior door and headed back upstairs for coffee.

Half way through my coffee I put my cup down and looked at Mitch.

"Problem?" he asked.

"How'd the Weka get in the garage?"

"I don't know," he said setting his cup down. "Neighbours probably opened the door for something ..."

That seemed reasonable.

"So, the beach?"

"Definitely the beach. You want to finish exploring the house first?"

"I think so," I replied. "You could show me to my room?"

He bit his bottom lip. "I could."

"Did you get our bags?"

"Yes."

I didn't see them anywhere.

"Mine is?"

"In your room."

"Thank you."

Maybe I should go find out where my room was by myself. I mentally ticked areas of the house off a list.

What was left? Up. My gaze shifted from the coffee on the table to the window as I tried to determine time of day. Afternoon. But what day?

"Mitch?"

"Tuesday about three-thirty in the afternoon."

This time I didn't question how he knew what I was thinking. Where Mitch was concerned just-go-with-it seemed to be the best philosophy.

A yawn escaped unchecked. Mitch smiled. "Tired?"

"Little bit."

"Been a long two days."

Been a long life.

Another yawn crept out.

"Why don't you go have a nap?" Mitch said. "Your room is upstairs on the right. You'll find everything you need in there."

Everything? I doubt that.

"I think I will. What are you going to do?"

"Think I'll sleep too."

I stood up, placed my cup in the sink and found my room.

I rolled over, light peeked through a gap in the curtains. Life sang outside. Beautiful songs I'd never heard before.

I was beginning to see what Mitch travelled all the way out here for and why he referred to Marlborough Sounds as paradise.

The clock on the dresser said five-thirty.

I'd slept for two hours and felt fantastic.

With no place I needed to be I rolled onto my back and attempted more sleep. Half an hour of tossing and turning later I lay still and stared at the smoke alarm on the ceiling. Counting seconds between flashes of the tiny red LED that said the alarm was operational.

Counting to occupy my mind.

It failed. My brain was already thinking about Mitch. Was he asleep? I could go make coffee. He might be awake by now? Could I go make coffee? What if he wasn't up? Take him a cup and wake him up? Risky.

The internal debate raged until I heard a door open and close. He was up. I hit the shower, cleaned my teeth, dressed in fresh clothes, and casually walked down the stairs. I paused at the bottom. Left or right?

Mitch's bedroom? No. The living area. I turned right. When I opened the door I could smell the coffee. Mitch looked over from the kitchen.

"Morning, sleepyhead."

Puzzled I joined him in the kitchen.

"Morning?"

"Yes."

"I woke at five-thirty in the morning? That's a little more than two hours sleep."

Mitch grinned at me. "You slept like the dead."

No wonder I felt so good.

"You know this how?"

"I checked on you a few times," he replied. "Breakfast. Coffee. Then we'll go for a walk."

"All planned then?" I laughed as he poured cereal into a bowl and pointed to a chair at the table. I sat down.

"Breakfast," he said, setting the bowl in front of me.

"Thanks."

Breakfast carried on, amicable, chatty, fun. All the things I associated with Mitch.

"Beach?" Mitch asked taking keys from the counter near the back door.

"Awesome."

We left the house via the back door. I didn't want to go back down the internal stairs to the door at the bottom. Something about the cold air down there made my skin crawl.

We passed the garage and carried on down the steep driveway.

At the bottom was an upside down dingy. We carried on following the driveway to the left. Climbing over driftwood.

We stood on the gritty sand. I breathed. Deep breaths. Across the sound a bush-clad mountain rose from the still water.

Paradise.

Mitch walked up the beach. I watched him pick his way around rocks. The tide was out.

"You coming?" he called.

"Yeah," I replied. Just enjoying the view. Seemed best to keep that to myself.

I caught up with him.

A familiar smell wafted on the light breeze. Once you've smelled a decomp you never forget it. Dead fish maybe? Hopeful. I knew it wasn't fish. My stomach churned as I scanned the tree line and the beach. I saw the cause lodged by a tree at the edge of the beach.

"Mitch..." I moved toward the trees. The smell

grew stronger and completely over-shadowed the clean sea air. Bile rose. By the time I reached the tree I knew I was right. A body. I struggled not to retch as I saw maggots writhing and wriggling as they fed on the person's face.

I spun around as Mitch came up behind me.

"Don't, you don't want to see this," I cautioned. "Does your cell work?"

He nodded. I could tell by the look on his face that he'd glimpsed the body.

"On my beach?" he mumbled, dragging his cell phone from his jeans pocket.

"We're going to need police."

He made the emergency call.

I crouched by the body and began a visual examination. Female. Slim build. Light brown shoulder-length wavy hair. Obvious facial wounds. I looked at her hands, no abrasions that I could see. She was wearing a diamond engagement ring. I moved around her, stepping with care. The back of her hair was matted with blood and sand. The body didn't appear waterlogged. Maybe she hadn't been in the water or if she had she wasn't in it long? She was wearing jeans, sneakers, and a fitted tee-shirt. Her clothes appeared dry. I patted my own pockets expecting to find latex gloves.

Nothing.

Damn.

Vacation.

"Hey, Mitch, you don't happen to have a first aid kit down here anywhere?" Ever optimistic. First Aid kits usually contain latex gloves. I didn't want to contaminate the body by searching for ID without gloves on.

"Isn't it a bit late?"

"Not for her. I need some latex gloves." I had another thought. "Can I use your phone, please?"

Mitch half-smiled. "Sure." He threw it to me. A thoughtful look crossed his face. "Actually, yeah, there's a first aid kit under the dingy. I'll be back." He took off at a run.

While he was gone I photographed the body and surroundings with his phone.

There was a two foot long broken branch a few feet behind her that interested me.

Hair and blood stuck to it, I only noticed because I got close, the blood splatter and hair strands looked like they were mostly under the branch and divided by a break.

I looked from the wood to the body.

Did she fall and smash her head on the branch? Hopeful but not likely. The way the branch lay, it had been thrown or dropped. Could be a murder weapon. I took a series of photos of the branch and the body.

Mitch appeared next to me with latex gloves.

"Thanks." I swapped the phone for gloves and pulled them on. I had to search the woman's pockets and clothing for anything that would tell us who she was. I don't like unidentified bodies. I like to know who I'm dealing with. She was wearing a backpack. I could clearly see the straps over her shoulder.

"Supposed to be a vacation," I mumbled and then gave the woman my undivided attention. I rolled her toward me. Maggots fell to the sand. I supported her with one hand and inspected the back of her head. Looked to me like she'd been hit with force. Bits of bark were lodged in a large wound, there weren't maggots in that wound, yet. I tried to free the backpack with the other. It was quite a struggle. Dead people are heavy. Dead weight is a truism.

I tossed the pack out of the way once it was free and lowered the body back down.

Moving away from the smell I sat on the sand and opened the bag.

It was a daypack.

Snacks. Change of clothes. Suntan lotion.

Tissues. A phone. I set the phone aside. A wallet. A passport. As soon as I pulled it out I knew it was American. My heart sank a notch or two as I opened the passport and recognised the woman on the beach.

"Nancy Medina," I whispered.

"El?"

"Mitch, she's American. Her name is Nancy Medina and she's twenty-three years old."

I set the passport aside and checked her wallet.

Cash. Credit cards. Travel card. A university identity card. Not a robbery then. "College ID, she attends Caltech."

I put everything back in her wallet. "Can you photograph the pack and contents, please?" I asked Mitch.

He took his phone back out of his pocket and did as I asked.

I pulled the gloves off, balled them up and dropped them on the sand.

"Okay, done," Mitch said. "You okay?"

Until he asked I hadn't realised I was frowning. "Yeah, just, you know, supposed to be on vacation." I shot him a smile.

"What do we do now?" Mitch asked sitting next to me in the sand. "I'm presuming our day just got screwed?"

"Pretty much," I replied. "I'm going to use your phone and call a friend, then we'll know."

Mitch passed me his phone. I called home. Well, not home exactly but Iain Campbell's cell phone. I needed to talk to someone in the State Department.

"Hey, It's Ellie Conway," I said as he answered. "I got a messy problem."

"Thought you were on vacation?" he replied. "I'm off tomorrow, good timing on your problem."

"I am on vacation." I remembered the conversation with Mike. "You climbing?"

"Yes, heading down to Ecuador tomorrow. Now about this problem ..."

"I'm in New Zealand." I'm at the end of the world and still shit happens. "Just found the body of an American woman on a beach. What now?"

"Seriously? What is it with you?"

"I dunno," I said with a hefty sigh. "What now?"

"I'll contact the embassy, we'll send FBI. You want to work this or walk away?"

I looked at Mitch. I wanted to walk away but I wasn't sure I could. I could try walking away.

"Send agents. We called local police. I'll hand over to them and FBI can pick the case up when they get here."

"Address?" I gave the address and Mitch's phone number, just in case. "Enjoy your vacation."

"Yeah, you too."

I hung up and this time gave the phone back to Mitch.

"Do we have to be here by... Nancy?"

"Yes. But not this close. We could move back down there," I pointed back down the beach to the jetty. "Should also have a quick look for other victims or the person who did this."

Mitch touched my arm. "It wasn't an accident?"

"I don't think so."

He breathed in sharply. "She couldn't have fallen or died of an illness?"

"Maybe, but I don't think so. I think, someone hit her across the back of the head with a branch. And hit her hard enough to snap the branch. I also think the person turned her onto her back. She fell forward, hence the scrapes and wounds on her face. She didn't put her hands up to save herself. Either it was a fatal blow or she was unconscious and died later. Whoever did it, then rolled her onto her back."

"Why?"

"Check she was dead? Looking for something? I don't know. If we find whoever did it, we'll ask," I said with a smile. "Shall we?" I pointed to the jetty. "Close enough that I can watch this area, but far enough that Nancy isn't our only focus."

Mitch nodded.

He stood up and brushed sand off his jeans. I followed suit.

I sent Mitch ahead of me, then turned back and had a quick look around the area, just in case there was another body or someone lurking. Nothing. No footprints, no sign anyone else had been in the area.

Catching up to Mitch I asked, "How many properties can access this stretch of beach?" I could see rocks and unfriendly coast line to the east and west. Estimating about a quarter of a mile of accessible beach frontage from the land. The sea was a different matter.

"Four, I think, yeah, four."

"Don't suppose you know if any of your neighbours rent their houses out or run bed and breakfast accommodation?"

"Sorry, no."

"When was the last high tide?"

We sat on the jetty. I could see how high the tide rose by the line of driftwood and marks in the sand. Didn't look as though it went up as far as Nancy's body, but maybe far enough to wipe footprints from the sand. Hers weren't there.

Thinking aloud. "She could've come off a boat with the Unsub."

"Unsub?"

"Sorry. Unknown Subject."

Mitch smiled, nodded, and checked a tide timetable on his phone.

"Twelve twenty-eight this morning. Next high tide will be twelve-forty this afternoon."

"So if they came ashore from a boat it was before the high tide or during..."

"No footprints," Mitch said, nodding.

"How long before police get out here?"

"Nearest cop is Havelock, forty-five minutes away,

give or take." Mitch checked the time on his phone. "Should be here soon."

He bumped my shoulder with his.

"Want something?" I asked nudging him back.

"What will happen when police get here?"

"We'll give statements. I will hand over the crime scene and we'll get on with our vacation."

"Can you walk away?"

"Yes." Wow, that was definite. I was just a little impressed by how sure I was. That was new territory. Life with Mitch in it had a different focus? "Yes I can walk away. Our State Department will have contacted local police and let them know that it's my scene until hand over – and who I am. And that FBI agents are on the way from Wellington to assist in the investigation."

Mitch said nothing. He smiled but he said nothing. We sat, our legs dangling over the water, and waited.

I was conscious that the body was degrading as the minutes ticked by and become an hour in the hot sun. Eventually I heard gravel crunching under foot and two police officers emerged from the end of the driveway.

We stood up and waved. They acknowledge us and

waited as we clambered back over rocks to greet them.

"SSA Ellie Conway," I said offering my hand.

"Senior Constable Simon Curnow," the first officer said shaking my hand.

The second nodded and shook my hand next. "Constable Jack Barron."

"This is Mitch Iverson —that was his driveway you came down."

They shook Mitch's hand.

"The body is over there," Mitch said pointing down the beach past the trees. "If you don't mind I'll wait here."

They nodded.

I led the way.

"The body is an American citizen, have you been briefed?"

"Yes ma'am," Curnow said. "FBI are expected to take charge sometime today."

"If you can take it from here... I'm on vacation," I said.

"Go right ahead, agent. Just as soon as you've given me a complete statement." He pulled his notebook from his pocket.

The other officer followed suit and went back to Mitch. Made sense.

Ten minutes later I was signing the statement in his notebook and ready to leave.

Back at the house I asked Mitch if I could use the computer in the living room and uploaded the photos from his camera.

I scanned through them quickly, then paused on one, and scrolled back to the previous two. All three photos showed more bush than the others.

"Mitch!"

He appeared next to me. "Yep?"

"Look at this picture, what do you see?" I zoomed in on an area in the bush, the foliage was thick but there was something else there.

"A hand?"

"Yeah, that's what I thought," I replied.

"There was or possibly is someone else down there?" Mitch did not look pleased. "Dead or alive?"

"Alive maybe? We have to warn those cops."

I emailed the photos to Caine and asked that he forward them to whoever had the case in Wellington then looked at Mitch. "Don't suppose you have a rifle?"

He nodded. "For rabbits."

"Can you get it please?"

He disappeared then returned empty handed. "It's gone."

"What?"

"The gun safe is empty."

Not good.

"Ammunition?"

"Two boxes, last I checked. They're gone."

"Where were they stored?"

"Gun safe is in the bottom garage. Ammunition in a cabinet in the garage up top."

"Someone knew? Doesn't sound random?"

"Must've, nothing else is moved or gone."

Potentially there was an armed Unsub on the property and I wasn't.

Vacation?

I should just give up all notions of ever having a vacation. Yeah I was going to make it all about me. I thought for a few minutes. I had to go warn the police officers, that was a given, what about Mitch?

"Okay, we're going down to the beach. We cannot leave those officers alone knowing someone was in the bush and that a gun is missing." And I didn't want to leave Mitch alone either.

He nodded.

We locked the house, just in case it made a differ-ence to the Unsub and hurried down the steep stony driveway. Near the bottom I announced my presence. Sneaking up on police wasn't smart.

Mitch's hand sought mine.

"Stay together," he whispered.

Okay by me.

One of the officers met us by the driftwood pile. I spoke to him quietly, telling him about the photos, showing him the pictures on Mitch's phone and then about the missing rifle.

"Not good news," he said. "I'll call it in."

He walked toward the jetty, far enough away from the bush clad area near the body that no one could over hear him.

Minutes passed.

He beckoned for us to join him. Walking toward him I saw him talk into the radio on his shoulder. "Jack is coming over to join us," he said. "FBI have landed at Woodbourne airport and are on the way out here. I've asked for AOS support."

"AOS?" I asked.

"Armed Offenders Squad... our SWAT."

I nodded. "There is no real cover down here. If that person is still in the bush and our Unsub, potentially they're armed."

The cop looked around. "The boat shed?"

"It'll have to do, we'll sit it out over there."

I heard movement. The three of us looked up at the same time. Constable Jack Baron was walking toward us. Two shadows fell on the ground. He stepped sideways just enough for us to see a woman behind him and a rifle barrel.

"Ellie?" Mitch whispered.

"I see her," I replied. "This isn't ideal."

"No kidding," Mitch whispered. "Now what?"

"Well, it's tricky but not impossible."

I leaned toward Curnow. "That a Glock 17 on your hip and is there a round in the chamber?"

"Yes to both questions."

"How good are you with that?"

"Proficient," he replied.

Yeah but I'm probably better. It's how it is.

"Ever fired at a person?"

"No."

"Give it to me."

He started to shake his head. The woman called out. Kiwi accent. "I'll shoot him if you don't let me leave."

I whispered to Curnow, "Would she expect you to be armed?"

"No."

"Give me the gun."

Mitch moved in front of me. Curnow reluctantly handed me the Glock. I shoved it in the back of my jeans.

Then stepped away from Mitch and Curnow. I smiled at Jack, using my left-hand I tapped my head and pointed to the ground then held two fingers up. Hoping like hell he'd understand. I needed him to drop and cover on two. I still held two fingers up. Jack watched my hand.

"No one is stopping you," Curnow told the woman. "Let my constable walk over here and you go on up the driveway. We'll stay here."

I didn't want to speak and give away my nationality.

"I'm taking him with me," she said. She was calm. Calm is good, less chance of accidental gunfire.

Even so, I couldn't let her take Jack up the driveway.

"You don't need Jack, let him stay here," Curnow said.

I reached behind me and grasped the grip of the Glock.

As I pulled the gun free of my waistband, I closed my fist.

Jack dropped. I fired as soon as he moved. My bullet hit her in the shoulder. My preference was head but this wasn't my country.

No second chances.

The woman's face registered surprise for a moment, the rifle fell from her hands as she sank to the ground. Jack scrambled to his feet, taking the rifle with him and ran over to us.

"Okay?" I asked him, my eyes focused on the woman, the gun now aimed at her head.

"Yes," Jack replied. He didn't sound it.

"Curnow, you got cuffs? Now would be a good time to use them," I said. "Just don't cross in front of me, go around."

He did. He cuffed the woman, inspected her wound, and called for an ambulance. I lowered the gun and handed it to Jack. Mitch grabbed the first aid kit and gave it to Curnow. He dressed the wound.

A conversation ensued between me and the woman.

Her name was Rachel Bridgeman; she was a New Zealander and studying at Caltech.

"All right Rachel, let's talk, shall we?"

She shook her head. Then changed her mind. Wise.

"You shot me."

"That was unfortunate. You are ruining my vacation. Tell me what happened here."

"She was my best friend," Rachel said making an attempt at sorrow. I wasn't buying.

"Usually people don't shoot their best friends. Waiting for an explanation here," I rocked on my heels. "And getting bored. You don't want that to happen."

"He asked her to marry him!"

"Who asked her?"

"My ex-boyfriend," she said. "This hurts."

"Yeah. It does hurt when you get shot. Moving on. Paramedics will be here eventually." The police officers watched as I continued. "Why was Nancy Medina here?"

"We were holidaying together."

A horrible feeling swam up my spine and entered my brain. It sloshed about, whipping itself into a frenzy before falling off my tongue as words.

"Your ex-boyfriend is here isn't he?"

Her eyes widened.

I glanced at the senior officer. "Do we have another victim?" he asked.

A sick little smirk tweaked the edges of Rachel's mouth. She didn't say anything.

"How did you get the gun, Rachel?"

"My parents look after Mitch's holiday home for him. I know where everything is."

Nice.

"Where are your parents?"

I hoped the killing spree stopped with the boyfriend and best friend.

All the colour ran out of her face. She waivered. Her body swayed. I reached down and pinched her arm.

"Ouch," she squawked.

"Focus. You don't get to pass out before I'm done talking with you," I said with a growl. "Where are your parents?"

"Nelson. They won't be home for a few days."

"I'm sure they'll be thrilled when police find them and tell them what their delightful daughter has done."

A tear slipped down her face. Must've been hard to force one out. She didn't look at all remorseful.

"I told Nancy not to date him!"

"You can sit here and bleed while Constable Barron watches you. Senior Constable Curnow and I are going to search the property. What'd you say your ex's name was?"

"I didn't. You can't leave me here," she whispered.

"Yeah I can. Who are we looking for?"

"Jerry Ryan," she replied.

It took us fifteen minutes to locate the body of the fiancé in the potting shed by Mitch's garage. It was cooler in the potting shed, his body smelled less, and thankfully there was less bug activity. Single gunshot wound to the head.

Rachel provided us with a time line of events. She killed the fiancé first. Nancy tried to run away, that's how she ended up on the beach.

The double murders took place about eight hours before Mitch and I arrived in the Sounds. Rachel said she saw us arrive. We didn't leave the house until morning and she followed to see what would happen next. Really? What did she think would happen?

Guess she didn't expect to get shot. Pretty sure no one expects to be shot at the end of the world.

She stopped talking when my FBI back up arrived.

Mitch and I finished writing additional statements for both the FBI and police, an hour after everyone arrived we grabbed our bags and drove away, intent on a vacation no matter what.

Edited by Darren Pulsford for Fox Spirit Books: Girl at the End of the World. 2014.

Seat next to you

I stretched my arms up over my head, letting the stretch ease through my body. A couple of bones clicked. Kurt smiled.

"You heard that?"

"Yep."

I rotated my shoulders forward. The ensuing crunching and grinding felt audible. Less noise rotating backwards. Relaxing my shoulders I breathed out. Rolled my head side to side, and felt relief that there was no noise. I half expected to hear my brain slosh around. Breathing deeply I relaxed my upper body.

"Ready?" Kurt asked, checking his weapon.

"Yep," I replied, seating my Glock comfortably in my right hand. We walked together along a corridor in an apartment complex. I checked numbers on the doors we passed. "Next apartment."

Kurt stopped before the apartment door. I walked to the other side of the door.

It was open.

I looked again.

It was missing.

Two fast hand signals relayed my concerns to Kurt. He gave me a thumbs up. I held up three fingers.

Kurt pushed off the wall. Silent count.

One, two …

I swung into the empty doorway, weapon at the ready.

"Three," Kurt whispered, with his left hand on my right shoulder.

His fingers squeezed. I moved left, he let go and moved right. I felt him move but didn't look. Not my job. Focused on the left side of the room, I scanned for trouble. Nothing.

"Clear."

"Clear," Kurt repeated.

I moved to a closed door at the far end of the room. Kurt followed. I signaled my intent to open the door. He nodded. My left hand curled around the doorknob. Deep breath. Sharp twist. Locked. I took two steps back, braced myself, and aimed a power kick just below the doorknob. Wood splintered. I stepped forward and pushed through the door. Left. Movement.

"Freeze!"

A male stood slowly from a crouched position near an unmade bed. His hands came into view. My eyes rested on his, taking in the gun in his right hand with my peripheral vision.

"Drop the gun," I instructed.

His fingers moved.

"Now!"

His grip tightened. I squeezed the trigger. His gun fell as his shoulder jerked. Kurt moved up and kicked the gun out of reach. I breathed. Slow. Steady. Just breathe. Every inward breath dragged a mixture of garbage and something disgusting but familiar with it. My eyes scanned the rest of the messy room then stopped. Sitting on a cluttered dresser I saw a paper band with 'Federal Reserve' written across it.

"Where's the money?" I asked as I holstered my weapon and pulled latex gloves from my pocket.

He didn't speak.

I pulled the gloves on and walked over clothing and assorted trash to the dresser. I showed him the reserve band.

"Jog your memory?"

He shook his head. His squalid existence didn't seem improved by the four million of dollars in cash stolen from an armored car.

"Cuff him ...," I said, as three more federal reserve

bands fell from a tee shirt I moved. There was still a familiar odor. Cloying. Unpleasant. Damp with a hint of rotting food and general filth.

"Oww," the man squawked as Kurt pulled his hands behind his back. "My shoulder!"

"Could be worse," I replied using my pen to lift clothing items and move them. More wrappers fell to the floor. "Really, all that money and you live like this? Never thought, to hire a cleaning a service?"

"I don't know what you're talking about."

Of course not, they never do.

I found two passports. They both bore the same picture. Our man.

"This apartment is leased to Neil Crandon. According to the system you are him. Mind explaining why your picture is on these passports with the names Alan Grisham and Derek Faulkner?"

He shook his head.

"They're not mine."

"Yeah, thought as much."

"Let's go," Kurt said giving Crandon a shove toward the door. "Seems to be some confusion over your identity and the reason there are Federal Reserve money bands in your bedroom."

Kurt escorted him out. I made a call.

"It's SSA Conway, we have a potential suspect in the federal reserve armored truck robbery."

The voice on the line faltered twice before speaking, "Thank you ... how?"

"A CI of mine gave him up. Meet us at George Washington emergency room for hand over."

"You okay?"

"Yeah, yeah, your suspect requires attention."

"I appreciate your help, Conway."

"Happy to help, Dan. I'll secure the scene and post a guard."

"Tequila?"

"You know me well."

I hung up and made another call. "Sean, I need a scene guard."

"Sure, now?"

"Yep." I read out the address. "Handing over to Secret Service."

"I'll have a guard there in five minutes. You waiting?"

"Yes."

I hung up. Kurt waited in the living area. The combination of various unpleasant odors lurking in the stale air were starting to give me a headache. I needed to get out.

"I'll run down and grab the tape," I said, waving at the empty hole where the front door should have been. Turning to Crandon I asked, "Where's your door?"

"Dunno," he said.

Kurt took a look around, dragging Crandon with him.

"It's here Conway, behind the sofa."

Joining him I noticed it was lying on something. Lifting one corner exposed a black sports bag. Flies crawled in and out of the partially open zip. That didn't bode well. Money doesn't attract flies.

"What's in there?" I asked Crandon, pointing at the bag.

He shrugged.

I touched the bag with my foot. A waft of decomposing meat met my nose as I batted flies away from my face. My mouth filled with saliva. My brain took over and propelled my legs out the door.

Behind me I heard Kurt and Crandon. I kept walking until I hit fresh air. Leaning on the building to steady myself I filled my lungs with clean air. The words 'not our case' repeated in my head. Grateful that I didn't have to deal with whatever was in that bag in the room, I took another few breathes of clean air. Kurt marched Crandon out the door and shoved him into the back seat of our car.

An unmarked black Suburban pulled up behind our car. I pushed off from the wall and greeted the man who emerged from the car.

"Hi, Trent. It's all yours," I said, shaking his hand.

"Thanks, I think," Trent replied, looking past me toward the door of the building. "In there?"

"Yeah but I would stay outside if you value your lunch."

Trent grimaced. "That doesn't sound good."

"There were two bank robbers but we only found one, alive."

"Thanks for the heads up. I'll definitely stay out here and wait."

"You're welcome. Secret Service will be here soon. It's their case."

A smile settled on my lips as I waved to Trent and got in our car.

One and Only/Ellie

"You're smiling," Kurt said settling into an armchair in my living room. He'd said he wanted to chat and we really hadn't found time to catch up since my impromptu vacation. "After the day we had, you're smiling. What gives?"

"Nothing."

"Of course," Kurt replied leaning back in the chair and regarding me with interest. "What else would you say?"

"Why such fascination with my smile?" I asked resting my head against the back of the couch and closing my eyes for a moment.

"It's become a rare and wonderful thing," he replied.

"I'm enjoying the moment, that's all. We had a day and now it's over."

He shook his head. "This isn't you, I'm not buying it."

"It's not that hard to imagine." I looked at him sideways. "Don't shake your head like that. It really isn't that hard to imagine."

Suspicion shot across his eyes. "You don't usually let go that quick."

I shrugged. "Well today I am."

"All right, gimme?"

"Gimme? What are you, two?" I asked with a smile as I checked my wrists for a hair tie. There wasn't one so I twisted the length of my hair and pushed it behind my back.

"Yeah sometimes. Tell. Wow me with your observations," Kurt said. "Tell me all about Mitch, I just bet he's behind this smile."

I leaned on the arm of the chair.

"I'm going to need coffee."

Kurt rocked forward and lurched from his seat. "Be right back."

I watched him go. My phone buzzed. I glanced at the screen. Butterflies danced in my stomach. False alarm, not Mitch. The butterflies stayed regardless. I replied to the work email and dropped my phone into my lap.

Kurt came back carrying two mugs but I couldn't smell coffee.

He passed me a mug. I spied milky brown liquid. It

wasn't coffee. Milk in coffee is an abomination. Tea? I sniffed at the contents of the mug.

"Tea, really? We still on that?"

"It won't hurt you. Now talk."

I set the mug on the coffee table. "See that?" I pointed at the table. "It's a coffee table, not a tea table."

"Ellie ..."

So hard to keep a straight face.

"Kurt ..."

"Last nerve Conway. Just tell me, where'd you meet him?"

"The first time?"

He nodded.

"I don't know. Shortly after he was born probably."

Kurt smiled and raised an eyebrow.

"Skip ahead. Where'd you meet him more recently, when did this glow thing you've got going start."

Glow thing. I'm glowing now? Proof I'm an alien?

"All right. Jeez." Time to suck it up and talk. "I picked Sam up from the hospital. You'd finished up. Lee was in recovery or ICU." I stopped talking to make sure that sequence was right. Was it? No. "I'm wrong. You were still in theater with Lee. I picked

Sam up to help me rescue Tierney's wife."

Kurt stretched his legs then adjusted his position on the couch. I sensed his impatience and it amused me.

"Okay, I know what happened to her." He used his patient voice to good effect. "Where did you meet Mitch?"

"We rescued the hostage and were on our way up the escalator at Rosslyn Metro. I stepped off the top and Mitch was there. Or nearby. I dunno. I was aware of the crowds and that we were escorting someone to safety but not much else."

"And?"

"I heard someone say Gabrielle."

"He used the G word? And he's still alive? Must be love."

"Shut up."

"Carry on ..."

"I'm not sure what to say now. He was there. Hadn't seen him since Carla's funeral and before that we hadn't seen each other in a life-time."

"What was happening in your head?"

I frowned. My phone buzzed. I checked the display. There was no stopping the smile.

"Okay," I said, looking from the screen to Kurt as I replied to the email. "What was happening in my head ... I was stunned?

I think that was it. Something clicked or snapped into place. I can't explain it very well."

"Try harder. This guy has you all turned around and as much fun as it is to watch I want to know more."

"All turned around," I whispered. "You got the wrong girl. That's not me."

Kurt's right eyebrow rose. "And now you see why this is so fascinating." He grinned. "Yes it's you. Keep talking."

Not about what was happening in my head. I needed to avoid that. Until I knew for sure what was happening in there.

"I was dressed in a SWAT bullet proof vest and carrying an assault weapon and I couldn't get one of my cards out of my shirt pocket. So, he slipped his card into my jean pocket." My eyes met Kurt's. "I really know how to make a great impression."

Kurt laughed. "Yeah you do."

"I carried on with the day, it was shit. I think you caught up on it the next day, yeah?"

"Yes. Fissile material and a rouge agent turned terrorist. Big fun in D.C."

"Once I had all my ducks in a row, I called Mitch to see if he wanted to meet for coffee."

"And?"

"He did. We did. He came over. He brought a chicken with him."

"I have to ask, an eating chicken or a laying chicken?"

"Eating."

"The man is not stupid."

"We spent a few hours talking, cooking and eventually eating."

"You're smiling again. I haven't seen a smile like that since ..." He stopped. I could see the cogs turning. "I've never seen you smile like that."

I ignored it.

"Then he left."

"He left?"

"Yeah."

"And?"

I shrugged. My phone buzzed in my lap. I could see the email icon flashing. My finger touched the screen. Another email from Mitch waited for me. Just knowing it was there was enough. I chewed my lip, tried to hide the smile I couldn't stop.

"And ... we talk every day. We see each other when we can."

Kurt watched me for a moment. I knew we weren't done yet.

"And you went away together to New Zealand on vacation?"

"Yep."

"And?"

I shrugged. "And nothing. We went away."

"We haven't met him?"

"No, you haven't." But Sam did briefly.

"That's not like you, what's going on?"

Oh, I see. This is about them not meeting him.

"You drew the short straw then?"

Kurt nodded. "Why haven't we met this guy? He's obviously important to you. You left the country with him."

"He's important. He's not like Mac or Rowan. He's a regular guy."

"Or us presumably?"

"Nope, not like us. Has a real job, you know, not a crazy one. No one shoots at him. People like him ...

He's my safe place. Okay, there I said it."

"Your safe place?"

"I have to explain that?" I asked.

"Please ..."

"I can talk to him about anything and everything, and he's okay with it."

Kurt grinned at me. "Trying to get my head around you talking ..." He took another sip of his tea and waggled his finger between us. "... Because this is more like interviewing a hostile witness than talking."

"It happens. I talk, sometimes."

"And this whatever it is with Mitch works for you?"

"Yes, it works for me."

Kurt nodded, finished his tea and set the cup down on the table. "Don't you think you should invite him to the next team dinner, so he can put faces to the names?"

"Because you're so sure I talk about you three?"

"Do you?"

"Yes. You've come up in conversation."

Kurt's smile was way too knowing for my liking.

"Bring him to dinner, Conway."

"So you three can interrogate him? I don't think so."

"Conway, if he can't handle a little light questioning ..."

"Have you met yourselves?"

Kurt laughed. "Sam did a background check, you know that right?"

"Yes, and that's my point. I like him, Doc. A lot. Don't scare him away."

"If we can do that, then he has no business being here."

Oh good grief.

"We're not dating."

Kurt's face registered surprise. "All this," he said waving his hand at me. "And you're not dating. Okay now I get the cat thing."

"About time."

"You were away together and nothing happened?"

"Uh huh."

"How is that possible?" Kurt smiled, his eyes flicked up to meet mine. "He's gay?"

I laughed. Nope he really isn't. I chose not to answer his question about Mitch's sexual orientation.

"I've been away with you plenty of times and nothing's happened."

"Away working. Not away vacationing," Kurt

replied, sinking into the chair and stretching his legs out.

"He's my best friend. Nothing happened."

"Conway, he's way more than that or you want him to be."

Biting my lip did not stop the smile. "He's my safe place. What I want may never happen."

I watched him trying to digest that. It was entertaining.

"That being said, serious question for you ... birth control?"

"Really?" Didn't expect that.

"Really. Do you need me to write you a prescription?"

Not a conversation I wanted to have. At all.

"We're friends."

"I know. I see friendly and I raise you – birth control and I know you're not on the pill."

He was right. Rowan was never around long enough to make long term birth control an issue.

"Okay, write the prescription but we're friends."

"I know, Conway. I know." He reached down beside his chair and rummaged in his bag. Moments later he lifted out a prescription pad and a pen, he also dropped a box of condoms on the coffee table. "Just in case."

I was pretty sure he didn't usually walk around with a box of condoms in his medic kit. Time to deflect.

"You know that both Sam and Lee are seeing people right? And I know that there is someone in your life … but I just freaking bet, they don't know that."

"And your point is?"

"My point is … we all have a life outside of the team. And if you want to meet Mitch then y'all need to be up front and bring along your significant others." I leaned back in my seat and picked up my phone. If we were going to do it, it needed to be now, before I backed out. "Shall we do this, T.G.I. Friday's tonight?"

Kurt nodded. He dropped the prescription on the table then pulled his phone out of his pocket. He text while I made a call.

Mitch answered on the second ring.

"Hey, are you busy?"

"No."

"Wanna go get a drink tonight?"

"Sure, name the place."

"T.G.I. Friday's."

"You okay?"

"Yep. Time you met the team. Let me apologize in advance."

His voice never faltered. "Sounds like fun. I'll pick you up."

"I'll be waiting."

I hung up and turned to Kurt. "Done."

"Everyone will be there. Lee and Tara, Sam and Sandra, and Rachel."

"I'm going to change." I extracted myself from the chair, unwrapping my legs and stretching them before I stood up. "Let yourself out and we'll see you and Rachel tonight."

One and Only/Mitch

I leaned back in my chair. Coffee time maybe. I looked at my watch. Had it really only been forty-five minutes since my last break. Hopeless.

All day focus had been hard to come by, so not like me, hence I was still at work and everyone else had gone home.

Where had my reliable work life balance gone? Usually I was heavily weighted toward work with a little life.

Today, the last few weeks even, life fought back with vengeance. Even winning the internal battle if that was possible. Ever since returning from our vacation my thoughts never strayed far from Ellie.

I got a coffee and sat down at my desk. Without conscious effort, Ellie was again the center of my thoughts. A strange shiver ran down my back. I smiled and took a sip of coffee. Hot. Nice.

My fingers tapped away on my keyboard.

Missing you appeared on my screen. Great start. Now she'd think I was stalking and needy.

Delete? I thought for a second. I wanted to be strong not needy. Was I needy? Probably. I could feel the smile on my face. That certainly wasn't helping. Ellie was strong and surrounded by strength.

I took a breath and made a decision. I was going to be strong. I was not going to delete. I was strongly going to be myself or the new me that came from somewhere.

That felt like a good compromise.

My keyboard started to tap again.

'I'm having another coffee. Living on the edge, I know. Cheers Ellie, hope you're having a nice day.'

I pressed send and waited ... knowing that sometimes timely replies from Ellie weren't guaranteed. Could be hours, or even days.

Bing ... as I sipped and stared blankly at my screen a reply bounced back. Ellie said she was having tea with her work mate Kurt.

Hmmm, what was that about? She didn't like tea. Tea felt like a code word for a fact-finding mission. Work mates asked questions. I considered that was especially true when cups of tea were involved. And this workmate was Kurt.

I'd heard a little about Kurt. He was the other SSA

in Ellie's team. She trusted him with her life. They were close.

No problem with that, but I still wondered what they were talking about. What was Ellie saying? About me?

Crap, I'd become the stalking, needy, paranoid type. That was not me. That couldn't be me.

Brain in gear. Now would be good.

I replied to Ellie. 'How's the tea? Anyone in particular being discussed or is it work stories? Smiley face.'

Okay, that still sounded a bit needy. I hoped the smiley face made up for it.

I sat back and waited for a reply. My mind slipped away into a silent drift. Smiling. Why do I keep doing that? Ellie's face appeared. That was why.

There'd always been something about Ellie. Something comfortable when we were together, but there was something else. She lived inside a protective shield. I wasn't convinced it was just a figurative shield either. It was hard to break through but when we chatted and laughed there was a glimmer of what lay beneath. Cracks in the surface that widened with each conversation. I smiled again. One day, maybe, she'd let me in. No rush.

My phone rung snapping me back to the present.

There was no shaking the smile on my face.

Ellie's name appeared on my screen. I fumbled for the buttons as quickly as I could.

"Hi."

Some Nights

The darkness edged in slowly at first, I hardly noticed. By nightfall the pace increased, faster, deeper, darker, and unrelenting. My mood plummeted. It wasn't a migraine. That much I knew. What was it? What was this thing that took over my mind?

I pulled my legs up underneath me and curled into the living room sofa. The dimming light pulled shadows from the corners and set them free. I took a breath and held it. Exhaling I counted to ten. And repeat.

It didn't help.

Images bounced across my mind, jumbled, confused. Flashing pictures on a screen. Voices collided with one another. They didn't match the images. Not out of sync but didn't go with the pictures I could see at all. Confusing.

Cold swirled around me.

I blinked hard. The pictures wouldn't leave and I didn't want to see them. Been there, done that, have the scars to prove it.

As more images pounded my mind it became harder to breathe. Murder victims. Body parts. Blood. So much blood. Crime scenes. Mac lying on the wet ground. Windows breaking, glass flying past me.

Something hit me.

Darkness fell, then broke wide open.

Images gave way to sirens, screams, loud voices, gun shots. More blood.

My hands shook. Icy blades burrowed into my bones. Grabbing the throw rug from the back of the sofa, I wrapped it around me. Shivering. So cold.

An ache traveled my right arm from my inner wrist to my elbow, then became a throb. I tugged my sleeve up revealing a gaping wound. Blood ran over my hand and off my fingers. Drips splattered onto the blue leather sofa. Confusion reigned.

Unsure reality became a crazy glued dream. A glimmer of sanity asked one question, why was there pain? Unable to answer my own question I stared at the wound. It wasn't right. I'd been there before. It looked real. It felt like now. It hurt.

The fingers of my left-hand wrapped around my right forearm and squeezed the edges of the wound together. The blood flow slowed.

Breathe.

I looked at my arm again. How? My eyes closed. This wasn't good. A black sharpie wrote words across kitchen cabinets. 'Darkness folded images like cloth. Wrapping the past in a gilded bow.'

Familiar words.

I let go my arm and leaned over the side of the sofa. Fingers searching for my cell phone. Finally finding it and bringing it into view. I pressed the bottom on the top of the screen. The phone sprang to life. I swept my finger upward, unlocking the phone and then swept left revealing favorite contacts. Kurt, Lee, Sam, Dad, Caine, Mitch.

A voice in my head told me to call Kurt. It sounded awfully like Mac.

My finger hovered over the icons. Mac was in front of me, lying on the ground, paramedics kneeling next to him. He turned his head and looked at me. "Call Kurt."

"Dead men can't talk. Shut up!" I watched him splutter blood. "Dead men can't talk."

My finger shook then touched the image of Mitch on the screen. I waited. Mac faded into a reddish puddle and washed down the gutter.

I waited.

Images slid across my line of sight. The many faces of the dead, so many faces. I knew all their names. I didn't forget anyone.

Pain came in waves. Blood ran from my right arm. Blood dripped down my face, obscuring my vision. Blood trickled from my upper left arm. I wiped a hand over my eyes. Red droplets flicked across the room.

Maybe I should've rung Kurt.

"Ellie?" Mitch said.

I stared at the phone in my hand. I could see his picture but his mouth didn't move. Did he speak? Other voices smashed into me, they screamed, cried, pleaded, gurgled last breaths. Underneath the cacophony was the one voice I needed to hear.

"Ellie?"

"Hi." That was all that fell from my lips. Words eluded me.

"You all right?" he asked, then changed his mind. "You're not. Where are you?"

Concentrate. Stay with his voice. Don't let go.

"Home." Tears spilled over my eyelashes. No amount of blinking or squeezing my eyes shut would stop them.

"El?"

He was moving. I heard his footsteps. "Hang on, putting you down for a minute."

I said nothing. Listening to him moving around was oddly comforting. It took a lot of effort to stay with him.

The room shimmered. Stones, sand, a river. A marine barreled toward me with a KA-BAR in his hand. I really hate knives. I ducked sideways. He missed, over balanced, regained momentum and came back at me. Mitch's voice from the phone stopped the marine in his tracks. He melted into the sand.

"El, I'm on my way," Mitch said. "You want to stay on the line?"

"Yeah." Speaking felt out of my reach. Everything was out of my grasp. Tears fell. I tugged the blanket tighter around myself.

Mitch's voice soothed the rising panic.

"Honey, can you tell me what happened?"

"I need you." Couldn't, can't. It's not real. "Mitch ..."

Terror pounded, keeping time with my heart.

"Right here. On my way."

Traffic noises. Dread filled me. He was going to be

too late. The noises in my head dragged me into an image that wouldn't let go. Cars flew past on the highway. I saw a woman standing by her car. The hood was up. She seemed distressed. I pulled over.

The smell of exhaust fumes hit me as I climbed out of my car and hurried to the upset woman on the side of the road.

A small child in the car cried. Something felt wrong. I dropped one of my cards on the shoulder of the road and stood on it.

Hoping that if anything happened to me, she'd pick it up and make a call.

No one knew where I was. A series of images bumped the road sideways.

Suddenly I was in the back of my own car.

Handcuffed.

Tape across my mouth.

Unable to move. My head hurt. Thoughts crowded me. I knew where we were headed. Fort Belvoir. I doubted I'd survive whatever would happen next or that the woman found my card and called for help. Memories stolen by the night. Time sliding dividing light. Who I was suddenly died.

I closed my eyes. It didn't help. The phone fell.

When I looked for it there was no phone, no carpet, and no living room. Trapped inside a horror show. My world imploded. I ripped a shower curtain back revealing Roy's headless body swarming with flies. Blackness punctuated by bright yellow devoured me.

From behind somewhere I heard a noise. Glancing over my shoulder I saw nothing but dimming light. Pinned under something heavy, I struggled to move. Sam's voice broke through and expanded to fill the small gap around me. The world shook. A hard wave of air hit me, knocking me back. Voices yelled in my ear. A fine red mist covered everything. The weight above me lifted. A mask. Oxygen. I could breathe again. Kurt peered into my eyes. Something caught in my throat. Coughing. Blood.

We missed something. Sinking into the red vapor my eyes closed.

Everything hurt. Everything.

Carla screamed. I blinked to clear my vision. She was in front of me. Taped to a headstone. A man with her. I fired. He dropped. Bits of brain sprayed across the ground behind him.

The next thing I knew I was kneeling next to my own body, it felt bizarre, but I wasn't dead.

If she was Gabrielle Conway then who the hell am I?

No one.

A figment of someone's sick imagination.

I moved and something pressed against my hip. My hand sought the object and closed around the grip on my Glock.

A sigh of relief escaped. I was armed.

No one else was going to come for me. Sliding off the sofa still clutching the blanket with one hand, the Glock firmly seated in my right hand, I crawled into a space between the sofa and one of the big blue leather armchairs.

Never again. Flashing pictures on a screen. Unsure reality dripped through a dream. Shadows deepened all around me. Some moved. Some didn't. All felt threatening.

Noises bombarded me. Images swirled, taking pieces of my life and throwing them into a jumbled heap. A ringing fell upon the voices then stopped.

Gunfire echoed into a cavernous space. I glanced left, Sam fired the shotgun at the door in front of us. Three breaching rounds. With a small kick the door fell inward.

I racked the slide on my Glock.

In the distance a metallic knock resounded. Someone was there.

My breathing slowed as I raised my arm and aimed at a shadow moving toward me from the darkness.

A flashlight beam played across the walls. Then moved in a sweeping motion across the floor.

Voices hid behind the light.

The light hit my face. My finger slid onto the trigger.

"Conway?"

Conway? It felt familiar. Who called me Conway like that? Kurt. Kurt did.

Turning my head to where Sam was a few moments ago I saw nothing but the blue of the sofa.

"El?"

Another voice. It rolled around in my head then cemented. Mitch.

"Conway, put the weapon down." Back to Kurt.

Weapon? I looked at my hand. Weapon.

The air pressure changed. I twisted but wasn't quick enough. A hand closed over mine and gently took the Glock from me.

"Chicky Babe, we're here," Sam crooned.

We're here? His words felt warm like they should mean something.

"Where am I?" I asked, as Lee helped me to my feet.

Mixed emotions. Confusion reigned.

"At home," he replied. "You're at home. Mitch is here."

"Mitch?"

"Right here." The main lights flicked on. Mitch wrapped his arms around me.

"Right here," he whispered.

Lost in time too tired to run. A safe place came to be.

Pictures of You

My eyes flicked open. The clear image in my mind expanded into a full-screen video clip of Mitch. Watching internal footage wasn't exactly new for me. I considered it the next step from hearing songs no one else could hear. A tired sigh escaped. There was someone who could hear my songs. We found that out by accident. Mitch.

He stirred in his bed. As I watched, he rolled over and picked up his phone. The glow from the screen lit his face. Sleepy but not asleep. He put his phone down on the nightstand and rolled onto his back. For days, I'd been seeing images of Mitch doing various normal things. Every night for a week, he woke me at the same time and I watched him check his phone.

Every night I wondered what he was looking for.

Was he checking the time?

Was he expecting something?

I rolled over, picked up my phone and noted the time. Three-thirty in the morning, as usual.

With a sigh, I flopped onto my back, the phone still

in my hand. Staring at the ceiling in the dark did not help. The pictures stayed.

Mitch drifting but not asleep.

I closed my eyes. Still there.

I gave it a minute and just watched.

The big difference between viewing Mitch and seeing images at a crime scene or during a case was the level of darkness and fear.

There was no fear or darkness associated with images of Mitch. Nothing bad was happening or going to happen. I scrolled through my contacts until I found his number. Okay so not a bad thing? But something was going on, something that woke us during the night.

What?

Why?

How didn't concern me. It didn't concern me because it was the very tip of an ever-expanding iceburg. Best not to start down that track. How did I hear songs? How did I hear dead people? How I smell scents no one else could?

Three-forty. My index finger tapped the green phone icon. The wait seemed excruciatingly long. Meanwhile his picture was there on my screen smiling and in my mind I saw him fumbling his phone, half-asleep and disheveled in the best possible way.

"Hello." Groggy. Sleepy. Warm. His voice changed a little more awake. "El?"

"Hi." I wanted to apologize for waking him up but I wasn't sorry. "Sleepy?"

"It's late," he stated. "I was asleep." A smile edged into his voice. "What's up?"

"Me."

"You're funny in the middle of the night, huh?"

His hand reached out and turned the lamp on. How did I know that?

"You weren't asleep. You were drifting. As long as we're both awake ... fancy a visitor?"

"You're coming over?"

The image in my mind changed.

I could see the smile spread across his face. I expected surprise not a smile.

To be honest I didn't expect to be able to see him at all. But I could. There he was lying propped on his left elbow, phone in his right hand, smiling. Shirtless, the bedding resting across his hips. A warm yellow light from the lamp bathed him in a soft glow. Something very odd was going on. Odd even for me. I was seeing him in real time?

"What's with the smile?"

I heard his voice falter and saw his expression change to confusion then back to the familiar smile.

"You, you make me smile." He laughed lightly. "How'd you know?"

"Same way I know you're leaning on your left elbow and holding the phone in your right hand, and have the lamp on. And that every night you wake at three-thirty and check your phone."

A frown creased his forehead. He reached over the side of the bed and picked up a book.

"What'd I just do?" he asked.

"Picked up a book," I replied. The image settled. I could see the title. "How to be a supernatural lover by Sherron Mayes."

Really? He did this?

"Yes. That's the book," Mitch said, a smile floated in his voice.

"Do you think this is what the author intended that book to be used for?" I asked, watching him thumb through the pages and chew his lip at the same time. "Waking me up every night for a week?"

Waking me up was one thing, but being able to see

him like I could.

That was fascinating.

"Maybe not. But who knew it would work?"

Mitch put the book on the bed next to him and lay back, one hand behind his head. Relaxed. Comfortable. Smiling. Being able to see everything he did wasn't just fascinating it was disconcerting and yet not. Complicated. "You coming over?" he asked.

"Yeah and you can explain the book and this waking me up thing you've got going here."

"You all right?" His voice was laced with amusement.

"I think so." Or completely insane, could go either way. "See you soon."

I hung up, rolled out of bed and hit the shower. Five minutes later, I was in my car heading to Mitch. Music loud. Thoughts halted. Images still right there.

As I walked to the front door of his house, I knew he was walking down the hallway to the door. I saw him so clearly it was like looking through a glass door and not the solid wooden door in front of me. His lean muscular body, shirtless, wearing jeans, belt open, top button undone, bare feet. My heart pounded.

I didn't knock. I paused. The door opened. The image from my mind stood in front of me, this time he was real. With a slight shake of his head like he didn't quite believe I was there, he smiled.

"Come on in," Mitch said not moving from the doorway.

I couldn't step around him.

"You're blocking the door," I whispered as my voice failed me.

"Got a plan?"

Hell yeah I had a plan. No, I really didn't.

"You could move?" Faced with the living breathing image that resided in my head, all bets were off. My brain was going places without me. I needed to catch up.

"Or?"

I took one-step; it brought me within three inches of him. My eyes wandered down his body to his open belt and back up. Mitch's blue eyes filled with amusement. My right hand slipped around his neck, my left was flat against his chest. My lips barely touched his when his arm snaked around my waist and pulled me closer. Three steps forward and the door closed behind me. His fingers slid inside the waistband of my jeans, the button released.

"Can't believe it took you a week to get here," he whispered.

Starting All Over Again

Mitch's mom hugged me hello. We walked into the house arm in arm. That's how it was my whole life when I was with Joan. Easy. Relaxed. Part of me wondered if things would change now it was me and Mitch. Now I wasn't just Simon's daughter. The aroma of chicken roasting filled the air. I pushed the crazy thoughts aside, everything felt right.

"Come into the kitchen with me," Joan said giving me a squeeze. "Mitch is running late."

I got the memo. Something came up at work and he'd be late but not too late. Usually it was me running late. So this was new.

Joan's kitchen filled me with joy. Warm, delicious smelling, comfortable. I sat at the kitchen table and watched her check on the cooking chicken.

"Anything I can do?"

"No, all taken care of. You can tell me about your day?" Joan replied, placing a bottle of pinot noir on the table and two glasses. She sat opposite me.

"Two glasses? Where's Alan?" I asked realizing I

hadn't seen him when I arrived.

She smiled. "He's over at your father's. He's been there all day. He'll be in later."

Joan poured the wine.

"How was your day?" I said sipping the red liquid and enjoying the sensation of warmth that followed.

"I had a lovely day." Joan took a sip of her wine then placed the glass back on the table. "Tell me about your day."

Images from my day flashed in my mind, I discounted the first four. They were not things that should be discussed before, during, or anywhere near a mealtime. The next image was Mitch smiling at me. That one would do nicely.

"Mitch and I went for a run at lunchtime. We ran along the river." I sipped more wine. That wasn't all we did at lunchtime. I knew there was a smile on my face and could feel Joan's eyes on me.

"That sounds a nice way to spend a lunch break," Joan said. Smiling she leaned on her elbows. "How often do you see each other?"

Her question threw me. It felt a little like a left-fielder. Daily. Sometimes twice a day. If we were both in town. If not, we talk every day. I bit my lip. We were almost living together. Perhaps I didn't hear the question correctly. I was pretty sure Joan knew how much time we spent together.

"Sorry what was the question?"

"How often do you see each other?"

"Often." No need to elaborate.

"We were talking about you last night," Joan said.

I knew they were. Mitch was at my house talking on the phone to his mom for over an hour. Sweet. I loved how close they were. Mitch and his mom. My Dad and me.

"Really?"

"You knew," Joan said with a smile. "He adores you, Gabrielle."

He's either got taste or he's insane. Maybe a bit of both? Gabrielle?

"Yes, I did know you two were talking last night."

She nodded, smiled, sipped her wine and then spoke, "Does he stay over a lot?"

I felt my eyes widen. Not really wanting to take this conversational path but knowing I needed to answer her question.

"I suppose he does," I replied. The floor could open up anytime now, I'd be quite happy to be swallowed before she asks anything else.

Joan sipped her wine and regarded me with inquisitive eyes. The look faded and was replaced with a softer expression, as if she thought better of following her curiosity.

"You make him very happy," Joan said.

I felt tension leave my shoulders. "He makes me happy."

"Do you know what we were talking about last night?"

"No." That was the truth. I left him to his phone call and didn't ask afterwards, beyond my usual questions about how his mom and dad were. Mitch told me we were invited to dinner tonight and that he'd said we'd be there. A smile edged over my lips. I liked that he was able to do that, because he knew my current schedule and he knew how much I loved being at his parents place.

"He's going to ask you Gabrielle ..." The look Joan gave me said she thought I knew what she was talking about.

My mind stalled. Ask me what?

I gave the thought a kick and it rolled over.

Oh, ask me.

I had an urge to look in the oven and see how big the bird was ... just in case it wasn't just us at dinner tonight. My eyes drifted down my shirt. Pleased I'd had time to go home for a shower and clean clothes. My heart pounded. Another sip of wine helped steady the sudden nerves. Surely she didn't mean tonight. Maybe I got it wrong. Yeah. Wrong.

"Ask me?"

Joan's eyes widened, she smiled in a knowing fashion. Panic surged through me. I took a big sip of wine.

"Ask you. What will you say?"

Time to play dense.

"Depends on the question ..."

Joan sighed, smiled, and said, "To marry him."

No mistaking what she said that time. Just like that, Joan changed in my eyes. She went from a loving caring mother and someone I'd always felt comfortable with to a potential mother-in-law. Bubbles of terror burst in my mind sprinkling everything that was good with bloodied confetti.

Images of my last mother-in-law crammed all available space in my head. Memories of Mac's mother made me feel ill.

More terror bubbles exploded.

There she was, Beatrice Connelly, smoking up a storm, swearing and cursing at the world while a big cloud of evil encroached upon her fragile mental state.

More confetti fell as she made ginormous wooden bows to decorate the outside of the house at Christmas time; and overloaded the electrical circuits with a hundred strings of fairy lights.

She spread misery like a thick blanket smothering everything within her reach. She hollered about how useless her husband was and how Mac was just like him.

 Rampaging through my mind casting aspersions upon my character. She told anyone who would listen how I was out to ruin her family. Me! She couldn't understand how being near her family made me physically ill and how I didn't want to ruin them, I didn't want anything to do with them. Well apart from Bob and Mac.

Bob was still in my life and I was pretty sure Mac would always haunt me.

Another image surfaced, Beatrice sat in her rocking chair on the front porch with a six-pack of Bud and her rifle, shooting squirrels. She picked them up by their tails and flung them into the woods behind the house. Dead squirrels hung like macabre Christmas decorations from the tree branches as the air filled with her crazy cackle. I knew my mind wasn't done with the joys of Christmases past.

Rolls of wrapping paper dropped in front of me. The specific wrapping paper that we had to use each year and the screaming fit that ensued because she changed her mind once about the wrapping paper and didn't tell anyone. Then I saw the seven Christmas hams Bob bought because she wasn't happy with the shape of them.

I watched in horror as she hacked one of the hams to pieces with a large knife, then turned on Bob. Mac restrained her while Bob disarmed her. Sedation followed and a quiet afternoon ensued. A bottle of vodka sat on the counter in her kitchen. She drank vodka like water, a trait she passed on to her oldest son, Eddie the 'tard. A shudder shot through me.

The mother-in-law from hell. I could hear her screeching at me down the phone about how it was my fault Carla committed suicide.

Yes, mother-in-laws invoked terror, much like mothers did.

Joan's hand touched mine. I jumped. She laughed and gave my hand a warm squeeze.

"Gabrielle?"

I swallowed hard, and then took another sip of wine while I tried to convince myself Joan was the only mother who could call me Gabrielle without it sounding like a precursor to an interrogation. My mother favored water-boarding. Or at least that's what it felt like, and it always began with my full name. I hadn't heard my real name since her death, well, until Mitch said it once at Rosslyn Metro. He quickly accepted I preferred Ellie. Oddly, I'd never asked Joan to call me Ellie. I couldn't understand that.

"Joan?"

"Are you all right?"

I nodded.

She smiled.

I smiled back. "I'm fine."

At that moment, the backdoor opened and Mitch walked in. He kissed his mum's cheek then leaned over the table and kissed me on the lips. Long, slow, warm, he was home. A hole opened in the air above the table, swirling black clouds sucked the images of Beatrice Connelly from the room then dissolved.

Leaving the air laced with roasting chicken and a hint of Mitch's cologne.

I breathed.

A chair scrapped on the floor. Joan busied herself at the counter.

Mitch slid into the chair next to me.

"Hi," he said, smiling, and bumping me with his arm.

"Hi," I replied, bumping him back.

He picked up my glass and took a mouthful of wine. "This is nice. Do I get a glass Mom?"

He handed me my glass and read the label on the bottle.

His mother set a glass in front of him, and rubbed his shoulder.

She didn't hit him. She didn't scream. She didn't belittle him or accuse. She openly adored her son.

"How was your day?" she asked and actually wanted to know.

"Good. Busy," Mitch smiled. "Tell me about your day?"

"Just the usual," Joan replied. "Until Gabrielle arrived." She walked behind me toward the refrigerator, pausing to give my shoulder a squeeze. "Lovely having you here early," she said then carried on talking to Mitch while she moved to checked on the cooking process.

I watched them for a few moments and remembered why I loved being around Joan so much as a kid. She was the mom I always wanted.

Joan looked at me, she smiled and said, "Remember the question?"

I grinned. "I'd say yes."

Confusion crossed Mitch's face and made us laugh.

Burning Bridges

I rested on the doorframe and watched him work for a few minutes. It soothed my soul in ways I couldn't explain. Today he was working from home. My home. Nice.

Mitch looked up and smiled. "Can I help you or are you lurking for fun?"

"I like the view but yeah, you can help me," I replied crossing the room and perching on the edge of his desk. "I need a favor, Mitch."

"A big one?"

"Yeah."

"Shoot."

Let's hope not.

"I've lost someone and I need one of your toys to help me locate this person."

He leaned back in his chair and regarded me with what I deemed to be curiosity.

"You want to use one of the Iverson drones?"

"Yes."

"To find someone in The District?"

I nodded. "We've done it before."

He shook his head slightly. "You can't get FAA approval for a one of the CIA drones can you?"

Am I that transparent?

"No. They're screwing around and I don't have time." I chewed my lip.

"What else?"

"My actions here are conusable by an oversight committee. I can't get this wrong."

"And the only way you can find your target is with one of my birds?"

"No, I just would like to have a better view."

I could see his mind working on my comment. No need to explain, he was getting there on his own.

"You're tracking an agent?"

"I'm tracking an agent." An agent who likes to blow things up.

"I think I can help. There's a prototype drone in my office. It's so small it doesn't need FAA approval." He held his index finger and thumb apart about an inch. "It's the size of a sparrow."

"The size of a sparrow?"

"Yep. There is a catch, like the humming bird, the range isn't great. We're not going to be flying these things in Iraq from here."

"That's the only catch?"

"Not exactly. I'm looking to field test the sparrow so data would be collected by us."

"And if someone spots it and swats it against a wall?"

"We'll find out if the Kevlar it's wrapped in protects it or not ..."

"That seems fair." My quarterly budget sprang to mind smashing the little drone would blow a big chunk in that and take the budget for the rest of the year with it. Another thought ebbed in. "Who'd control it?"

"I would," he replied without hesitation. "It's a prototype, can't let anyone outside the company control it."

"And you have to follow it?"

Thoughts rolled around in my head, we'd been here before. I didn't like it last time and I didn't like it this time.

"Yes, it's a limited range vehicle."

"You'd be in the field with me again?"

"Yes."

That was another scenario filled with potential hell

and fiery death.

"You okay?" Mitch asked draining his cup.

"Not really. I'm not keen on you being in the field with me. Too many variables."

"It's surveillance. I'm not going to be entering any unsafe situations." Mitch mustered the same patient voice he used last time we had this conversation. Last time D.C. exploded and nearly took him with it.

Life had a way of fucking everything up.

I shook my head.

"It's surveillance El, I won't be in the line of fire." His tone was reassuring. "And anyway, I know you'll be there."

I didn't like where that was going but nodded.

"I'm concerned I won't be as focused with you in the field, and to be honest the last time you trailed a drone it didn't go so well."

The patient voice continued, "Remember that situation a few months ago?"

"Situation?"

"Hostage thing ..."

"Yes, I remember."

Lunatic with a hostage. Good word situation.

"What were you thinking about when you entered

that building? Honestly."

"You."

"Uh huh."

"That's not the same. You weren't in danger."

"No, but you were and you still focused despite me being on your mind." He smiled. "You can do this, El."

"I can do this. If you get hurt ..."

"I'll be out of the way, flying the drone, nowhere near the targets." He smiled. "Kris and Jerry made good minders, would you be happier if they were with me again?"

"Marginally."

An hour later I briefed my team with Mitch. I borrowed Kris and Jerry from SWAT to babysit Mitch while he flew the sparrow. Just in case seemed like a smart way to play the situation. There was nothing worse than a rogue agent with an agenda. We were after a guy who had nothing left to lose and the desire to inflict pain as retribution for imagined wrongs. He'd gone off the reservation and sent threats via email and text message to various important people, some within the FBI, a few Senators, and two Congressmen.

My priority was finding and stopping Joseph Rosenbaum before he committed one or more acts of no return. I was kidding myself. He already had. There was no coming back for him.

"What Intel do we have regarding his whereabouts?" I asked leaning forward in my seat at the table.

Lee shook his head. "He ditched the last surveillance team in Georgetown. He's contacting people via burner phones. Each time a different number."

"So we can't pinpoint him using cell towers?"

"Not effectively. Do you know how many burner phones are active in D.C. on any given day?" Sandra said. "I can work magic but I need something to go on or a pattern."

D.C.: a hot bed of intrigue and bullshit. Burner phones were standard fare.

I mulled that over and came up with an idea.

"We need to get the word out to Rosenbaum that I want to meet with him."

Heads shook all-round the table.

"He's got a screw loose El," Mitch said. "This doesn't make me happy."

"It's my job, Mitch." I smiled. "Badge, gun, can do

attitude." Rogue agent to apprehend.

Lee grumbled then asked, "How do we reach him?"

"Social media," I replied. "Sandra?"

"On it."

Half an hour later Sandra reported contact and a meeting place.

"For us tactically, this is a shit meeting," Lee said, looking at a Google map of Rosenbaum's chosen area. "He's got multiple entrances and exits, not to mention vantage points."

Lee pointed to several places Rosenbaum could use to carry out his own surveillance and check that I am alone like stated in the request to meet.

"Yeah, it's great for him," I replied. "I want him to feel as though he has the upper hand here." I turned to Mitch. "We haven't got long. How fast can you deploy that drone?"

"I need ten minutes."

"Okay – you need to be out there in five to allow for your deployment time. You're riding with your old buddies Kris and Jerry from SWAT. You do as they say."

Mitch smiled.

"I'll be fine."

"Yeah, and they'll see to it." I stood and paced for a moment. "He'll get there early and set up. He's going to be watching. I need you to find him in the crowd or in his temporary hide."

"That's what this little sparrow is for, finding people who don't want to be found."

"Okay go. I'll follow. I'll be close but you need to guide me. Anything that looks or feels wrong and you get the hell out. Got it?"

"Yes."

Kris stood. His chair scraped across the floor. "We'll get him out at the first sign of anything hinky, Conway."

Mitch picked up a metal case from the floor by his chair and walked to the door. I hugged him.

"Be careful out there. Rosenbaum is a loose unit."

A clawing cold enveloped my gut. Mitch smiled as Kris and Jerry escorted him out of the room.

Lee and I followed a few minutes later. Kurt and Sam would be nearby. Sandra stayed in the office, at her computer, available to offer us whatever sort of digital help we required. We hoped to nail Rosenbaum without any fuss.

Chances were beyond slim.

Mitch called my cell.

"The drone is up. I've swept the entire area. No sign of him."

"He should be there by now." I paused. "You sure?"

"Yes. Nothing."

"Can you see us?"

"Yes."

"Give him a minute."

I hung up.

My phone rang. No caller ID.

"SSA Conway."

"Go to 3rd Street NE."

Rosenbaum.

He hung up.

I called Mitch back. "Mitch, he's changed the meeting point. 3rd Street NE. Go. We're on our way."

"It's a long street, anything to narrow it down?"

"Not yet, I'll let you know."

I called the office as Lee and I ran back to our car. "Rosenbaum changed the meeting place, 3rd Street, NE. We need to clear the area as much as possible."

I had a horrible feeling this was not going to go well. Although, being in a crowded place like we were could be worse.

Half way to 3rd Street my phone rang again. No caller ID.

"There's a traffic cone in a car park near the East Capitol Street and 3rd Street intersection, park there and walk toward the church on the corner of 3rd and A."

He hung up again.

"It's pretty much all residential up there," I said, relaying the instructions to Lee before calling Kris and Jerry to let them know. My next call was the office.

"Sandra, he's sending us to a residential area. Wants us to walk from East Capitol to A Street. Get as many people off the streets as possible. No marked cars. I want this guy in custody."

"Consider it done O Genie of Capitol Hill. Want Capitol police involved?"

"Yes. Once we are inside the area, they can shut the streets behind us."

"Stay safe."

I saw the traffic cone and hung up.

"That must be for us," I said, pointing to the cone. He'd been in position long enough to get really comfortable and set us up. I breathed a few deep breathes and stopped my thoughts spiraling to the dark side. Every breath I took reminded me I was wearing a bullet proof vest.

Lee stopped close by, I jumped out and hefted the cone off the parking space and onto the sidewalk. They're deceptively heavy.

He parked. Cars lined both sides of the street. We walked up sidewalk toward the A street intersection. My heart pounded. I ran my damp palms down my thighs.

Something whizzed past my head. I grabbed Lee by the arm and pulled him down behind a parked car. The phone in my hand flashed. Incoming call. Bullets hit the car next to us and then the wall on the other side of us chipping chunks of mortar. I answered the phone.

"Stay down, manoeuvring the drone." Radio silence punctuated with gun fire followed. "I have a location. Shots are coming from the church. Looks like the bell tower."

Lee was on his phone before Mitch stopped talking. I could hear him as bullets hit and more mortar and chunks of concrete fell onto the sidewalk.

"Agents under fire. Stay back, make sure the area

is locked down."

I ducked lower as more pieces of building chipped and fell. Not listening to Lee's voice or Mitch I crept around the car we sheltered behind. A bullet lodged in the metal near my head. Breathing hard I crouched lower and edged back to Lee and more cover.

It had to be Rosenbaum. Must've changed his mind about coming in.

Ambulance sirens wailed. Coming closer. I hoped Capitol police or one of our cars would intercept and divert so they didn't get caught in our situation.

Kris's voice erupted from the phone in my hand. I'd forgotten the line was open.

"I'm coming for you. Jerry is with Mitch."

"No."

"Conway, I'm at the edge of the block, turn around."

I turned, a dark shape waved once from the corner of a building. Deep shadow. There was no way he'd be able to get close. Bullets peppered the road. From the bell tower, Rosenbaum had a three hundred and sixty degree view. Any minute an innocent person could caught up in the situation. Back behind Kris, I saw rolling red and blue lights in the middle of the road.

Down the intersection I saw more rolling lights. All I could do was hope they'd warned as many people as possible and that most people were at work and not in the houses nearby.

"The church?" I said to Lee. A gunman in a church tower, it'd been done before. Not exactly inventive.

"That church is closed for renovations. No one in there but our shooter."

"You're sure?"

"Police confirmed the church is empty."

"Kris is trying to get to us ..."

"Then let's distract the idiot with the rifle," Lee said. "How good is Rosenbaum with that rifle, you think?"

Probably not as good as me. I kept that thought to myself.

I smiled. "Let's distract him and find out."

Lee tried the car door of the car next to us, locked.

"Let me," I said, pulling a tactical pen from my jacket pocket. I hit the upper corner of the window with the sharp end of the pen. Glass shattered and fell over the seats of the car.

"Nice," Lee murmured, brushing glass away from the top of the door so he could unlock and open it.

"It writes nice too." I stuck the titanium pen back into my pocket. I knew it'd be handy one day.

Gunfire erupted again. I glanced back and saw Kris had moved, he was maybe ten feet closer. Almost at our car. I crouched by the open car door. Lee reached for a bottle of water in the footwell.

"Thirsty?"

"Distraction."

"A rifle would be handy."

"Better than a bottle of water."

A rifle would be super handy. We were a block away from our car and my rifle. Fuck this shit.

I jammed my phone in my pocket. "Our keys."

Lee gave them to me. I took off with the keys in my hand. Tiny speeding projectiles smashed into the brick on the buildings and cars next to me, chasing me to my car. I fumbled the fob in my hand, a round whizzed by as I wrestled the back door of the Suburban open. My windscreen disappeared. Glass hit me. I wiped fragments off my face and dragged the gun case across the back of the car, flipping the locks open. I hauled the rifle from the case. Adjusted my grip to the weight, took a handful of rounds from the box and dropped them into my pocket. Chambering one.

A voice next to me made me jump.

I swung the rifle around.

Kris.

He gently pushed the muzzle away.

He pointed up. I shook my head.

"I'm shooting from closer, line of sight isn't good enough down here."

My phone buzzed. Kris took it from my pocket and answered the call. "Mitch, get that drone working, will ya."

I couldn't hear the response. More glass fell as another bullet hit my car.

I shoved the backdoor shut, the back window blew out. Shaking glass from my hair I ducked and ran, cradling the rifle in my arms. I used my shoulder to wipe moisture from side of my face. Moisture. Blood and sweat. Once back with Lee, Kris and I looked for the best return fire position.

Mitch gave Kris a clear account of the shooter and his position. A flash in the sky above the street and an exclamation of anger from the phone in Kris's hand told me the drone took a bullet.

Dammit. That'd cost the division a bit.

Kris pointed to where Mitch told him the shooter was, confirmation that he was in the bell tower. I needed to be higher than I was but not much higher. Without thought, I charged through the door of the closest building. In the foyer I scanned for stairs. Wiping my face with my shoulder again, I pulled open a door marked stairs. Two floors later, out of breath from running upstairs with the weight of the rifle, I pulled open another door and entered a spacious office. Howls of surprise echoed across the wide space. Someone screamed. I imagined my appearance was less than comforting. I felt blood drip down my face and figured it was leaving stains on my shirt collar and the front of my jacket. Always a good look.

"FBI, get out," I said, adjusting my hold on the rifle. "Go in the hallway, shut all the doors. Do not leave the building."

People moved with quiet speed, skirting me and my scary looking rifle. The door behind me opened. I swung around to see Kris holding the door. He spoke softly and with practiced calm. When the door closed it dropped a thick silence over the room. I found a window that gave me a good angle and clean line of sight through my scope. Kris cleared a desk by sweeping his arm over it, and dragged it to my chosen window. I hooked a chair with my foot and pulled it to me. Kris leaned across and slid the window open. Using the chair and the desk, I settled into a semi-comfortable shooting position. Good enough. Wasn't planning on being there long.

Kris called Lee and asked him to start throwing stuff out of the car into the middle of the road. The water bottle exploded in midair. I trained my rifle on the origin of the shot. Blood trickled down the side of my face and dripped onto the desk.

"Got him?" Kris asked. He wiped blood off my forehead with his sleeve before it got to my eyes.

"Yep."

I took a deep breath and held it, counting in my head. I saw the flash as he fired again. I exhaled and squeezed the trigger. The round hit the wooden frame next to him. Crap. I reloaded, took a deep breath, lined him up, and fired again. This time, the gun fell sideways. I watched through my scope. No movement. I couldn't see the floor inside the tower. He could've ducked down.

Kris was on the phone telling police and SWAT to

move in.

Still watching for signs of movement. I breathed.

A deep voice behind me said, "Everything okay up here?"

"Yeah," I replied. "You all right Lee?"

"Never better, Chicky."

I didn't turn around, instead I continued watching the tower for signs of life.

Kris spoke, "SWAT entered the building and bell tower. Police are on the ground. Ambulance en route."

A face appeared at the top of the tower. "Tell me that's SWAT," I said, flexing my trigger finger.

Kris held a phone to my ear. "Stand down Conway, the shooter is deceased," a familiar voice said.

"My bullet?"

Andrews laughed softly in my ear. "Head shot Conway, who else's would it be?"

"Confirm identity."

"Sending you a photo now."

I loosened my grip on the weapon, and placed it on the desk. Kris dropped the phone in my hand. A text with a photo arrived.

Joseph Rosenbaum.

One less loser in the world. A large drop of deep

red plopped onto my phone screen. I wiped it away with my fingers, smearing my blood across what was left of Rosenbaum's face.

Lee ripped open a dressing pack and handed me several pads of gauze.

I pressed dressings against the cuts on my face.

Lee grinned. "Paramedics are on the way up. Mitch and Jerry are waiting downstairs. Despite the amount of ammunition Rosenbaum fired into the street no one was killed or wounded."

"Good result."

That was a win for the good guys.

Bed of Roses

"Today sucked and gave change," I said to the old cat curled at the end of my bed. He didn't care. I pulled my boots off and let them drop to the floor. My right shoulder ached. "Maybe I need to live in a warmer climate." Weariness enveloped me like a blanket as my words collided with the mirror on the wall and bounced into oblivion. A little green flashing light on my phone caught my eye. I picked the cell phone up from the bedside table, the screen woke, and the reason for the little green light became apparent.

A text: Now as you close your eyes, know I'll be thinking about you. M.

I wanted to reply to Mitch but I didn't know what to say. Felt like I should start with sorry. The day hadn't gone to plan. Not my plan anyway. I'd missed our morning run. I'd missed our lunch. The case I was on caved in and caused utter chaos. Didn't even have the chance to tell him I couldn't make our run or lunch or even text to say hi. Every time I tried something or someone interrupted me. I read his text again.

"Why does he put up with me?" I mumbled to the cat.

Shrek meowed, twitched, and rolled over.

Not the answer I was looking for.

Mitch's text was still on the screen when my phone rang.

An image attached to the caller flashed, the text disappeared.

Muscle memory kicked in. My finger swept across the phone.

"Conway, we have a lead," Kurt said.

I hesitated for a fraction of a second. "Is it good?"

Fair question. This case was weird. Leads led to nothing. Minimal light shone through frosted windowpanes. Doors opened onto brick walls. We needed a wrecking ball to make any progress, and not the Miley Cyrus kind.

"Yes. You all right?"

"Uh huh. Where are you?"

"Almost at your place."

It took much effort to stifle a sigh. The phone call confirmed my suspicions. The universe was conspiring against us. Maybe me and Mitch weren't meant to be?

"See you soon."

I hung up, dropped the phone on to my bed, and stood up. Sadness barreled headlong toward me causing me to do a quick sidestep. The sleep I needed would have to wait. The life I wanted faded into the night. So much for having a work/life balance.

The cat stretched along the end of the bed and looked up at me.

"Maybe it should just be you and me, Shrek," I said, patting his fuzzy head. He rolled over exposing his stomach for scratching. "I'm not silly enough to take the bait." One stroke of his stomach and he'd close his claws and teeth around my hand like a bear trap. No thanks.

I showered fast and dressed in warm clean clothes.

A hot shower was almost as good as six hours sleep.

My eyes rolled at my reflection in the bathroom mirror. An uneasiness crept over me. Where did it come from? I searched my mind for an answer.

Something was tweaking in my gut but it didn't feel like a work thing, considering the day and the total lack of balance in my life that was quite surprising.

Breathe.

What did I feel? Anticipation? Nerves?

It felt like something was going to happen. I gave it a minute. The feeling settled into my bones but it didn't feel bad. Not bad in an imminent death type way. Wandering through thoughts helped narrow the feeling to a person.

Mitch.

I sent a quick text.

Sorry, today was shit. On my way back to work. Talk soon. E xx

By the time Kurt arrived I was waiting outside the front door wearing an FBI jacket, zipped against the biting cold. I climbed into the warm car.

"All right?" Kurt asked.

"Uh huh." I couldn't say anything. All I had was a weird feeling of anticipation and nothing to base it on. My gut was traditionally more intuitive than that. Usually a song pointed me in the right direction. The deviation perplexed me.

"You sure you're okay?" Kurt asked flicking his headlights onto high-beam as he pulled out of the driveway.

"Yep."

"Conway?" He glanced at me. "What's up?"

"Nothing. Let's just get this over with. Where are we going?"

"Reston," he said. "Our suspect was last seen entering a large property in Reston."

"His? A Friends? He's trespassing? The story is?"

My cell phone buzzed in my pocket. I wrestled it free and read the text.

Call tonight if you get the chance. M.

I stared at the screen and the text. The feeling was back. Butterflies? Yes. That was it. Something was up. Maybe it really was over.

"Problem?" Kurt asked. "You want to talk?"

I took a breath and swallowed. The butterflies flapped around in my stomach. My head shook. That was not what I wanted.

"I need ..." I looked at my phone in my hand. It buzzed again.

Another text. It's important. M.

"... I need to go to Mitch's. Now," I said.

"Is there something wrong?" Kurt asked, tapping the turn-signal and taking the next right. "Conway? Is there something wrong?"

"I don't know."

It was something, I suspected it might not be good but I couldn't say it was wrong.

"What is it?"

"My heads not in the game. You need me to be focused and I can't right now."

"You're not making a lot of sense Conway. This isn't you."

I glanced down. Looked like me. Pretty sure it was me. Moving on.

"Lee and Sam?"

"On their way to the last known sighting of our suspect."

"Can you three cope without me?"

My eyes were drawn to the dark world outside the car. I recognized an intersection. This wasn't the way to Reston.

"Yes, we can cope, Conway," Kurt said as he flicked the turn signal again, this time a left turn. "Hence, I'm driving you to Mitch's place."

Ten minutes of silence later, I stood on the curb outside Mitch's house and watched Kurt drive off. He was right, this wasn't me. Ditching my team in the middle of the night without a damn good reason was not something that happened in my world and I never had a problem concentrating.

Darkness shrouded the house. For a split second my unannounced midnight arrival seemed like a bad idea. He could be asleep? Maybe he sleep texts? People do all manner of weird stuff when their brains switch to standby mode. So sleep texting, was a possibility.

A deep breath shuddered through my rib cage. Just get it over with.

He might not be alone. I frowned. Did I really think that?

"Shut up," I muttered. "You're not doing yourself any favors thinking stupid shit."

I walked up the grass next to the driveway to muffle the sound of my cowboy boots. Quietly opening and closing the side gate. Security lighting flicked on illuminating my way to the second gate. Beyond that was a large flagstone patio, swimming pool, and the back door.

So much for being quiet.

The protective steel heel and toe taps fitted to my cowboy boots made sure silence wasn't a thing on hard surfaces – sparks occasionally were.

My boots clicked and tapped across the flagstones.

Another set of security lighting flooded the area, the pool water appeared inky in the night. A shadow from inside the house fell across the ground by the back door. I took a breath, reminded myself I wasn't at work, and released the grip I had on the Glock on my hip. Love the way my body reacts without conscious thought.

The door opened.

Mitch stood bathed in electric light. Tousled, shirtless, wearing jeans with his belt open. Smiling.

"Hi," I said trying to settle my nerves and convince myself his smile meant it was going to be all right. My stomach twisted into tight knots.

"Late for a visit," he said.

"I can go ..."

Mitch shook his head, his smile never faltered.

"I'd like you to stay," he said ushering me through the door. "Feels like we'll get early snow." Mitch shivered.

The door closed firmly behind us. His arms wrapped around me.

"Missed you today," he whispered.

With my head on his shoulder I drank in the scent

of his skin. Feeling his heart beating through my jacket. Or maybe it was my heart?

"Missed you too."

"It's nice that you miss me," he said. "I think I like being missed."

I started to relax, maybe it was going to be okay.

"Were you in bed?"

"Yes."

Something red on the floor caught my eye. Petals? A hallway strewn with rose petals?

"Mitch?" I pointed to the trail that led down the hall and out of sight. "Expecting company?" I glanced at his face.

He bit his lower lip as he nodded.

"Yes."

I pulled away. "Is this what you wanted to tell me?" The knots in my stomach were back. Tightening until I could hardly breathe.

He shook his head, his hand grabbed mine. "I was expecting company. You."

I forced air into my lungs while I let his words sink in.

"Me?"

"Yes."

"How did you know I'd come?"

"I know you," he replied, wrapping his arms around me and pulling me close. "I know you."

Arm in arm we walked through the house, following the flower petal trail to his bedroom. The only light in the room was the soft flickering glow emanating from several lit candles. The warm mix of roses and candles reminded me of long summer evenings by the pool.

On a small table under the window stood a large vase of long stemmed red roses. Next to the table - a bottle of champagne and two glasses.

The butterflies were back, dancing in my stomach.

I saw Mitch's laptop open on the bed amidst more rose petals. "Not sleeping then. Were you working?" I asked even though it didn't look like he was working.

He closed the screen and moved the computer to the dresser, rose petals tumbled to the floor.

With a smile he said, "No, I was emailing you. And here you are."

Synchronicity. He was good at tuning into me.

"What'd you say in that email?" I sat on Mitch's bed and watched him walk toward me.

"I said I couldn't sleep ..."

He was in front of me. I hooked a finger into the waistband of his jeans and pulled him a little closer.

"Did you have anything in mind that might help you sleep?"

He nodded. His eyes sparkled. Mitch plunged his right hand into his pocket, he pulled his hand out and then dropped to one knee.

My moment of confusion was replaced with surprise.

Oh, we're here. I felt my eyes widen. We're here?

My heart caught in my throat. I swallowed hard hoping to force it back into my chest. "Gabrielle Rylie Conway will you do me the honor of becoming my wife?"

Stunned.

He took my left-hand and slid a diamond ring onto my finger. Three diamonds.

Mitch's voice crumbled a little as he said, "A diamond for your past, a diamond for the present, and a diamond for our future."

My eyes looked deep into Mitch's and found everything I'd ever needed, wanted, and hoped for.

"Yes."

Mitch leaned down, his lips met mine, softly at

first then firmer with more intensity, pressing me back onto the bed.

Dying Ain't Much of a Living.

I read the article from the Miami Herald with curiosity. Naked man killed by Police near MacArthur Causeway was 'eating' face off victim. If I hadn't gotten home so late from finishing up a ton of paperwork from a case I wouldn't have read it at all.

The twinges in my stomach were not curiosity; they were the early beginnings of fear.

The police suggested the man was suffering from a cocaine psychosis.

Cocaine psychosis my ass. I smelled a big fat conspiracy.

The naked man did not attack the homeless guy and eat his face due to a cocaine psychosis. It didn't take six rounds fired by a police officer to kill him because of a cocaine psychosis.

Meth maybe, but that didn't feel right either.

Twinges became outright terror as scenarios I didn't ever want know were possible spiraled out of control in my mind.

I picked up my phone from the coffee table and

made a call.

While I waited I checked my watch, just in case morning had snuck up while I wasn't looking.

It was still the middle of the night.

To be more accurate it was three in the morning.

What was I even doing surfing news articles at three in the morning? Innocently waiting for sleeping. That's what. On the fifteenth ring my call was answered.

"It's Ellie. Did you see that piece from the Miami Herald?"

A sleepy reply came back, "You'll have to be more specific."

"Trust me, if you'd seen it you'd know."

He sighed. "When was it reported?"

"Just after two this afternoon, they reported a naked man was killed by police while eating the face off a victim."

As I uttered my next words, I knew we were probably too late to contain this. Thirteen hours and counting.

"How many shots fired?"

He sounded fully awake now.

"At least six."

"Crap."

"They're saying cocaine psychosis ..."

"Good that'll keep the media busy for a little while, where is the body?"

"I don't know. Talk to Miami Police."

"Where was it?"

"Florida, near or on MacArthur Causeway off ramp. Google it."

"Any idea if the fatal was a head shot?"

"No idea, but it would be my guess. I thought you had people trolling for this kind of event?"

"Yeah me too. I'll call you back."

The call ended.

I jumped to my feet and flew through the house, gathering important things together.

I packed clothes and bathroom items in record time.

From the closet I took a gun case and lay it on my bed. I flipped the locks open and checked the contents. The case contained an SG 551 and extra magazines. From my office I took a shotgun and a box of 12 gauge shells and another box full of ammunition for the SG. I took the guns out to the truck. I put the SG case on the back seat. The shotgun I left on the passenger seat and put the box of shells on the floor.

Back inside I put on a shoulder holster. In the shoulder holster I had my Glock 17. Extra magazines slotted into pouches on my belt. I took a drop leg holster that held another Glock 17 and put it in my pack. I pulled a jacket on and zipped it up half way. My pack lay on my bed; I added a new box of 9mm ammunition. A first aid kit sat next to the pack with my badge hanging from a chain lanyard sitting on it. I put the lanyard around my neck and tucked the badge inside my jacket.

I took both bags to the truck and threw them in the back.

Quickly I went back into the house and gathered my phone, a car charger, flashlights, emergency radio, and laptop and power cords. I scrabbled through my desk until I found an adapter for the laptop which would allow me to charge it from the car. We may end up without power. I figured sooner or later we'd end up without internet too but while we had it I was going to use it.

Next I scooped up two boxes one at a time from the bottom of the pantry and set them on the counter top. Non-perishable food items and bottled water. I dropped packets of cookies, chocolate, nuts, and cereal from the pantry shelves into the boxes. It all went into the back of the truck. Along with a camp stove and extra gas from the garage, a tent and sleeping bags.

Before I left I set the security system to fortress.

That armed the mines around the perimeter, activated the cameras, and tracking lasers, turned the alarm on - the alarm was designed to disorientate and it was very effective. If anyone breaking in didn't hit a mine or be zapped by a laser then the alarm would turn to a quivering vomiting jellified mess. Over kill? Some would say yes, but I'd hazard a guess that they haven't had two of their houses blown up, they also probably haven't considered apocalyptic scenarios as reality.

It's not paranoia when you know what I know.

I locked the house and the garage. The gates, razor wire, and security system would protect the house for a while. At least until the power failed. Even then, the mines were armed. If you didn't know they were there you couldn't avoid them and I was the only one who knew.

Worst case scenario.

Always plan for the worst case. Ever since meeting Obadiah the worst-case scenario was never far away. I'd managed to keep those thoughts under wraps until now. Now the duct tape holding it all together was losing its stick. I set my phone in the holder on the dash and called Mitch.

"Sorry, I know it's late. This is important," I said as soon as he answered. "Just listen. Something bad is happening. I'm picking you up in ten minutes. Pack fast."

"You all right?"

"Yep." But the world as we know it might not be. "Get ready. I'll explain on the way."

I ended the call.

My phone rang as I pulled out of the driveway. Obadiah's face flashed at me from the screen. I answered it while I waited for the gates to close behind me.

"Got anything else?" I said to Obadiah.

"Body is in the county morgue, I'm having it shipped to our facility," he said.

Our facility. I was a hundred miles away from that facility in Virginia.

"I'm on my away down. I will be arriving plus two."

"You need a respirators," Obadiah replied.

"I have them in the back of the truck."

Always.

Worst case.

"Put it on before you enter the facility - to be safe do it at the twenty mile mark."

"Hazmat suit?"

"Not at this stage, if it's what I think it is, then it's airborne, it spreads just like a flu virus, via droplets from coughing, sneezing, talking. This contagious period only lasts a few days. We believe the virus mutates once contracted and then as it takes hold of the person it is spread by virus containing saliva."

"Like rabies?"

"Yes, the initial infection causes rabies like virus in the victim which then has a similar effect on the brain."

"Timing?"

"The virus incubates in the body for up to fourteen days then when it reaches the brain symptoms appear, and they're akin to rabies and by then the virus is present in the saliva and transmitted via bites."

"Survival?"

"Nil."

Curiosity got the better of me. "What was the shot that dropped it?"

"A head shot. He took five shots to the chest and kept on eating."

"How many infected?"

"No way of knowing. Haven't determined where he came from. I have the CDC onto that task, they're helping local LEO's."

"What's the cover story?"

"Drug induced psychosis possibly due to bath salts."

"That doesn't explain the CDC involvement."

"I told the local LEO's that the bath salts probably contained another substance and that the CDC were the best people to investigate it at this point. DEA are assisting to lend credibility."

"What about the victim?"

"Being transported to our facility. He's critical and won't live, but for research purposes we want him with us."

"Anyone else sick?"

"Not that we know of." He sighed. "If this is what I think it is, then the biter was infected about two weeks ago, there could be a steady stream of infections now coming to the fore."

Fourteen hours and counting.

"See you soon."

I touched the end call icon on the screen of my phone, and drove south.

At the gas station, I set a timer on my phone - to remind me to put my respirator on at the eighty-mile mark. That would put me twenty miles out. No sense risking contamination.

Neither of us had said it but we both knew what we thought it was.

Two years ago two viruses went missing in New Zealand. They were intercepted and hidden by an intelligence officer. Unfortunately he had been exposed to both viruses. Another kiwi operative found the viruses still contained in separate safe containers. We never found out how the first officer became exposed. The kiwi operative also located his body and watched as it reanimated. It was put down by Obadiah. The incident area was sanitized.

Baptism by fire.

The containers were brought to the United States and stored in a secure facility in Florida. Secure right up until they fuc'n weren't.

Two viruses. Alone you get a nasty flu. Together you become a blood hungry warm flesh-eating monster, all reason gone, and only basic animal responses left. We don't even know if they feel pain. It's supposed to be theoretical.

Some smartassed sicko in New Zealand at the Investigation and Diagnostic Center in Wallaceville, Upper Hutt developed the viruses then tried to sell them to a known terrorist group until his plan was foiled. Now we have the viruses and someone had potentially become infected.

How?

Pulling into Mitch's driveway I called Obadiah back, don't panic, hands free.

"How did someone become infected?"

"I don't know yet, no reports of any break-ins at the Florida facility."

"I'm sending Delta."

"Level A."

"I know."

I hung up, parked and called Sam.

"Chicky?" He answered on the first ring.

"Don't you sleep?"

"Not tonight, problem?"

"Yes. I need you and Lee to get your respirators and head to Florida. Use our jet."

"What's up?"

"Potentially world changing situation. Level A. Need to know only. I'll authorize the jet. You're going to a government storage facility to locate two viruses." I paused. "You're looking for Tminus4 and Tminus6."

"Got it. Has this got something to do with the face eater?"

"Yes. When you locate the viruses call me. I will be at a facility in Charlottesville, Virginia."

Sam paused. "A what where?"

"The National Guard Armory, only it's not just that. It's a secure underground facility, I'll be there. Peregory Lane."

I was quite pleased that I didn't call it what I usually did.

"Purgatory Lane?" Sam asked.

I smiled. "Yeah, that's what I usually call it."

I always figured if I ever needed to go there for anything it would be purgatory and we would be in dire need of purification. I wasn't wrong.

"I'll get Lee you get Kurt. Let's do it."

We hung up. I made the call to Andrews. "This is

SSA Ellie Conway authorization code ..." I pressed seven numbers into my phone then the hash key.

Seconds later a human voice spoke, "What do you need Agent Conway?"

"The Delta jet for a flight from Andrews to Florida then Florida to Charlottesville. Two passengers no crew apart from the pilots. Strict quarantine procedures to be implemented on the Florida to Charlottesville leg."

"Yes ma'am."

I hung up.

My headlights illuminated Mitch as he locked the front door of his home. He hurried toward me with a backpack slung over his shoulder. I reached over and unlocked the passenger door. He tossed the pack into the back and climbed in.

"This isn't good is it?" he asked.

"No, this isn't good." I pulled out of his driveway and headed north again. "We're picking up Kurt."

Nothing was said until I made the next call from outside Kurt's home. I wasn't going without him. No way was I going to face this without my entire team and Mitch. Stopping for Mitch and Kurt would only add fifteen minutes to the journey. Two hours and fifteen to make it to purgatory.

"Wait here, I'll be right back," I said to Mitch.

I knocked on Kurt's door and waited as sounds of wakefulness crept along the hallway lit by the soft glow of lights flickering on.

The door flew open.

I smiled.

"Hey, up for a road trip?"

"Conway, it's nearly four in the morning, what the hell?"

"We have a situation..."

Kurt was standing in the doorway, shirtless, barefoot, wearing jeans with his belt undone and half asleep. I knew Lee and Sam would already be on their way to Andrews.

"A situation?"

"Yes. Mitch is in the car. Hurry up."

"Come in," Kurt said. "I'll be five minutes."

I wandered into the living room and tossed myself onto the leather couch to wait. Four minutes and fifteen seconds later Kurt emerged fully clothed and carrying two bags.

"Let's go."

I filled Kurt and Mitch in on the way. We stopped

for coffee once. Fifteen hours and counting.

Kurt opted to drive the rest of the way after our coffee break. Mitch rode shotgun. His silence was unusual but considering the circumstances not surprising.

"Did you get any sleep at all?" Kurt asked adjusting the rearview mirror so he could see me in the back.

I could've lied but what would be the point?

"No, was still winding down when I saw the story."

"Get some rest. We'll wake you before we get there."

"When my phone alarm goes - we need to put on the respirators," I replied with yawn.

"Okay, sleep."

My eyes did not need to be told twice.

The alarm woke me before Kurt could. He'd pulled off the road ahead of schedule and was getting the masks from their cases in the back of the truck.

I looked at my watch. Sixteen hours and counting.

Kurt opened my door.

"Wearing these into town, even inside the truck, is going to cause a stir," I said. I took the mask he handed me and set about getting into it. "It's also going to be ridiculously annoying."

"Better than being ridiculously dead," Kurt replied.

Good point.

We checked the fit of each other's masks and climbed back into the truck.

Within minutes, I started to feel overheated. I consoled myself with the thought that it could be worse. I could be wearing a level A Hazmat suit or even a full-face mask. The half-face mask seemed a little less cumbersome and claustrophobic after that.

We could still talk and understand each other. In one way we would've been better off wearing the full suits, they had an inbuilt fluid dispenser. The masks did not. Drinking would only be an issue if we had to wear these masks for extended periods.

"Remember to drink," Kurt said. I heard the amusement in his voice.

"Yeah, remember to drive," I replied.

Mitch laughed breaking any tension we'd felt wide open.

My phone rang. Mitch handed it to me. Good thing I'm used to having my phone in front of me and not at my ear.

"How far out are you?"

Obadiah.

"Almost there."

"Just got a report from New Jersey. A man disemboweled himself and threw his guts at police."

Holy crap. You couldn't make this shit up.

"Dear God."

"I have people at that scene now."

"The police could be infected."

"We're tracking those cops and cleaning up after them."

Cleaning up after them sounded ominous because it was.

Anyone they came in contact with would be cleaned up as would anything. The fires would be burning in New Jersey today.

"Why no reports of this kind in Georgia, North and South Carolina, Virginia or Maryland?"

I knew the answer. Someone flew infected.

"The man flew to New Jersey from Florida last night," Obadiah said.

"Newark?"

"Yes," he replied.

"We're fucked."

"Probably."

Probably? Yeah, nah, we're screwed.

"We're here, bring us down," I said.

Kurt drove onto the site. In front of us a large steel door slid sideways. As we drove down a ramp, the steel door closed. The area below us was well lit. Kurt followed the roadway down two more ramps. Obadiah was waiting, wearing a respirator mask like ours and directed us to a car park.

I noted the absence of a Hazmat suit on Obadiah. I don't know why I expected him to be wearing one when we didn't have too, but I did. In the movies everyone is always wearing Hazmat suits at these kinds of facilities.

The voice in my head reminded me that this was not a movie. There was no happy ending looming. The guy would not get the girl and no one was going to ride off into the sunset. I grabbed Mitch's hand. That wasn't entirely true. We could be a happy ending or at least together at the end.

Customary greeting followed. I introduced Mitch. We followed Obadiah to the elevator. We were going deep underground.

The elevator opened into a small room, beyond the glass doors was another small room and another set of glass doors. Airlocks. We stepped into the first room and waited while the elevator doors closed. The glass doors in front of us opened letting us through. Again, we waited while doors closed. There was a hiss and a rush of air. Moments later the next doors opened and we were free.

Obadiah took his mask off. "You can breathe safely down here. Air does not come directly from outside. It's filtered and purified before we get it."

It was a relief to take the mask off. Obadiah pointed to a set of empty cubby holes in an alcove. He dropped his mask into one with his name on it. I placed my mask in one and used the black sharpie I saw on the top of the shelves to name my cubby. Kurt and Mitch followed suit.

"Where is the victim?" I asked.

"Quarantined on the next level down."

"Will he make it?"

"No."

"Any chance of an antidote or at least a vaccination?" Kurt asked.

"We've been working on that for over a year now."

So they've been working with the viruses. Why not just destroy them so this this can never happen? Because they're a weapon. Humanity deserved to be annihilated; we created these viruses to use against others.

Live by the sword die by the sword.

"How far has it spread?" I asked.

"Reports are now coming in from all states on the eastern seaboard."

We're out of time.

Obadiah indicated that we should follow him. He took us to a comfortable lounge room complete with large leather couches and the smell of fresh coffee.

"These are our living quarters. This is the communal living area, the kitchen is through that door," he said, pointing to a large door on the right of the room. "Over there." He pointed to the left. "Is a hallway that leads to twelve bedrooms all containing their own bathrooms."

"Water?" Kurt asked.

"Underground wells and again purified before we get it by our own filtration plant. The whole complex is fully self-contained. We even have gardens on a lower level to provide our fresh vegetable and some fruits."

"How long can people survive down here?"

"The plan was always to stay underground for seven years."

"That's the plan, what's the reality?"

"Ten. Twenty-four people can live down here for ten years."

"How about maintenance?"

"We have two maintenance engineers on site at all times."

I sat down on one of the couches and considered the predicament we were now in as humans. We were facing the end of life as we knew it. I had no idea how to feel about that. My life to date had been pretty clear cut. People do stupid shit, I arrested them, we made our case, lawyers got involved and often screwed things up but more often we won and the bad guys went to jail. End of story. I couldn't arrest a virus. I could arrest the shit for brain tard that released it, but that wasn't going to help. My traditional skill set of investigation and resolution was not applicable here.

Yet here I was. Why?

Because Obadiah and I worked for the same person once upon a time and Tierney wanted me and Delta here in the event of a catastrophic world event. And I was lucky enough to be allowed a plus one. Life without Mitch would be unbearable. Tierney would be in his own bunker with other so-called valuable people, specialists in survival, intelligence gathering, and various support people. I wondered if Iain Campbell made the cut. I hoped so.

The kitchen door opened. Sandra came out carrying a tray of coffees.

I jumped to my feet. Kurt took the tray. I hugged Sandra hard.

"Thank God," she said returning my hug. "I didn't know if you would make it in time."

"How did you?"

"Tierney sent someone to get me."

A shadow fell over the kitchen doorway. From the shadow came a familiar voice which in turn became a familiar man.

"Iain!"

"The gangs all here," he said with a grin looking around the room. A frown furrowed his brow. "Not quite, where are Sam and Lee?"

"Retrieving the viruses unless of course someone else took them first," I replied. They should be at the facility by now. I checked my watch. "Hopefully they're on their way up here soon." They hadn't checked in.

A cold feeling of dread stirred amongst the icy feelings of doom. It was hard to distinguish cold from ice but it was there none the less.

I looked at the display on my phone.

No missed calls.

No new messages.

I made a call.

Their phones went unanswered. Iain used his phone and called Tierney. Moments later he had our pilot on the line. Sam and Lee never returned to the plane. The pilot was locked in the cockpit. He reported chaos on the runway and from what he could see in the airport buildings. Carnage and chaos.

I sat on the nearest couch.

It had happened.

We were done.

Life underground was the new normal for however long it would take before we were safe above ground again.

About the author:

Cat Connor is a prolific crime thriller author hailing from New Zealand. Her expertise in the genre is reflected in her engaging and suspenseful narratives, which have garnered a loyal following. Her work is known for its intricate plots, dynamic characters, and relentless pace, keeping readers on the edge of their seats until the very end. She has authored multiple books, including the popular "Byte" series, which follows the exploits of an FBI unit that investigates serial crime.

Cat's passion for crime and espionage is evident in her writing, as she strives to create a world that is both authentic and thrilling. Her meticulous attention to detail and extensive research have won her critical acclaim and accolades from readers and peers alike. In addition to writing, Cat enjoys speaking on topics related to writing and publishing. Her talks are known for their candidness, humour, and practical advice. With her unique blend of talent, expertise, and passion, Cat Connor has established herself as one of the most exciting and accomplished authors in the crime thriller genre.

Her other passions include music, reading, tequila, red wine, coffee, and chocolate. When she's not writing she can be found binge watching TV shows and spending time with her much adored animals; Diesel the mastador, Patrick the tuxedo cat, Dallas the tortie Birman, and Jimmy the thug.

You can follow and contact Cat at the following places:

Website: www.catconnor.com
Twitter: @catconnor
Facebook: @cat.connor
Instagram: @catconnorauthor
Bluesky: @catconnor.bsky.social
Threads: @catconnorauthor

Also by Cat Connor:

The Kiwi set Veronica Tracey Spy/PI series:

[Nothing happens here] -2020

[Lure the lie] - 2021

[Leave a message] - 2022

[Whiskey Tango Foxtrot] - 2023

[Foxtrot Mike Lima] - 2024

The FBI based Byte Series:

Killerbyte - 2009

Terrorbyte - 2010

Exacerbyte - 2011

Flashbyte - 2012

Soundbyte - 2013

Snakebyte - 2013 (novella)

Databyte - 2014

Eraserbyte - 2015

Psychobyte - 2016

Metabyte - 2017

Qubyte - 2018

Cryptobyte - 2019

Vaporbyte -2020

Raidbyte - 2021 (collection of short bytes)

Cachebyte -2024 (collection of short bytes)

Whispers in the water - the poetry of SSA Conway and SA Connelly

9MM PRESS

www.ingramcontent.com/pod-product-compliance
Lightning Source LLC
Chambersburg PA
CBHW020417030726
47495CB00006B/1544